Sarah Hall was born in Cumbria in 1974 and now lives and works there. She has written three previous novels. Her first, *Haweswater*, was published by Faber in 2002 and won the Commonwealth Writer's Prize for Best First Novel. Her second, *The Electric Michelangelo*, was shortlisted fro the Man Booker Prize 2004. In 2007 Sarah won the John Lewellyn Rhys Prize for her most recent novel, *The Carhullan Army*.

Praise for *How to Paint a Dead Man*:

'Sarah Hall writes a fine, vivid prose of exceptional poetic intensity and there are passages in this novel . . . of luminous beauty.' Jane Shilling, *Daily Telegraph*

'Her characters are sharp and hauntingly memorable.' Katy Guest, *Independent on Sunday*

'Elegant and poetic . . . Captivating.' *Marie Claire*

'Finely crafted . . . Hall accomplishes the conceptual ambitions of the novel with great skill: it is a tough and unsentimental exploration of the way art feeds on the dead.' Jonathan Beckman, *Independent*

'In four threads of looped and echoing stories, Hall uses the effects we've come to find more appropriate in so-called genre fiction – suspense, shock, romance, eroticism and terror – to create a world that questions life's biggest, most painful matters. All this while she entertains and challenges. To read this book is to rediscover what the novel is made for and of what it can be made.' *The Australian*

by the same author

HAWESWATER
THE ELECTRIC MICHELANGELO
THE CARHULLAN ARMY

HOW TO PAINT A DEAD MAN
Sarah Hall

faber and faber

First published in 2009
by Faber and Faber Limited
Bloomsbury House
74–77 Great Russell Street
London WC1B 3DA
This paperback edition published in 2010

Typeset by RefineCatch Limited, Bungay, Suffolk
Printed in England by CPI Bookmarque, Croydon

A CIP record for this book is available from the British Library

ISBN 978–0–571–22490–6

10 9 8 7 6 5 4 3 2

For Jake

'Things are not what they are, they are what they become.'

GASTON BACHELARD

The Mirror Crisis

You aren't feeling like yourself. You haven't been feeling like yourself for a while now, not since the accident. More accurately, not since the moment you heard about it. That morning, that minute, holding the phone to your ear and hearing your father say those horrific words; it was then you felt the change, then when you were knocked out of kilter. You're not sure what's wrong exactly; it's hard to put your finger on, hard to articulate. It isn't grief. Grief would be simple. Something internal, something integral, has shifted. You feel lost from yourself. No. *Absent.* You feel absent. It's like looking into a mirror and seeing no familiar reflection, no one you recognise hosted within the glass.

You're not crazy. You must emphasise this point and remind yourself of it. You are not crazy. And you're not being coy, or difficult. This isn't about fashionable social detachment, the current trend for woe-is-me, or wanting to be the cool detached outsider. You can't quite catch sight of yourself as you go about your life, that's all. Your body doesn't contain its spirit, just as the mirror has relinquished your portrait. You are elsewhere.

You used to feel something similar as a child, but it was less empty, less lonely then. Your brother was the same. The pair of you had a peculiar sense of each other, not as separate people but as doppelgängers, symmetries, which is quite common in twins of course. You weren't formed from a separated egg – you weren't identical, not a common gender, John and Jack, or

Ruth and Rita. Still, there you were, together, from the very beginning. You linked fingers in the womb. You shared a pillow of placenta, pedalled in tandem against your mother's belly. You heard concurrently the wet chamber music of her body, shared nutrients, and dreamt the same hermetic dream. After you were born, pink then blue, you then Danny, your existences were still pegged closely together, like your newborn hats on the washing line.

Later, it was as if you were sitting with him on the sofa, at his exact coordinates, when really you were sitting opposite him at the table, making potato prints with your mum. Sometimes you felt you were more at his location than you were at yours. Ulterior proximity, it's called. When you waved it wasn't to your brother, it was to yourself. Nobody ever worked that out, not even your mum, who said, *Wave to Danny again, sweetheart, he's waving back.* You were placed in separate cribs, but the heat of him still kept you warm at night. He still tugged the blanket away from your cheek when he tucked it up under his own. At least, that's how it felt.

Inevitably, you learned to talk. This is when things got tricky. You developed a method of speaking on behalf of the displaced you. It was logical, in a way. At first they thought you were speaking on behalf of your brother, as bossy, older siblings often do. *You want juice please*, you said, and they gave it to Danny in his chewed sippy-mug. *And would you like some juice too, Suzie-Sue,* they crooned. *Such an adorable bond*, people said. *So unusual.* There were lots of baby photographs taken with you looking quizzical, frowning at items around the room or at the adults posing with you. Your brother was quiet, quieter than you, and always smiling, as if he knew a secret.

The situation became worrying. Playgroup was a minefield. Nobody could really tell who you were talking about: yourself or Danny. The subjects of your speech were often confused,

4

and you and your brother babbled privately together, making up names for spiders, stomach aches, and rain. You did not make friends with the other children at first; instead the two of you played hoops and balls together and swapped beakers of milk; there was a system of cup colours to be observed. There was talk of educational retardation, developmental limitation, which shocked your mum and dad. There were visits from the healthcare worker, District Nurse Lane. You remember her rigid triangle skirt and her bleached cuticles. She wondered about this inseparability, this double-speak. She wondered if, rather than being delightful, it was abnormal to possess a psychological satellite. She wondered how healthy the relationship really was between Danny and you.

Enter Dr Dixon, at the paediatric clinic in town. Because you seemed to be the one in charge, because the sibling unity was too powerful, you were going to have special lessons with him, to help you 'be more comfortable'. The building had a brass bell, and an old wooden revolving door wheelchairs couldn't fit through: the first time you went you watched a girl with callipered legs being lifted up and carried through. It looked as if she were being fed into a giant grinder, and when it was your turn you had to be cajoled and encouraged into the blades. The carpet inside was made of tiny blue plastic threads. After you'd walked across it there was enough static to make a little jolt of electricity crack from your fingertip when you touched the table. There were anti-smoking posters with cloud-skulls floating above people holding cigarettes. Dr Dixon kept a tank of stick insects in his reception for the kids to look at. Sometimes they shed, leaving their skins behind on the aquarium trees where they dried and curled like thin spun toffee. It made you feel queasy to see the brown husks hanging off the forks of bark.

The doctor smelled of pencil shavings and peppermints. He

spoke very slowly, very deliberately. His teeth looked white and strong. For a while you thought he was a dentist, but he never asked you to open wide. Instead he held you gently by the shoulders and asked impossible questions. *What do you think is the best way to answer this question, Sue? If I took away your mother and father, and then I took away your brother Danny, what would you be called?* The last proposition always made you furious, and you scowled yourself into a headache. He asked you to paint pictures of your family. *Who do you see here, here and here?* You were encouraged to play by yourself each day, without Dan, without dolls, or books. It seemed particularly unkind to your brother, who looked crestfallen whenever your mum said it was time for you to go upstairs for 'special hour'. Only once did Danny come to the clinic. The two of you were put in an observation room and left alone. You endured six months of Dr Dixon. It felt like years. Then the whole thing was over. Only later, when you were a teenager and you asked about those memories, was it described, apologetically, as treatment. Now you can't pass by the old sandstone clinic at the top end of your hometown without hearing that man's relentless nasal parroting. *Say I do, Sue, say I do, Sue.*

But it worked, you suppose. You learned to communicate normally, like the rest of the psychically circumscribed automatons of the world. You looked at yourself in the mirror Dr Dixon gave you to hold. You repeated the words until they stuck. *Me, me, me. I, I, I.* You wound back into yourself, like the reversing spool on your mum's sewing machine. You became a separate unit. You were cured.

Now here you are again, dislocated, remote, spilling your essence out into the void.

You've been thinking about this. You've been wondering if you are really so different from everyone else in the massive, grinding city where you live. You look at the variety of faces opposite you on the bus; listen to the conversations. Everyone seems to be in crisis. *You just want to get out of the financial mess,* a man in a grey suit says to his black-suited colleague. An oily teenager yells into his mobile phone: *You can't help feeling like a bastard for wanting her to get rid of the thing. She was the one who forgot to take the fucking pill!* An Asian woman with a nose piercing softly confides in her friend: *You get sick to death of his moods. You want to kill him. You really do.*

Nowadays, people often don't say *I,* as if they don't want to be involved in the desperate act of being. No one is contented dwelling inside their existence any more. No one is secure. Identity can be chosen. You can be whoever you want to be, which means you should consider all the options before selecting yourself. People are aware of the heart, slopping about like a piece of lively meat inside the chest, as if it isn't snug, as if it hasn't been fitted right. They are constantly told that a better incarnation lies just over the horizon; all it would take to be joined with that preferable version is beauty, money, weight loss, fashion, confidence, talent, surgery, cosmetics, gymnasiums, a cordless drill, a new microwave, more sex.

The ruthless calibration of consumerism. For if this is all you've got, this single chance, this brief, blemished simian posing opposite you in the mirror, then hadn't it better be refined, hadn't it better be romanticised? The self is no longer made to measure. 'I' is simply the wrong size. If only that better, happier edition could be purchased and possessed. But it ghosts around out there, tantalising, beautiful, erstwhile. Meanwhile London is filled with laterals, crowding on to trains and buses, talking different languages, avoiding free newspapers. They tug at their exteriors, wrestle with their features, and recast themselves in conversations. They are trapped inside the dull, deficient hides that Nature has unhelpfully allocated.

7

You are not yearning for improvement. You don't want to be reborn from a womb of material idealism. You don't wish to emerge, perfect and bright, out of the modern western chrysalis. You are not interested in living magnificently and utterly, certain that in this life you have triumphed. All you want is to be yourself again, because the identity that was once yours has vanished. Though a familiar face is reflected in the mirror, its anima is missing. *You* are absent.

There's no real mystery of course, no complicated reason. The nub, the crux, the heart of the matter is this: Danny died a month and a half ago. You've lived six weeks, fourteen days, and several minutes longer than he.

Translated from the Bottle Journals

Today a journalist from the city came up here and admired the view and asked me why I paint these objects on the table. They are so plain and ordinary, he said. Why do you paint bottles and bottles and bottles? The same painting, over and over. What does it mean? He asked this of me as if it were answerable, as if it were important. And I said to him, I do not paint bottles. The man must have thought me mad or obtuse or cunning perhaps. He will, no doubt, blame the rustication of the place where I live, or my absence from the galleries and salons. He does not see choice. He does not see beyond the quartet of fruit in the dish, such as it is presented – a plum, two apricots and another plum. On the canvas he sees only the surface: the green paint and the grey and the white, which will not pass over a border unless it is directed. He considers quaint the long shadows taught to us by the academies.

To him, the painting on the easel is a funeral. It is careful and uncluttered, and it is not loud enough for him to understand. He does not have the practical training to recognise the discreet layers of vermilion used, their illuminating effect. If he had turned to the west during our conversation, he might have seen the sun setting behind the mountains, he might have seen the radiance of the sky.

But I am not whom he expects, this young traveller with his recording device and his pressed suit. He tells me he is sorry to hear of my ill health. He grieves on behalf of Italy. Then you must have acute indigestion, I said to him, and you will surely need some Averna to restore the balance. I assured him that I am quite well, merely old. I do not know who makes these reports, in which I am lying on my deathbed. Next week, he told me proudly, he is going to Milan to hear Miles Davis play his trumpet. How wonderful, I said. Now he has gone away, back to his apartment in the street with its commotion and motorcars and thin girls selling chips of ice. And he will write in the magazines and tell his friends that I am an artist of great simplicity and a man of great complexity. He will say that I like to make a joke when the issue of mortality is raised, and my body is profoundly stooped, and I show no sign of enlightening the world about the subject of my work. He will say that the paintings have a strange luminosity, but it is meaningless. The meaning is unavailable; it cannot be grasped. And they will photograph these bottles of mine for the exhibition catalogues, and in America I will upset the critics. They will say it is deliberate.

Look, I told the man, look again, because he had driven a long way to get here.

Theresa visits me once a day, sometimes twice if there is a delivery or laundry to be done. She brings my cigarettes, onions and anchovies, the usual things. She will let herself in without knocking and call out because she imagines one variety of noise disturbs me if I am at work in the studio while another does not. In her there is the bustle of the market where she has been shopping. Hurry is in her hands as she turns items over in the sink to rinse off the soap. There are tremors in her flesh from the broom's short strokes. If asked she will turn the earth and uproot my garlic, some of which I give her to take away. I tell her to step over the basil, not to water it until it has parched completely, though she will often water it. The tomatoes she likes to bring inside, yellow-red, and she puts them in bowls against the walls, like ornaments. The lizards she sweeps into a pan, flicking them outside with broken tails. They scurry back into the house to begin their campaign again. She might think I want to paint her. I do not know her thoughts. In the winter she comes less often. The hill to Serra Partucci is too steep.

I receive other visitors, and more frequently than has been supposed. Antonio has begun keeping tabs on me. He would like me to move to a house less like the house of a peasant; he would prefer me in the apartment on the Via Fondazza in Bologna where he can call round regularly. The journalists are nervous if arriving unannounced. I do not believe it is stealth but perhaps they feel they will catch my true self. Then the enigma will finally be solved. Perhaps they think they will see me wearing a uniform, or performing a curse, or talking to the objects in the studio. They say the unmade roads remind them of the weddings of their cousins. They leave their motorcars down by the cypresses and walk up the slopes. If a bird skull or an iris catches their eye they will always pick it up and arrive holding it like treasure. Nature is found particularly in single objects here, though it is all around. For city dwellers Nature is invisible, located inside the weather brought to their towns, or inside their bodies when they visit the doctor to hear of its errors. To collect bones and items of colour is instinctual. They practise the language of still-life as they approach.

I like to be surprised by visitors though I can often hear the engines labouring and cutting out and the vehicles reversing back to the bottom of the hill, so I am not truly surprised, just anticipating the appearance of a face at the window. I always have the coffee ready to make by the time anyone arrives. Oh, you take honey to sweeten your coffee, they always say, how unusual, is it not unlucky? It is better not to begin debates about the importing of sugar, and from which states, so instead we talk of bees labouring in our golden fields. I put their stems in a basin to keep fresh and I put their bones on the kitchen table. Other times there will be a letter of inquiry first, with particular mention of this composition or that composition, or the old party, or a new theory, and I write back of course, come, but not on Thursday. On Thursday, if I am well, I teach in the local school. Such courtesy is not necessary but I can instruct them not to attempt the hill. If ever a car makes the climb all the way to Serra Partucci then I will be absolutely surprised and I will enjoy asking the driver of such a fine vehicle if they would like some coffee.

My dog Benicio died a year ago in the summer. I miss his warm presence in the house. He was a loyal dog with short brown fur and he was run over and could not be saved. In the afternoons the sun is very strong, I think it blinded him on the road or he was sleeping on the warm dirt. His back legs were injured in a difficult way – they had already been broken once before. I wish in mercy that he had died more quickly. A companionable dog cannot be replaced for many years. I do not need one for hunting or digging for truffles but have always enjoyed the easy fellowship of dogs. In any case there are too few years for another, so I have taken to finding company in other ways, such as the radio and writing. At the house now there is me, an old man who does not paint bottles, the little broken lizards, and Theresa, installing her red tomatoes.

To begin each day there is only the wind, asking to come in from the north before even the daylight. It is a rolling wind, excitable as it prepares to leave the continent. Some mornings I will accompany the wind to the road above the town. It helps me to unstiffen. There is sciatica in my legs and my breathing these days is somewhat impaired. Really I can do no more than amble. The land often seems like an ocean below – the hill moves through leaves, wheat, lavender tides. It never reaches the mountains on the horizon, but still we can hope. Heat arrives after the wind has passed over the bricks. Then fire blooms across the tiles of the town. The flames of the sun turn back the petals of the flowers in the gardens. It is as if the ground has secreted embers overnight. If I knelt down and cupped my hands to my lips and blew perhaps the day would start early.

There was no decision made to never leave this place, though it has been said that I renounced everything, that I suffered a great dismay and withdrew. Or that I was possessed by art, removing my heart to paint its space, its absence. This is said because of my wife and child. I am a brute and the work denotes much calculation and control. Old news. When I hear such things I do not ask for sympathy. Whatever sins I have committed exist beyond me now. I will let Nature alone judge me; she will abominate me if it is her finding.

We should not forget that when we limp away afflicted through the spirit, it is not to the factory gates or to the corporate steps we pilgrimage. Instead we go to the sea for its salt. We find shade under the sycamores on the great avenues. Or we go to the rivers where water tells us modestly of its own sickness. I cannot say that I have found peace now. But I have never loved with greater strength than in this place, with its earth the colour of *verdaccio* and its generous fruit.

Sometimes I long for the wind in the studio, to harden the tips of the brushes if they have not yet been cleaned, to ruffle these pages, as if in answer to a question I have posed. But the studio faces south and its shutters are quite secure. The work must not move or display movement, otherwise I might try to turn the house and gratefully receive the wind. Then the easel would tumble over and the bottles would sing at their necks. This of course is the alternative, which we must all imagine from time to time.

Benicio used to bite the wind. Poor confused dog! If it came suddenly through the trees and assailed the house, if it tugged his ruff and made balloons of his ears, he would snap and snap his jaws. He did not understand that to lean back against the current is to have a firm friend. Instead he was followed by it and it stroked his coat in the wrong direction and it unsettled him. He would consider no truce. But the invisible enemy always prevailed, surprising him from east and west. He snapped and snapped. Then the eating of air inflated his stomach and made it creak, and he would look very sorry for himself. Sometimes his growling and shouting at the wind, or the wind's retaliation, disrupted the boar, and Benicio's adversary was finally made manifest, squealing and grunting as it charged. Then retreat, retreat, back into Serra Partucci! The wind, the dog and the boar; it was such a comedy, like the American brothers.

Today I have also received a letter from England, forwarded by Antonio at the agency. It is a delight. A young man called Peter is asking technical questions about a still-life of 1959. He asks about the placement of the china rectangle, the way one side is favoured slightly in the composition and rests against the left-hand vessel. He does not believe the rectangle is tucked behind its neighbouring box, as the artist seems to imply, but that it exists in the frontal plane, its angles shortened. He mentions the white piping through the vase and its relation to a mathematical scale. He asks, am I the inventor of negative space? He writes in English, with regret, and I am able to translate most of it. For that which I cannot, I have asked Theresa to retrieve a dictionary of phrasing from the library. This has displeased

14

her; she does not approve of ferrying intellectual books in the basket of her bicycle. Is *L'Unità* not too heavy for you to cycle with, I ask her, and she clicks her tongue. We must not talk of politics or newspapers, Theresa and I.

In the letter the young man says he does not know where the artist of the piece could have been standing during its production, such is the 'almost independent but myopic' perspective of it. There is, within his letter, the subjective mania of the youthful mind. Alas, he is too excitable, for there is no address to which I might return his correspondence. The painting was sold to a private collector; perhaps the young man has seen a reproduction, or perhaps the original if it is on loan. I do not always know the whereabouts of the paintings, though Antonio keeps good records. Peter tells me he is a student of art in Liverpool and he is eager to learn. From the slope of the lettering, and the dragging of the palm across the ink, I can see that he is a left-handed scribe, like Leonardo. His wishes are kind in conclusion. His signature is flourished. Peter; I will remember his name.

And I will test myself with the questions posed. The piece was completed six years ago. It contained the tall blue bottles, a hatbox, a china receptacle. In 1959 the red towers of Bologna were still standing impressively, having survived the war. Wine was less expensive. Cardinal Montini kissed the reactor at Ispra and we entered the new atomic age. Benicio was troubled by his hindquarters, and was limping. I was troubled by arthritis, and dropping things. There was a ladder placed against the rear wall of the studio. First I worked on its third step, with the easel set at its highest bolt. Further away to achieve detachment: the vantage point of a ghost. Then I set the easel an arm's length from the objects and in this way found greater detail.

* * *

15

Of all the conditions we experience, solitude is perhaps the most misunderstood. To choose it is regarded as irresponsible or a failure. To most it should be avoided, like an illness. Inside solitude people see the many compartments of unhappiness, like the comb of a pomegranate. To be emptied from the world, to be cast away and forgotten – is this what we fear most? So we must shake hands and pass money and hear talk of society and talk of our families and our selves. We must move in and out of doors, press buttons for lifts, catch each other's colds, laugh and weep, and contribute to the din and the restlessness. We must dance and sing, and visit the courts. We must make these daily contracts.

But if it is embraced solitude is the most joyful of commitments. In the grace of these quiet rooms I know far better the taste of each day. How well I know life. I understand water in its glass. As the afternoon circles, shadows move behind the objects on the table. There is a pinch of cinnamon in Theresa's lamb casserole. Such acceptance! Such intimacy! The paint on the chassis of the easel is as thick as guano on the cliffs where seagulls nest.

I am not lonely, but receiving such a letter reminds me of the other souls in this world whom I might have liked to meet.

The Fool on the Hill

Peter's first rule of practice is that a canvas should fit into the boot of a car. It's a simple rule: size dictates size. A commonsense policy, the best kind. He's been telling his daughter for years she should adopt such measures in her work, and in her life also, but she won't listen. 'Dad,' she says, 'you should expand your mind. You don't have to think small any more.' No, no. Children are not interested in the wisdom of fathers. He can hear her creaking around in her room now, treading the oak boards, hauling up the sash window to let the dewy, laundered air in; dragging her enormous portfolio around. Always an early riser, Suzie, like her mother. And always contrary. A mystery where that particular attitude comes from.

He on the other hand is not what we might call lark-like. At least not today, on this late-summer morning with its light like ageing copper, and its insistence on no more than his being in the world. The breeze is thick and green in the trees outside the window. He casts a long leg outside the quilt to cool off – hot under the covers now the sun is beginning to magnify through the glass pane. He should get up. He should get up, have a cup of coffee, a glass of water and a rolly; get going for the day. He should swing into action, yes indeed. And if he were a man of greater resolve, if he were a man of veritable habit, perhaps he would do that. But it's tough, this whole business of entering the world. Pondering the opposing poles of rules and daughters is enough to be going on with just now, never mind tackling burnt toast scrapings in the sink, hardboard emulsion, and all else the risen must contend with.

With a bit of luck Lydia might fetch him up a brew and deposit it on the bedside table. With a bit more luck she might be inveigled back under the covers and they can put the morning glory to use. Unlikely. She knows better than to enable his inertia. Better to tempt him out of his comfortable pit with the grinding of coffee beans, the black aroma wafting through the kitchen and up the stairs, and with the frazzling of wheat crumbs under the grill. Better to torture a fellow with unavailable pleasure; she's got that one right, his wife. Just another five minutes or so, maybe then he'll be fit for employment; then he'll spring up, 'ta-da', and surprise them all.

He tucks the leg back under the quilt, folds the cover down off his chest to cool his upper body. Nope. Children never listen to the rules of their parents. It's like advising a horse to saddle itself. Nor did he give much credence to the laws and logistics of his old man. Neville Caldicutt had routines they could set the Metro clock by. Off to Shildon club on Wednesdays and Saturdays, partaking of not more than three pints of stout and a finger of Grouse for the road. Bed at a good hour on weekdays so as to be up at five the next morning to catch the colliery bus. Fish on Friday when the pay came in, no matter the catch, no matter the monger's chalkboard list and the bad bloody north-east tides. NCB coat to be worn winter and summer, bonfire night, and election day. Union votes. Coronation mugs for visitors. And a halfpenny tossed off the bridge into the river after church, as alms for the Lord. Because Neville Caldicutt would not put anything into the cloth collection purse passed up and down the aisles; he was averse to new vicarage roofs, but was a God-fearing man nonetheless, and the river seemed as likely a channel to charity as any. 'Heads for the Holy Ghost, tails for the fishes,' he would say to them as he spun the coin off his thumbnail into the cleggy water. That was a genuine bit of daftness, Peter always thought. That was enough for two liquorice laces, one for him and one for his sister Hillary. Or maybe it was the price to pay for not being sent to Sunday school.

His father used to bring him a cup of tea and a biscuit in those unoccupied, dogwatch hours, before he went off to the mine. It was the pitching of the mattress that always woke Peter, not the chirping of the outhouse door or the shuffling of the tartan slippers on the stairs. Neville Caldicutt would leave the light off, and would sit on the wire-sprung bed, and talk softly about this, that and the other to his son. He would talk about working men's politics, right and wrong, about school, and his great hero Bevan, and places to which he had never been but had always hoped to go. South America. Australia. Brighton pier. 'That'll be me then, lad,' he would say a few minutes later as they heard the old grumbler stalling on the corner of Alnwick Street and the doors on the terrace shutting, one by one. And the bedsprings would squeak and rattle as his father stood up to leave.

Peter would switch on the light for a few minutes, drink maybe half the cup of tea, to the third blue line painted round its inside. He'd nibble the digestive, then sleep again until his mother screeching the curtain rings woke him two hours later. 'Time to get up, Petie. Shake a leg.'

His father sitting in the dark: that's what he remembers. Those gloomy, unseen movements. That pipey underground voice, preparing for the day with inconsequential murmurs. And the malty crunch from a biscuit packet, and those cold-stove winter mornings, when men in the street rose before the birds' chorus and Peter waited for the next blue ring of daylight before getting up.

* * *

He's told the kids all this. He likes to talk about it when he's got them all home at the cottage and the fire is crackling and the homebrew is doing the rounds. It's good to recall the past and family. Good to know where you come from. Danny thinks it's hilarious – biscuits at the crack of dawn. Danny boy: never up until midday, then usually hung-over or coming down, and presently kipping, for some reason, in a jerry-rigged berth under the cottage stairs. But always amused by his dad when cogent, always willing to play a hand of nostalgia poker. Danny Dando, Two of Two. 'Was there an outside lavvy?' he asks. 'And bits of the *Sun* to wipe your bum on?' 'Yeah, kiddo, there was – not even Bronco.'

Susan smiles like the Sphinx during his chatter and busies herself with other things. Flicking through a book. Keeping the coal turned towards its orange industry in the grate. She looks away from the stories he tells, towards the embers, or towards the pages. Suzie-Sue. One of Two. She with her impatience and that daughterly tendency to spat with her old man. She with her fine eye and those gigantic sheets she likes, that cost a bomb to print and frame and have got her into Goldsmiths College. Here she is next door, creaking the floorboards, not lying in. Just finished her foundation year and straddled between home and a brassy move to the capital. She doesn't believe in his car-boot rule, never has, never will. 'What would Kokoschka have done with that kind of attitude?' she asks him, her brow pinched. Yeah, children always see the limitations of their parents. She'll find her own way, no doubt about that, he thinks, whenever her face disappears from him, whenever she turns a log in the grate holding the corner with her bare hand. 'Something wrong with the tongs, love?' He can't help asking, pedantic old bugger that he is.

Peter stacks all the pillows behind him and sinks his head back into the cotton swale. He switches the radio on. On the morning programme, a plum-tongued Tory is smarming about kids overdosing at warehouse parties, so he switches it off again. Could do with a piss – it feels like his bladder's begun shrinking at night. Time to think about getting up, seriously. Time to get organised and think about the doings and happenings of today. One – go for a run and clear the cobwebs. Two – bastard accounts. Three – ring Abbotsford and bollock them about printing the wrong dates for his talk (always getting the simplest things wrong!). Then do some clearing up in the studio maybe, though that would take a kind of mental fortitude probably not available today. No, he should make the most of this gorgeous fading season, get out and do something useful. He should use the light. He should go to the ravine with his gear and make some more studies. Remembering first to put some petrol in the car. And to look at the exhaust to see if it's coming unmoored from the chassis, as the recent grunting sounds would imply. He's loath to admit defeat just yet and condemn it to the great scrapyard in the sky.

His cars have always been one mile away from expiration it seems – cheap to buy, and cheap to run. They're usually crumpled European bangers, with slack steering and alarmingly high tickovers that suggest ambition to get airborne. There's a certain runt-like motor he favours – the no-frills variety. Cars with snapped-off window winders and hard, haemorrhoid-inducing seats. Cars with simple interior mechanics to tinker with and a recessed shelf by the oil reservoir to tuck in a rag. Often a boot where the engine should be. These ones are the best; he likes unloading paintings from the front end at the galleries. It feels like theatre, like a magician grasping a series of rabbits by the ears and extracting them from an improbable cavity. What's that called again? Counter-intuition.

It's not a question of money. They're doing OK now, better

than OK. There have been good years and bad years over the decades. In this profession it's always the way. There are things he'll blow his wad on – distilling equipment, limited editions, Indian black. Cars though, are not worthy of great expenditure; this is another rule of practicality he should make sure to pass along to the kids. So long as they get where they should be going and back again – that's what matters. It's about the skill of the driver anyway, not anti-lock brakes and air-conditioning and all that rubbish. At least he bloody well drives! Lots of his arty friends don't, or won't, or can't, or claim not to have any inclination to, especially the bloody poets. Donald doesn't, nor Robson. They take some kind of socialist pride in it, and at being able to expediently decipher bus and train timetables instead. 'The number forty-four will be here in eight minutes, comrades.' And they've developed a sort of royal posture and odd passenger tics. Reading the review sections and getting colicky rather than looking at the passing scenery for one. Dexterity with radio tuning, but an inability to locate the washer fluid if it's required while Peter's rolling a smoke and steering with his knees.

He'll be sad to see it go, this latest motor – a boxy, bug-eyed Daffodil – for the acquisition of which he talked the man in the dealership down to under two hundred pounds. Not a bad little deal. Then he sportingly upped his own price by a quid, saying the beast was on the endangered species list of cars and he'd better acknowledge it. And Jimmy Walton of Walton & Sons laughed and shook his hand, and was glad to see the wrecker trundling off the forecourt, whirring like a helicopter, and spotting on the ground. Another man might be embarrassed to drive such a car. Another man might consider it an inferior status symbol. Not Peter. Life's too short for material displays.

In any case the Daf does well on the hills in winter. Its thin rigid tyres suit the snow, slicing through it like knives through icing sugar. And its engine pitch clears hares from the road without him having to beep them back into their burrows. Two gears – forward and back, both as quick as each other – an ingenious system, if ever there was one. Steep gradients require agriculture-speed struggles, of course, but the thing usually makes it in the end. It's not often he has to leave it stranded at the bottom of the moor and walk home. Lydia uses her own car, a smart little Volkswagen Beetle, a dependable run-arounder. Susan says it's 'a false economy', buying cheap cars and having them conk out hither and thither. It seems whenever he arrives back at the cottage from a trip out these days, she'll be waiting, shaking her head, and ready with a stern lecture before he's even clambered out of the offender. 'Wilse', she'll say ('Wilse', not 'dad', not 'father dearest', but 'Wilse', the slang for all the local Peters), 'What a clapped-out old heap!' And just to make the case for her when he turns off the ignition some spastic belt along one of the engine cones will continue squealing. 'Look, kiddo, there's no point in getting a new Merc and having it lathered in shit from driving through the farmyard every day.' She'll roll her eyes, and kick the dinted hubcap. 'But the place looks like a wrecking yard, Dad.'

Touché, daughter. There is of course 'The Whale' – the enormous, filthy-white Volvo, his previous fin-de-siècle automobile, now parked up by the cattle-grid and growing over with ferns. An industrious branch of bracken has furled its way up through the rusty hole in the floor and is filling the interior, like a splendid Victorian glasshouse, with greenery. And yes, at some point it needs to be towed away to the scrappy. It's just that he's not got round to it yet. He's a very busy man. 'I think it looks adamantine,' he tells her. 'Like a Ted Hughes poem.' At which point she grimaces and stalks back into the cottage. Missy Miss. Suzie-Sue. 'Is that brother of yours in my pouch

23

again?' he calls after her. A bony shrug while she's departing. Stoner brother's not high on her agenda of reform it seems. Just crazy pikey dad.

That rich drift of percolating coffee is killing him, as is his walnut bladder. He can hear female laughter downstairs, and groaning. Lydia and Susan are trying to wake up the under-stair monster with a spritz or two from the watering can. 'Tip it, tip it, tip it!' Poor lad. Still, that's probably his cue; if the ladies of the house are feeling feisty he should surface pronto and avoid a dousing. He hauls himself up out of the bed's soft vegetation, straightens the quilt out with a flap, and goes for a whizz. Remember to put petrol in the car, put petrol in the car, he chants. And get a quote for a tow-away. Maybe.

In the bathroom the toilet looks a long way down; maybe it's been shrinking overnight too. Maybe there's a conspiracy of shrinking things. He puts a hand against the wall, leans over and unleashes. He starts, then stops, then starts the stream of yeasty yellow properly. Oh prostate, dear prostate. The Daf will cope, a good few months left in it, he's sure. Besides, you can't avoid the battle of machine against nature. Danny had a picture book called *Tractor Max* when he was little – Peter remembers the illustrations it contained. Those massive sweeping fells and turgid fields, vivid and sky-less. Human endeavour seemed diminished within the grandness of that landscape. Every time he read it to Dan at bedtime he felt something wobble in his gut from the sheer bloody tenacity of that little tractor hauling away. He felt like he might fall off the bunk bed. Yeah, that illustrator knew the score.

He pulls the chain on the cistern and water dumps down into the bowl. It should be another rule – a good image should tip you off your comfortable perch, stir up your notions of safety, and make you dizzy. Like vertigo. Like Rothko! He'll have to remember to tell the kids that one. He'll have to write these rules down or something, for posterity. It's useful information after all. He can hear Lydia calling 'Peter, Peter, are you . . .' as he pads down the hallway to the top of the stairs. Below is a strange scene. Danny is naked and curled against the bottom step, having made it no further than a few feet from his berth. His skin is glistening wet, his eyes behind his eyelids flickering. Probably still dreaming of that rave in the old art-deco hotel down the coast (hey, maybe he should pilfer some of Dando's little dove pills and give them a whirl, quid pro quo et cetera). His sister is standing over him with a primed watering can, looking lethal.

The Divine Vision of Annette Tambroni

In the cool back room of her mother's house Annette measures rose stalks with her forearm. The stems must be kept long, the length from her fingertip to her elbow. They must be trimmed under running water to prevent their white heads drooping, like nuns in prayer. She snips the stalks, one by one, then turns off the tap, closes and locks the blades and places the shears to one side. She arranges the roses in a pottery urn and takes it across the courtyard, careful not to trip on the uneven stones. She puts the spray into the back of the van, next to the freesias and the gaggles of narcissi, and closes the double doors with a *gong-gong*.

Maurizio is sitting in the driver's seat, eating a pomegranate for breakfast. Annette climbs into the cabin next to him. He sips noisily at the slippery fruit. 'You don't love me,' he says. 'If you loved me you would have given me a rose to wear behind my ear.' Annette smiles and tucks her chin on to her chest. Her older brother is a tease. He is always telling her she does not love him, when he knows very well she does. At the front door of Castrabecco their mother stands in her long shawl and a dark dress. She holds a crucifix between her fingers and rubs it from side to side along its chain. Under his breath Maurizio says, 'She will start a fire with that thing one day. Then she'll go up in flames.'

'Is Mamma waiting for us?' Annette asks.

'No,' he replies, then quite casually he says, 'I stabbed her and left all the pieces in the bathtub. What a mess. You're going to have to clear it up later, Netta. Then we'll run away.' His sister laughs, even though she knows it is a wicked thing for him to say. But Maurizio is a boy, and the rules are different. He is allowed to watch American films on Saturday night, and he is allowed to say wicked things, so long as he provides enough charm afterwards to make up for it. 'Is Mamma waving to us?' she asks. Maurizio turns the key in the ignition and the van shudders. 'Yes, with her bloody stump!'

The drive to the market only takes a few minutes and the streets are clear. A tide of mist has rolled up from the lake and lingers around the steps of the old town. Maurizio leans out of the window and folds the side mirror in with a squeak and a click as they pass through the narrow citadel and into the summer theatre. He calls out to the men at the pork stand. 'Too early! Too early, fatso!' Already there is the smell of *porchetta* and charcoal burning. The other vendors are busy preparing their pitches. Annette can hear chatter and gossip, the slamming of doors and the scraping of crates. From the back of the van, Maurizio takes out the containers of flowers. He bolts together the canvas awning of the stall, tightens the screws, and then puts a wooden stool underneath it. 'Your throne. Well, goodbye now. You will never see me again. Don't be ashamed that you did not love me enough to make me stay.' He puts his hands around her waist, lifts her and spins her round, six or seven times perhaps, but she loses count. The air rushes past. There is laughter close by, and she can feel her skirt billowing. When Mauri puts her down again she is unsteady on her feet. She reaches out and takes hold of the stool for support. 'Mauri?' He is gone. The gears grind as the old Lancia rumbles away. Elemme calls over from the thrift stall. 'Hey. Your brother is very good-looking. He looks like Mastroianni. He's got the chin.'

Annette arranges the bouquets so that the roses are at the front of the display. Today they are perfect. By tomorrow they will already have begun to fade. She must try hard to sell them. Her mother says the power of roses is that they make men who pass by want to propose marriage to their girlfriends. She says roses spread virtue. Annette bends down to neaten the posture of the little romantics. She is careful not to squeeze too hard, which could distress the silken petals and leave a grey mark. The roses contain a perfume that is almost too extreme for such slender creations, she thinks, as if it has been manufactured artificially and sprayed on to them. Her uncle Marcello could probably explain why, if she were to ask him. He understands aromatics. As well as growing the flowers for the stall, and the vegetables, he extracts oil from lavender and sells it to perfumeries in Parma. The soul of a flower is not its shape or its colour, but its fragrance, he often says.

Soon it is warm and the mist evaporates. A breeze comes intermittently through the market entrances, bringing with it the memory of wild herbs, lake rushes and cattle. At the café opposite chairs are scraped out from under tables and tablecloths snapped. Saucers chink as they are set down. At some stalls the haggling has already begun. The hotel kitchen boys are scouting for sweet onions to caramelise, good meat, and imported octopus to scare, once, twice, in the boiling pots, before it is submerged. Glass lids tinkle as they are raised to investigate spice; paper cracks like lightning hitting the surface of water as it is folded around ham and smoked fish. Voices crest and roll down the alleyways, there is rustling and gossiping. She can hear the tottering clogs of old women as they pass by and the narrow rasping heels of young wives. Someone is crunching a fruit rind. A loose tablecloth flutters. The summer theatre is open for business.

If Annette did not know what people looked like, if she had not ever seen them before, she would think they were fantastical compositions – part-insect, part-crockery, with wings made of gossamer or tin, with whiskers, hooves, and clicking lobster tails – so unlike tidy, soft-skinned creations do they sound. The heavy cassock of the priest brushes past like the stiff feathers of a giant bird. The tinkling of Elemme's earrings and bangles is an exotic percussion. At home, when her mother brushes her hair into the classic chignon, the bristles sound like a licking cat's tongue.

Often Annette wonders about Him. He is not a human. He is not made of hair and skin. But what does he look like? Does he have horns and a snout, the tusks of a boar, or the scales of a snake? Are his eyes out on stalks? Do his knees bend in reverse like a crane's, their hinges worn shiny as old leather? And is there a sharp grey tail, like pencil lead, like the severed re-growing tails of lizards? Perhaps in his mouth is broken glass, or two rows of teeth, with which he devours his meals? But what does he eat? She tries, but she cannot remember the image she once saw, and her mother will not answer questions about the Bestia. She snatches air through her nose and leaves the room when she is asked, and Annette hears her sibilant sleeve as she crosses herself, twice, even three times. Only when the headaches come, or the moods of passion, will her mother talk about his cloak of buzzing flies and his long red shadow. The fatal shadow that was cast over Annette's father as he died.

Annette knows he is there in the altarpiece of the church of San Lorenzo. In the painting is a vision of him that was said to have sent the illustrator mad, trying to tear his own eyes out, after its completion. 'I have opened the gate of Hell', he wept to the doctors. 'I have brought something unspeakable back with me.' How it struck fear into her when she was young, this haunted picture. In the dark varnish Christ was lifted tenderly from the cross by the faithful, and behind him was a terrible unholy face, a face that would not truly come into focus, but warped, as if pulled through water, as if the smudges of paint could never dry, as if the image were washing forever in torment. The demonic face was too terrible for her to look upon, even while she was able to look at the deep wounds of Sebastian mounted on the wall opposite, and at the intestines of the medieval martyr being wound on to a wheel by his persecutors. She knows he is still there in the church, leering at her as she kneels, and she cannot concentrate on her prayers. He is alive inside the ornate frame, alive and looking at her.

Here in the busy market, there are times she feels it too, a terrible gaze settling upon her, coming from a place at the very edge, by the furthest wall. It is as if the Bestia has stepped from behind the torrid robes and clay body of Christ and has walked from the scene of the Deposition into the street, into the summer theatre, looking for her. He stands watching, his mouth open and shining with its teeth in many rows, his inhuman eyes, and the meat of his forehead cast in primitive lumps. Then a cold wind passes, and he is gone, and the feeling is forgotten.

A man lingers beside her stall and asks the price of the white roses. He moves on without purchasing any, leaving only the drift of cologne. She can tell from the slowing of shoes and the speeding of shoes how people react to her prospect; who is interested in posies, and who only has money for the evening's meal. Like the other vendors she could call out, solicitous, inviting, and say that so many of the flowers at her feet are useful; that marigold is Roman saffron – each perfect golden bowl holding seasoning and dye enough for rice, cake and marzipan. That plum blossom can be made into tea. That rose petals dissolve so delicately on the tongue and can flavour gelato. But she does not call out.

In the school nearby a bell sounds. The Montessori children skitter up the steps like calves on a ramp. Her youngest brother is among them, learning to read, learning to write. How will they learn today, she wonders? Will it be a song, or a game of some description? What will Tommaso come home reciting and will their mother approve of his advancement or think it frivolous? She remembers when she attended school. She remembers Signora Russo, who was the headmistress, and Signor Giorgio, who visited the class and taught them to paint and was always kind to her.

There are casual heel-clicks making their way through the stalls, pausing at the cheese counter with its loamy globes, at the bead-maker, and at the bric-a-brac. A little distance away, footsteps follow, cautious, flat-soled. A lady is being followed by a shy admirer. He does not have the courage to approach her. The woman passes by; she has browsed, and made a purchase, and the package creaks inside her straw bag. There is the tonk of bottles. She has wine. They could share it at a table and talk to each other of how long they have wanted to meet. Annette reaches down and lifts a stem gently with two fingers under the petal bonnet. He approaches. She holds out the rose and it is taken from her hands, humbly, wordlessly, as if taken by a spectre. Now he begins to walk quickly, and now he runs. There is a small cry of surprise, and delight, and laughter. The footsteps together disappear.

In the late morning it thunders. Rain patters on the awning, plops into the puddles by her feet. It is like the sound Tommaso has learned to make with his lips, which irritates their mother. Annette pulls the buckets of flowers close under the shelter, rolls down the canvas sides. Uncle Marcello once told her in the greenhouses that when it thunders myrtle has been axed in half, and is protesting. When the sun comes out it is because two myrtle strips have been brought back together again. He is full of such lore. Her mother often thinks it inappropriate, and a contradiction to the supreme laws of God, but she is also very superstitious. She is superstitious about salt and numbers and animals. She does and does not approve of the little spirit-stopper Uncle Marcello has made for Annette to wear around her neck. Inside the pretty green vial there is concentration of rosemary. Rosemary: strongest of the charms against demons, holiest of the aromatics.

The Mirror Crisis

You've been trying to cope, for the sake of your parents. For the sake of your involuntary breath, and your heart, which bangs on without consent. To all intents and purposes, and to all appearances, you are functioning adequately. You get up in the morning, wash yourself, walk to the gallery, and work. You are not lying in your own faeces, howling at strangers in the street. You are accepting things. You even bought a book on bereavement. You found yourself in the self-help section of Waterstone's last week, pulling a pale pink volume off the shelf. The next thing you knew the salesgirl was running it through the till, taking your card, asking you to check the amount and type in your PIN. Maybe you thought this would provide the key to recovery. Maybe you thought it would give you a step-by-step approach to grieving, a register delicate enough to describe the qualities of your grief. It wasn't much use. None of it rang true. None of it made sense. The words passed in front of your eyes and failed to describe your position. So you got rid of it – gave it away to the Oxfam on the heath. What were you thinking? That you could study death as if it was a pregnancy, or a carpentry course? That you could find the 'lost fraternal twin' chapter and make notes in the margin? That it would actually help?

You want to be helped. You want to experience your life. You want to feel yourself again; the owner not just of muscles, connective tissues, nerve endings and senses, but of a soul, and a familiar personality. You want to feel inhabited. In lieu of this you'll take any transaction: pain, discomfort, cold, upset – anything. You've been trying to jumpstart your atoms; shock them into life again. It's what they do in hospitals after all – the gelid paddles on the chest, and then lightning shot into the unresponsive core. You've pinched your skin red. You've skipped meals, whole days without food, until you are starving. Only then would you eat; blue cheese, raw fish: anything with a strong taste. You've begun to eat meat again after a decade of being vegetarian. You eat it rare, savouring the wet iron on your tongue. Venison. Liver. In the grocery store your eye lingers over the stocky red slabs, bound with rind, vacuum-packed in white trays. When you arrive home, there they are at the bottom of your shopping bag, weeping pinkly against the plastic pane.

You've tried to provoke emotion. You've said cruel things to people you know – Angela, your colleague at work, and your partner Nathan – as if wanting a fight. You've seen the startled looks on their faces. Their expressions turning to pity. They hug you, and apologise, as if responsible for your outburst, as if excusing your behaviour. *You're hurting, aren't you,* they say. *You're missing him.*

You were offered time off from the gallery after the accident, which was kind of Angela, but you haven't taken it. Instead you've been erratic, not turning up, or giving short notice for impromptu trips back up north. And you've let your photography slide too: lucrative commissions remain unfinished, your Leica and the pricey digital sit in the kit bag in the spare room; you've lost money on the unused studio, and your films are tucked away at the back of the refrigerator behind the butter and bacon. There is enough art-world gossip for people to know what has occurred to your family, for them to extend consideration. Recently, Nathan told you that you'd woken up in the night crying, and hitting him, but you didn't remember doing it. The patience granted in the wake of Danny's death has been nothing if not remarkable.

You don't deserve it. You've behaved worse than this. You've found that there is something that can make you feel, and make you feel present: sex. Not the routine, dusk-and-dawn sex of a trusted, established relationship, but illicit, dangerous sex. Sex that is novel and leaves you sore; that is experienced in the gaps between your mundane, moral life; that is strange and breathless and addictive.

You have been seeing someone else. You've discovered this man is capable of creating that hot primary yearning from the cervix down. There have been several indiscretions to date. You want there to be more. You want the skin and the smell and the taste and the movement of him. His beautiful mouth, his top lip shaped like a bird in flight. The anise of his fluids. Him made hard and pushed inside you. You understand the risks, the damages, but they seem irrelevant. This is right for you; he lets you remember what it is to be human.

You and your partner Nathan have been together for six years. There are days you are sure you love him, and days you are indifferent towards him. Oddly, the moments of desire you have experienced with this other man are the moments in which you feel the most tenderness and compassion towards Nathan. As if only by hurting him do you make him relevant.

He loves you. He has not stopped loving you since you first got together. In the last few weeks he's been trying gently to manage you, trying to corral your grief, and provide support. He speaks quietly, as if not to spook you. He calls you regularly throughout the day, brings home flowers, cleans the house, cooks. He has not pushed you on any of the issues that must seem alarming to him as an informed observer. The meat-eating. The bitchery. The hours spent at the gallery in the evening when you should be home. The times you've gone running so hard on the heath you've made yourself vomit. He's worried, of course he is, about your health, your state of mind, the way your brother's accident has stripped you of your usual spirit. He's worried about the disappearance of the woman he knows. He doesn't say, *Darling, why don't you see someone about being depressed,* or, *Really, you should finish the work for the Trust,* or, *Susan, please come back to me.* Nor does he cry in front of you, though you know he loved your brother too, and misses the times they stayed up late drinking whisky and playing cards, or watching Bond reruns, the times they biked the trails, or walked either side of you up the fells. He has not unpacked his grief.

You exist just outside the life you have with Nathan. It isn't your life any more. Within is the choreography of eating and sleeping and paying bills, the mechanics of being together in a relationship, which has nothing to do with who you are. The man you live with is a kind stranger.

If Danny were told about all this, if by some miraculous paradox Danny could be drawn from the dark ether into which he has been vented and rearranged around his old anatomy and then told about your response to his death, he would get it. He would smile in that broad, puerile way of his, or laugh, or put his arm around you and say, *Lighthouse extinguished, Captain. The rocks! The rocks!* or something equally endearing and childish. The awful irony is that he'd be the one person to truly sympathise. By which you don't mean just accept poor old you, having it hard, missing him and messing up your life. No. Danny would have an exact perspective, a clear understanding of how it is to *be* you. If Danny were alive, he wouldn't need to be told what was wrong. He would simply know. Your little brother was cleverer than anyone gave him credit for. He didn't exhibit those unhealthy verbal symptoms or throw fits about swapping milk beakers. He didn't have to see Dr Dixon for any sessions. He was the quiet one, the dummy, 'the secondary'; in a way, he held all the power.

It's hard to explain this connection. Kids at school would ask you to read each other's minds. *What's Danny thinking, Suze? What colour are your sister's knickers, Dando? Woooh, can you levitate this pencil case between you? Can you feel her bits?* As if the two of you were holding private séances.

Maybe it's best described like this. You have always liked fire. In the cottage where you were brought up you were the one who kept watch over the hearth, clearing the grate in the morning, stoking the coals before dinner, and smooring the embers at night. You hated anyone else poking it, which your dad often did, as dads often do. He would tell you off as a kid for building the fire too high, being wasteful with the wood and coal, which he had to shovel, chop and stack. *You'll start a chimney blaze and kipper me paintings, Suze!* You weren't a pyromaniac; it wasn't about the thrill of conjuring up that thin, vigorous spirit and unleashing its ravenous appetite. It was the history you'd had with it.

You were never afraid, not since the moment you crawled over to the pretty sparking hearth when the guard was down, put one chubby fist in towards the flames and removed a burning stick by its un-charred end. You were still holding it a minute later when your mum arrived and dropped her washing basket. *Oh poppet, poppet, be careful*, she said, walking with soft haste towards you. As your head turned towards her the torch drooped and touched your leg. Then you understood what that red synaptic bloom was. It was pain, seen. It was how pain looked outside the body. There's still a scar, silky and white, like a spider's nest, above your kneecap.

It was your brother who cried the loudest and made the most fuss though. He squalled and wrung out his eyes in the next room, blind to the events but no less invested in the trauma. *Bur bur bur,* he yelled. *Suzeeeee.* He screamed and bawled and rubbed the wound until your mum went to him, lifted him up, and doused his knee with cold water. That was the first time there was clear evidence.

Afterwards, Danny was nervous. Any time a spark cracked in the fire and missiled out on to the rug, or later when a hot rock fell from a joint into his lap, he would stamp and flap and batter until the tiny smut went out. In contrast, you picked shooters up between your thumb and forefinger and flicked them back over the grate. At teenage parties you would pass your hand through a candle flame at the exact possible slowness for it not to burn you, while Danny panicked and clattered the wax stem to the floor. He was anxious, but giddy around fire. He loved it when you lit the whin bushes on the moor, or made bonfires, or held a lighter to the straw scarecrow belonging to the farm next door. He liked watching you lay fires in the cottage, aiding the draw with a sheet of newspaper, the orange eye brightening behind the events of the world. When the newsprint turned brown and flamed to life, you punched the paper up the chimney, and Danny blinked and blinked, and left the room, and then came back in.

Now he is gone, and you are here, trying to find yourself in the mess, trying to locate the intimate filaments of which you are comprised. So that from this chaos order is achieved. So that you might be restored. To summarise: you are, or were, a twin. You like fire, veal, the seagull-shaped mouth of the man you are fucking when it dips below your navel and preens in the emulsion of you. You don't find comfort in books. Your name is known in the art world, because you are relatively talented, and because you are your father's daughter. You have your mother's teeth, her black and topaz moles. You were the embryo on the left side of her uterus, the embryo fate was kind to. Your brother rode his mountain bike the wrong way up the motorway one night and was killed. You are alive, somehow, continuing to pulse, continuing to breathe.

Translated from the Bottle Journals

Theresa has brought a fine array of mushrooms this week and, as a special gift from her husband, Giancarlo, two good-sized truffles, which she has grated on to her omelettes. Their little dog has had a busy season in the forest so far. I was invited to the morning gatherings, but it has been impossible. My chest is suffering in the colder air and last year's cough has returned with renewed vigour. Soon I will need to use the oil heater in the studio. I miss such excursions. I've always enjoyed the muttering of the forest as it prepares to disrobe, and the smell of the old earth being turned when the dogs begin to dig.

The olive groves on the slopes have almost finished preparing their fruit. I can see the leaves fluttering – dark green, light green and silver. Soon they will be stringing the nets. Perhaps I might have gone with Giancarlo and the others. I should make an effort not to become sedentary. There is a paralysis of the mind that accompanies immobility. I have seen it in friends and colleagues; intellectuals who were once fierce and deft of thought, who later became lost in conversation and fixated on small, unimportant details or phantoms in the air before them. I fear this above all else. I find cigarettes to be the most useful tools for concentration, but in this matter there are arguments with Theresa. She would prefer that I took her breakfasts instead of smoking cigarettes. She believes passionately in their ill effect and is attempting to banish them from Serra Partucci. I have noticed of late the lady of this household is becoming disinclined to produce them from her shopping basket. Often she swears she has no knowledge of any new packet or any request for a new packet. She will hoist the shopping list into the air like a flag of victory and wave it in the face of her old ward.

It is played like a comedy, so familiar that I can step to the side and watch the performance. Giorgio puts out his finger. He is belligerent. He demands exactly the same amount of soft tobaccos each week, he says. He has his wits and would not forget to request such an essential. Then he snatches the list from Theresa's hand and strikes each item off the inventory as he finds it present on the kitchen table while she stands defiant, her arms crossed. There are no cigarettes, she says. Then it is not accurately taken dictation, he protests. It is slovenly! It is sabotage! How dare he call her slovenly, she cries; she is a woman of high virtue and cleanliness. And so, stalemate. The old man tries another tactic. He has depended on cigarettes for fifty years, to work, he says, and he has a certain image to uphold. When visitors arrive they expect to see their artist stooped in his winter overcoat, with his decrepit iron spectacles, and an eternal cigarette in his hand. They must not be disappointed. Such are his weaker arguments.

Eventually the tyrant Theresa relinquishes. The carton is ingeniously camouflaged behind her apron. Giorgio smokes in the terrible silence. He grinds out the stubs with extravagant force. Later, to make her begin speaking to him again, he engages her on inappropriate topics of conversation, such as the propaganda-filled newspaper her husband reads, her son's military service, the joys of the changing season, and her routing of the lizards. All she wishes to do is to proceed with her domestic duties in peace, if he pleases. He slinks away to the studio.

In autumn, the lizards all wear attractive green cowls. They take warmth from any warm surface, finding refuge from the bristles and the broom handle in the grooves of the shutters. Make room for me, little friends! Have mercy, Theresa, on such habitual creatures as us! Theresa and I are engaged in a masquerade – this is very obvious. The argument is not over cigarettes. There is occasional blood in my mouth from coughing. Theresa wishes for me to see the doctor. It is not a seasonal complaint, she insists. I suspect she has noticed the warnings they are currently printing on the packets and she is alarmed.

In the morning after listening to the wind kindling the daylight I listen to the radio. I enjoy new music and operatic. I remain interested in national events, the debates about divorce. The voices reporting are dyspeptic – the world can be a terribly bitter thing to swallow. We remain divided on many issues. There is still shame; until we are united it will never pass.

Many of the day's tasks can be done accompanied by the sounds of the radio. Reading. These journal entries. Letters to the bank, to Antonio, or a reply to an inquiry. I have been listening while putting glass tunnels over the basil – the radio casing is set on the windowsill and the dials adjusted. Sometimes I hear words coming from the radio when it is switched off, but it is only Theresa scolding the lizards for defying gravity on the ceiling where her broom cannot reach, or scolding her elderly ward dozing in an armchair for his tendency to leave the rind of the cheese in the drawer belonging to the cutlery. When I am in the studio I listen to the sporting events.

Though I have not felt inclined to join the truffle dogs at daybreak in the woods, I have been to the school this week. I should note that I was deceived into teaching there and I am now hostage to it. The mistress of the establishment invited me to lecture her class one Thursday last spring, and when I arrived she sent me home saying too many of the children were absent with colds. The following week I came again and she sent me away again for another reason, which I have forgotten; perhaps it was a holiday. She insisted we should try once more. On the third week I arrived earlier than any pied piper and I taught drafting and anatomy. By then I was used to the walk into town and the children enjoyed the lesson and Signora Russo asked me to tutor on Thursdays. I tried once to cancel the teaching and she became very annoyed and said duty and social contribution were essential for those in professions such as mine. I should consider the inheritance of our country and I should guide its young minds in beneficial directions. The economic miracle is oblivious both to our school system and to the arts, she said. She knows something of my relationship to the old government I think, and that I taught at the Academy, and the reasons I have extracted myself. She is versed in the country's history, as we all are, and has, no doubt, strong opinions. We have not had the opportunity to discuss this at length. I suspect, like much of the population here, she is Communist.

I do not begin the class until I have recited all the names of all the children to myself. They sit in alphabetical order, which is convenient. When they are concentrating they are very quiet and it is a briefly peaceful time for me. Their drawings are wonderful. Children have no conscious knowledge of talent until informed of it by adults and they will suffer no intimidation until then. Sometimes the mothers come to the school gates to collect their children. They look at the images and ask why they have sketched the root of a tree or a small stone, rather than painting family portraits and little Davids, and I say to them, in this class it is pertinent to select such material, and I send them away.

There is a young girl in the class who has a congenital disease of the eyes. Her spectacles have a prescription even stronger than mine, and they pinch red marks on to the bridge of her nose. She finds it difficult to read. It is anticipated that by adulthood she will be blind, but she does not seem to be afraid. Her left eye is the worst, wasted to half the size of the right through its white aspect, with the lid often closing of its own accord.

We will never truly realise what blessings we receive along with our losses. Annette has a gift for discovering invisible things. If positioned in front of flowers she can detect borders and colours very well. She makes compartments and then fuses forms back together. She is a true Impressionist. Her natural medium is watercolour. I find in her work the most observant understanding – it has taken me over sixty years to acquire such skill. It is as if she has been freed from the convention of what exists only to seek it out with more integrity. The children are not unkind to her. She will not waste a single visible day. What can we hope for but this? Annette's white peonies at rest in a vase. The white scent ends where the white page begins.

Peter has written to me again asking about the substance of shadows. A shadow can be one of two themes for a whole year in the Academy. He tells me he has been painting along the north-east coast where he is visiting his sick father and it is very cold. Peter imagines the rocks on the beaches have personalities. There is character in their detail, he says. Something peers out at him from within their forms. He wears gloves to paint. When the tide comes in he can hardly bend his fingers and wonders if the damp English air will one day give his joints arthritis. I should inform him that when he reaches my age it is certain to arrive regardless of the patriotism of the weathers.

Again his letter searches for clues. He has found a copy of *La Voce* in the university bookshop and he quotes Soffici: 'It is through still-life that one can establish the true essence of what painting is all about.' My friend, Ardengo Soffici, who I have not thought about for such a long time! I imagine Peter reaching out his cold hands. He reaches so much further than those who might more easily come here, to this hill, to this realm of discussion – those who catch trains from the capital, those who come to ask about my bottles and those who telephone Antonio at the agency in Bologna to ask about my health. From the distance of another country, from an old magazine with deep folds, which has no doubt been passed between many hands, his curiosity arrives.

Peter is accused among his peers of a disconnection from the modern world. He is warned of being labelled out of date. My friend, how well I know this charge! Even after all these years such notions are put to me. Is production of the still-life merely the ventilation of a dying genre? Is this lyricism and formality now redundant? Elsewhere artists swing paint cans tied to their hearts, people tell me, and these are expressions of the unbound spirit. I was told this again by the young journalist last week, as if I were a man in a cave kept in darkness. Of course, I said to him, it's like the incense swung by priests. This is neither a riddle nor an invention.

This is the age of abstraction and the split atom. And yet, as Peter writes, the infinite shoreline is so much greater than the reactors. He suggests that if I pass a hand over his letter I might feel the cold of the northern sea and that I too should wear gloves. Perhaps he is a fan of the 'marvellous reality'! In his spare time he is studying Fra Angelico and he hopes one day to walk the pilgrim paths in homage. He is saving money to visit Italy. He is working at night cleaning the stalls of the philharmonic orchestra. I imagine him standing against a great ocean, like the monk by the sea. I imagine his rock portraits. Bravo, Peter. Bravo!

I have collected each edition of *La Voce* that survives. The publication existed for less than a decade with only one thousand to each print run, but its influence has been wide. Like so many birds, its ideas have migrated to every corner of the globe. The theories of those brave editors have opened many minds. To be free of spite in such a century of hostility! To have unveiled eyes and no vendetta! To be radical and respectful, to know history and yet embrace the definite future! There is no comparable forum now. There are no independent voices and there is no comprehensive inquiry and it saddens me. The demagogues and the elitists prevail. It is as if we do not want to understand art, nor will we protect its integrity. Those editors were the finest thinkers, and perhaps the best men, of my generation. Some of the copies lie in tatters, their pages rubbed away from the thumbing and the words faded.

That which is radical is often that which is formal. Even the sea has its tides.

Today I have rearranged the objects on the table. Antonio will like the different symmetry I think – he will be surprised by my choice. The light in the afternoons has been good. If I finish a new painting before the snow comes perhaps I will spend some time in Bologna with Antonio. The truth is that winter here is particularly unkind to the old, but a long time has passed since I last travelled. Now there are unified passenger cars and the trains pass by at two hundred kilometres an hour. The Fascist emblems are gone. I could take my suitcase on the ferry to Sardinia or arrange rooms in the Vatican City. I have read that in Rome Howard Hughes keeps an aeroplane in a hangar, always fuelled. I suppose I could leave, and see some more of my country. It has been years since I attended the

Biennale and I have a liking for the salty fish of the Adriatic, which are pressed in oil beneath heavy stones until they become tender and the bones can be cleanly pulled. It is not Lent but Theresa might ask the market vendor if our fast trains have brought anything from the clear green waters of the Dalmatian. Then she might bake a flat corn bread on which they can be served.

The Fool on the Hill

Lydia is baking when he gets back from his run. He can see her through the open window, sifting clouds of flour. Her hair is caught up in a loose bun at her neck, which looks nesty and sparrow-built. Her elbows are patched with white powder and a white handprint sits above her rump on the brown twill of her skirt. Who is that lovely lady, he wonders. Who is she and what is she doing in this house? There is music coming from upstairs – one of the kids has the stereo booming and Lydia is sashaying a little as she works. 'Free from the filth and the scum . . .' There are moments when he catches a glimpse of her and she is not the woman who has given birth to their children. She is not the woman who squeezes the remaining toothpaste to the top of the toothpaste tube so it is gathered conveniently at the nozzle for him to use. She is not the woman who digs the vegetable patch over with a hoe, and takes punnets of redcurrants to the market. She is unknown, this apparition floating amid the bakery dust. She is the girl on the grass by the priory that he once lay down next to, all those years ago. Someone who revealed the workings of the hinterworld to him.

Light-headed, he needs to eat something. He's dragged the old bones ten miles – the whole loop of the valley – on a fag and an espresso, and feels like he's running on fumes now. His legs are brittle, knees like rusty hinges. It's not good enough, mister, says the voice in his head. Used to be able to do it nay bother. Then do it again. Howay, Peter.

He hefts his leg on to the window ledge, stretches the tendon, and peers into the cottage. Definitely some strange vapour in his noggin. There's river-life inside the house. Look, there. A dark scarf on the windowsill like an otter's pelt – did it move just then, did it stroke a whisker, flex a paw? There are sparks behind his eyes. The woman inside is waving a ghostly white hand. Hello, husband. Welcome to your disassociated reality.

Lydia bustles outside, tells him to take off his filthy trainers; in fact gets him to strip completely naked at the front door before he can come in. She disposes of the damp, splattered shorts in the corner, while he stands in the kitchen, red and steaming. 'Arts North West have rung again,' she says. 'They want to know if you're applying for a grant this year. If you are, the application's got to be in by Friday. It would be good to have your name, they say.' He huffs and tears a corner off the loaf on the table, chews through seeds and walnuts. 'Bugger them. Hey I tell you what though, Suze should go for it, shouldn't she? If she put in her portfolio? She'd bloody walk it.'

Lydia shakes her head, wobbling the fluffy bun. If there are any eggs tucked inside it they're in danger of rolling out and smashing on the flagstone floor. 'She won't qualify if she's in London. Peter! You've got mud, even in your beard.' He brushes breadcrumbs and dirt from his face and fills a glass of water at the sink. 'Well, it'll go to some winnety postgraduate who's painted a church floor with his girlfriend's tits then.' Lydia laughs, her head tipped all the way back. The eggs are safe. 'Go on. Get Danny out of the bath and go in yourself before you set like a clay pig. He's been in there an hour with his wacky baccy, steaming up the windows.' No, with my wacky baccy, Peter thinks; Two of Two's been raiding my stash again. Lydia puts a hand on his arm. 'I'm heading out. Yoga. Won't be too long. You should come – it'd be good for you. You're very

49

stiff.' She smiles with those two long incisors, dental pronouncements the twins share, and gives him a slap on his bare backside. 'Giss-giss then, pig.'

He goose-skins through the house. The cottage floor is even colder than the river ford. A pair of brown tights is hanging on the radiator: two dead moles on a fence. Danny's banged-up old steamer trunk at the bottom of the stairs looks like the cows' mossy drinking trough. The blue silk pincushion on the pile of mending: a waterbird. When he runs along the river it's always too fast to see kingfishers on the crooks of the branches. They flit away, turquoise, faster still.

In the bath, the mud on his shins slowly dissolves. His memories have started to do that too lately. Curse of breaking the half-century, he supposes. Unlike his formative years of coal dust and cod and library books, the spell in America is becoming worryingly erased. His early twenties – Susan and Dan's age now. Bloody hell. Where does the time go? Emigration. His first wife, Raymie. The transatlantic crossing – how many stops did it involve? London. Shannon. Gander. Boston. Music and bright times in Golden Gate Park. That insane army medical when he was drafted: a knock on the chest to test the heart, and please bend over, sir. And up into Canada to avoid reporting for duty. There are carefully edited notes about that period. There are yarns and inventions. Somewhere along the line the stories he's told have supplanted anything real. Sometimes he wonders, did any of it even happen? Was he even present?

There is a world. Who wrote that – was it Sartre?

Almost thirty years ago! The kids were enthralled as youngsters when he talked about San Francisco and Alphabet City. North Beach. Vesuvio. The Village. It was as if he'd been up the beanstalk and back down again, and true, he spun it that dark delighted way for them, exaggerating, ornamenting, giving it some welly. But he loved their wide and wonderful eyes. It was pure magic, the look on their faces – all Christmassy and open. He invented a whole treasury of fables just for them. It was over there he realised exactly why he should wear the artist's beret, because it was illegal not to if you were an artist, and they could throw you in jail. It was over there that he hung out with Brautigan, and things were pretty crazy, and the hippies came. Over there, he surfed in a tuxedo. Over there, he enjoyed the presentation, from the mayor himself, of a skeleton key to Frisco, which got him into the best joints, temples, and on to the ferries. He still had it in fact, here in his pocket (yes Suzie, coincidentally similar to the key for the cottage mortise). Over there, he drank absinthe, smoked opium, took excellent $5 acid (this one told a little later, after Danny had asked for poppers for his thirteenth birthday – 'I'm interested in getting out of body, Dad'). Over there he ate sea snake, mandrake, barbecued griffin wing, probably actually did without recognising it, those Chinese restaurants, ho-ho. San Francisco was psychedelic, man. New York, well it was just the bees' knees – literally – all the skyscrapers were built from giant insect parts, what, didn't they know!? They with their faces like open mouths, drinking his fantasies in. Those were the days!

Now Susan's been to visit these places with pals she made at college, to jewellery sales, Telegraph Hill and the Nuyorican café. She likes the New York dog-runs, she says, the égalitaire of canines. 'It's true democracy, Wilse, big ones taught to play with little ones.' A perverse dependence on therapists though, she says, scowling. The twang of touched nerves in his daughter. Should he feel guilty about that? Who knows. 'Hey, kiddo. If you were there in the sixties,' he tells her, 'you'd know. We were all into scrambling back then. Baby boomers have omelettes for brains.' Yeah, yeah, yeah Peter, the sixties, old hat, poor line. But you've got to keep justifying things. You've got to defend the imagination or the world goes under, of this he is sure. Meanwhile, the kids accept his blag now like they'd put up with a doddery relative's foibles; vowel glitches developed to cover the geriatric stutter, weepy drunkenness at weddings, the uncontrollable passing of gas.

He twitches the hot tap with a hairy big toe. Warm water streams in around his heels and the bathroom fills with humidity. He balances the bar of soap on his belly.

It's unravelled in their minds now, his exuberant, figmented past. It's been investigated, confronted, and vetoed. It's just shite, fertiliser for their cynicism to grow. 'You couldn't have been at The Six Gallery in fifty-five, Dad. You were only fifteen.' They believe none of it any more, not even the actual actualities. Oh! The pair of them! When did the growing-up happen! He only had his eye off them for a minute. It seems like yesterday they were in nappies, twittering on in that peculiar talk of theirs. They were both so pale as children that he could see through to the red scribble of capillaries in their cheeks and in their ankles. He could see absolutely how they were made, the remarkable pattern of cells. He would hold their bare, doughy feet as they slept in their cots and stare. Or he'd nuzzle up to their faces and examine the threads in their cheeks. 'Let them sleep,' Lydia would whisper from the nursery door. 'They're tired little things. Come and pour me a damson gin while I'm on boob reprieve.'

He never mentioned this fascination to anyone, not even Lyds, but it did occur to him there must be secret infant fascinations the world over. As they got older and ran about outside in the sun, their skin grew thicker, becoming less transparent. The bright alveoli patches disappeared. It made him sad really. There was something in the private display he had loved. He would peer at Susan's ankles all through her teenage years, until she got fed up with it and demanded he stop, saying that he was being a weirdo.

And there's the gist of it. All innocent mechanisms are muddied up with experience. Children become less and less translucent. Layers of guile and suspicion grow. It's the law of paternal disenchantments.

The fact is he can't exactly remember his legacy, can't entirely defend himself, and say, as a matter of fact, O petty disbelievers, O ye of bolshy attitude, I am telling the absolute truth. He has contaminated the water supply with piddle, so to speak. The Big Bumper Book of Peter's Life and Times is a white-paged, ad-libbed tome. But he does recall, with some clarity, the hot gothic stoops in the Village, the cooking summer steps against which they lolled, and the desperation for an old brass rotary fan found in somebody else's trash, saved and re-wired. In winter, the obverse, the necessity for several jumpers, apartments too cold even to piss in, and hot dumplings gobbled down at Vaselka to make them thaw. If he concentrates, he can remember the extraordinary districts of San Francisco. The Asian tattoo parlours. The views. Rivera's frescoes. He remembers the feeling of anti-climax when everything began to fade, when life began to look too real again.

And he can remember her. He can remember her long slim American legs. Her astonishingly clear eyes and her awful bloody temper. Her never going without a high for more than a day. The depressions that tasted nothing like apple pie, that tasted lysergic, like chemicals dripped on to paper. The clever Latin ink on her inner thigh: *Believe Not What You See*. This is what he's come away with, what he's managed to stash in the chaotic archives of the brain. It's not very pleasant, wouldn't be fun conveying it to anyone, the way the phantom friendship with Ginsberg is – that myth founded on a collision at a party and a brief exchange through untrimmed beards.

Raymie had legs like the spindles of the water towers, and she also was bursting with moisture; this he elliptically knows. But there are few cherished recollections.

Do his peers have the capacity to recall their former lives better than he can? Do they see fragments in the necklines of actresses in films, or find themselves wafted back by cheese or sandalwood smells? Is everyone in his generation taking gingko biloba, doing brain aerobics and writing pompous memoirs? Or are they all crumbling mentally, having heart attacks while shopping for tweed jackets, or banging their secretaries, or emptying their colostomies? Dear God, are they officially old?

What he needs is a smoke.

Beneath him the bathwater is turning tea-coloured, his balls float white and wrinkled in the stew. The room smells half of soap, half of Danny's pilfered ganja – he knows the good stuff when he sees it, does Master Caldicutt, wants none of the muck coming in from Spain these days. He'd reach for it himself while the rest of his filth slurries up the tub but the pouch is in his studio upstairs. Forgot to fetch it before getting in. Ho-hum. Pass the bloody gingko.

Yes. He remembers Raymie. Bleeding from her nostrils as if she would never stop. Narcotic pioneer, showing them all how it was done. Holding forth about post-modern art and the inauthentic project of being. Being thinner and more beautiful than all the other girls. Climbing the railing of the Empire State Building, her pale hand fluttering like a bird in the uproar. He remembers that night, before they bailed out of college, before they left merry old England for her home turf. The horrible *ménage à trois*. Him, their tutor, and her. The cuckold, the muse, and her new lover. Their bizarre agreement to share a human experience of loss and love and urges, to signal an end and a future between them. So he had to watch. He had to uncouple his primitive urge to smash in their skulls as she turned around on to all fours. And the man he had loved and respected like a father whispered to Peter, 'There, I've warmed the pearls for you, you bastard,' as he slid off the bed and left the room. Free love. More like a fucking disaster. There are some memories that won't leave, no matter how hard he coaxes them.

The mirror has disappeared under steam so a beard trim is out of the question. He'll just have to be a woolly old man for a while longer – wild man of the moors. He looks at his leg hairs swaying in the bath's current, like the manes of the fell ponies in the wind at the top of the valley. His cock hairs are turning grey, like the strands of fireweed caught in the elm trees in the garth. Crab ladder. Hernia scar. Patch of rabbit-skin glue. He twists the plug chain round his toe and lifts. The muddy drink begins to gurgle away. Jesus Christ, there were some casualties! Poor Brautigan. The man literally set the muzzle of the gun against his temple and blew his brains out.

The Divine Vision of Annette Tambroni

A tourist has become trapped under the flower stall for the duration of the storm. 'Hello', Annette says to her. 'Hello. The weather is bad. It is raining.' The woman is German. She has a phrasebook. Perhaps she is making a tour of Piero and Fiorentino. Perhaps she is seeing the ruins or the misericords. She has been separated from her travel companions – they have all ducked into cafés and under awnings, or they have gone into San Lorenzo to see the unusual altarpiece. The woman makes a selection – irises, freesias, and two roses. It is a hasty transaction – clearly she feels she is obliged to pay for being kept dry. 'Can you be able to make them?' she asks. She has noticed Annette's tilted face, her lost eyes. Annette smiles. She positions the flowers in complementary order, sorting through the leaves, pinching each stalk, and stacking the bouquet upwards, almost weightlessly.

'Can you see my colours?' the woman asks. 'Is the smell?' She is intrigued. Annette smiles again, and nods politely. She could tell the woman that the white iris of the Florentine has a scent identical to the violet. It is one of nature's comedic little duplicities, Uncle Marcello says. She pulls the thorns off the rose stems with a thumbnail so they will not prick the German woman when she carries them back to the rented apartment or the hotel. She fastens the arrangement inside a paper cone. The woman takes Annette's hand. Into her palm she presses three coins. 'That is true.'

It's easy for Annette to decipher the markings of currency.

She can run her fingertip across the franks and the corrugated edges, or weigh the coins, or Elemme might be called over to supervise the payment. But it is not necessary to make these checks. Even though her mother warns her some people will try to take advantage of her, even though at night her mother counts the money from Annette's soft purse, Annette trusts the customers. People seldom play tricks on the blind.

But the world of her mother's imagining is full of jeopardy. At home she tells Annette not to go further than the courtyard garden. On Sundays she is permitted to walk to the church, alone or with her brothers, and afterwards to the cimitero di campagna where her father is at rest, his photograph framed in the niche. At the market she must wait for Maurizio to collect her and dismantle the stall. She can purchase game or fish from the vendors who know her; she can go to the growing plots where her uncle works, with a new order or to assist with the transfer of seeds between mossy cases. Beyond this sanctioned territory, there are untold hazards. There are traps and snares, like the hidden rabbit wires on the hillside. If she is not careful she will trip, or burn herself, or snag her skirt on a piece of wood, a door handle, a buckle, or under someone's foot. She will become lost in the crowds, never to be found again. People will treat her with cruelty. They will corrupt her. There will be immorality.

Sometimes, as her mother braids Annette's hair, she issues warnings. 'Do you not see it? From a distance the boys will think you are attractive. They will whistle and flirt with you. Then when you come close they will see this,' she taps the bone around Annette's eyes, 'and they will laugh at you. There are so many other pretty girls. And I could not bear such cruelty against my daughter.' Her mother sighs. The braids are so tight that Annette feels the hairs breaking.

'In which ways might they find me attractive, Mamma?' she

asks. She has outgrown the last edition of herself she was able to see. Eleven years old, flat-chested, with spurs of bone at her elbows and ankles. Now she is older she has curves that she can feel with her hands. She has soft breasts, which are very sensitive, and silky little hairs. Inside she also feels different. Her mother will not answer such immodest questions. Instead she continues with her defence of the limitations she has imposed. 'In our home everything will always remain the same. Furniture will maintain its exact position – Marcello and the boys know better than to leave a chair out from the table. You can count the steps from the window to the cupboard and know there will always be this number of steps. Nothing will be rearranged. There. Doesn't that make you feel safe?'

She is no longer allowed to go to school. She has proved with her bruises and her laddered stockings that it is impossible for her to continue learning. And she is of an age now when others around her are beginning to wake from the sleep of innocence, her mother says. Her reputation might be insulted without her ever knowing it. 'Suppose you were to come home groped – how would we check? We would have to inspect you every night for marks, and take wire wool to you like a tarnished kettle.' Annette wonders whether Maurizio is patched and discoloured when he arrives home from the cinema after watching *The Sign of Satan*, or whether his eyes have turned black. She wonders whether his tongue becomes mottled when he talks about the heavy bosoms and long legs of the actresses, and when he dances with her in the kitchen singing, 'Sexy, sexy, yeah yeah, baby.'

If she protests, if she says that she would like to continue at school, or that she can still see the shapes of light and dark shadows, that she can hear traffic and can cross the street safely, her mother loses her temper. 'But you cannot read from the blackboard or even the pages pushed up in front of your nose, Annett-a! We have been through this! The doctors can do no more for you.' It is better for her to help with their family business. In this way she can be useful, and in this way protected. At the end of these discussions her mother takes hold of her hand and squeezes it hard. 'Listen to me. You don't know what is out there. You must resist succumbing to a wandering spirit, like that of the unfortunate Sicilians. Do you understand?'

Mauri often tells her that she is beautiful. He whispers to her across the table that she is the most beautiful girl outside of Paris. He kisses her cheek in the flower van, and when Annette asks Elemme if her cheek is black, Elemme says that it is not, and asks if Annette has been cooking squid or performing some other dirty occupation in the kitchen. The fish vendor and the butcher also call her pretty when she arrives for smoked eel and for pork. They often put aside the best cuts of meat for her family, or keep a handful of mussels on ice when they are delivered from the coast. At the fruit stall she presses fruit with a gentle thumb, smells the deep dimple at the stalk, or pulls out a leaf, and asks for a lower price if the fruit is not yet ripe. 'Yes. Of course. Anything for you, beautiful Annette.'

As she listens to the racket of the market she imagines the dark world beyond. Buses with no brakes to slow down for sightless, perambulating girls. Railings as sharp as pikes to skewer the skirts of the unsuspecting, or disembowel them like the spears of the Crusaders. And the notorious open drains, into which she could fall, and in which a breed of violent Southern men live – they who emigrated north twenty years ago and found it too cold to live above ground. But she cannot picture the immoral acts her mother suggests are happening on filthy beds in the dark rooms of apartments and in the bars, behaviour her older brother understands and can be forgiven for, but she cannot. And though she tries so hard, she cannot picture the face of the Bestia as he leers at her from the gateway of the summer theatre.

The day passes. The roses are bought and some are given to Father Mencaroni for the church. From the bakery ovens comes the smell of pastry. Annette asks Elemme to mind the stall for her. She eats a small baked crust. The Romany by the fountain gives her two long beans that have been strung with wire over his grill. Outside the high enclosure, she can hear the growl of traffic on the cobblestones, the zuzzing of mopeds, and the grumble of old farming carts as they judder and box their axle shafts. The pedestrian steps sunk into the Etruscan walls echo. A train rattles on its track as it arrives from the city. There are no screams. There are no alarms ringing, no calls of murder. There is no lewd breathing.

She returns to the flower stall and thanks Elemme for keeping watch over her trays of buttons and threads. 'I haven't seen your mother in a while,' says Elemme. 'Is she still unwell?' Annette inclines her head. 'Yes. Headaches. She gets them all the time.' Elemme says that she is sorry to hear this. 'But at least she has your brothers and your uncle to care for her, which is good.' 'Do you have brothers too?' Annette asks. 'I do. But they're in North Africa. They're unable to come here now. They are bullies but I really miss them. To have brothers is lucky. Especially such handsome ones as yours!'

Annette would like to ask Elemme about all the things she finds confusing, all the things she knows so little about and that have not ever been explained to her. Like the scenes cut out of the projector reels that Mauri complains about. Like the blossom she feels in her abdomen before it begins to ache every month. Once she asked Elemme if she had ever seen the Bestia, and Elemme laughed and said, yes, the night she got married. Annette asked what he was like. 'I can tell you that he was not gentle. He was quite wild in fact.' When Elemme said this she did not sound scared. It was like an amusement, and Annette wondered if perhaps in North Africa the Bestia was not the worst of all creatures. Whenever Annette asks Mauri about the Bestia he pulls her to the floor and says, 'It's me, it's me.' Then he growls like a dog and barks and pretends to be possessed by a demon. He digs her in the ribs and crushes her until she is breathless, or until their mother finds them and pulls Mauri off, slapping him and sending him out of the room.

Her mother will not be drawn on the subject – it is too upsetting. Her voice plunges into dark blue regions when she talks of it, like the reaches of water in the middle of the lake where no one swims. 'I don't know what he looks like, Annette! He looks like the most grotesque thing imaginable. A monster from hell! Your poor father,' she cries, 'he saw. He heard the flies swarming. He felt the red shadow falling over him. Why must you punish me with this question all the time?' She weeps and makes Annette promise not to let him take her away, not to make herself vulnerable or open herself to him.

Annette promises. She tries to picture this famous scene in the gardens, when her father died in the most terrible of circumstances, but the picture will not come. Uncle Marcello once let slip in an argument that there was also a woman present. Annette's mother became very upset, and said 'Never speak of that whore,' and Uncle Marcello tried to take her hand and comfort her, but her mother would not be touched. The mystery woman was not mentioned again. Annette wonders how her mother knew that her father heard flies swarming around the head of the Bestia when he died. He could not have told her so, because he was dead. Perhaps her mother was there in the gardens too. She says she was at home, feeling faint and asking God for forgiveness, as if she knew something terrible was occurring. By the time Uncle Marcello and the police arrived, the Bestia and the mysterious woman had disappeared, leaving only a pool of red evidence. Annette suspects that her mother has in fact seen the Bestia, and knows exactly what he looks like. The trauma was extreme and now she is simply too frightened to talk about it.

Annette wonders whether there is a strict tradition involved when it comes to the Bestia. She wonders whether other people hear flies and feel the red shadow before they die, or whether they hear and feel other things. Perhaps to some people the Bestia might, instead of flies buzzing, sound like Olivetti keys tapping, or a cat hissing, or a firework wailing into the sky. If they were expecting flies how would they know to run? How would they know to kneel and pray to be saved? It is a mystery.

The market begins to close. Behind her Maurizio steps up and hugs her fiercely. 'I've come back for you, even though you treat me with such contempt.' He puts his hands over her mouth. 'No, Mother, no one can hear you scream!' Elemme laughs and claps at the performance. Annette wriggles free. Her brother smells of musty potting soil and the vinegar solution with which he and Uncle Marcello have been dousing the greenfly.

The Mirror Crisis

Other than those strange six months with Dr Dixon and his creepy insects, your childhood was good. You liked being brought up where you were, in the border expanse. It was rural and difficult, and you felt hardy and capable because of that. You and Danny ran wild. The fells were on your doorstep, those brown and red massifs that your dad brought into his studio and undressed and made profitable. You swam in the rivers and waterfalls, made dens, climbed trees. You took over the tumbledown barns, swung off the beams, and reared yourselves among the bleating livestock. It was an exterior childhood, and you and Danny were exterior children. There were gales, floods, hardships, funerals; you were taught that this was nature, and you'd better respect it.

The north of your youth was practically pre-industrial. You are always amazed when you hear people's ideas about idylls and pleasure grounds, the myths of the sublime. Back then it was a landscape of filth loosened from fields, ringworm, walls of snow, and long, sickening bus rides to school. It was bad weather, burning carcasses, kids with disabilities, black-eye Fridays and badger baiting; collecting wood off the fell and trying to keep it dry under tarpaulin so the logs didn't fizzle with sap, hiss and blacken on the grate, because that was how you stayed warm. No Economy 7. No piped gas. Fowl were strung from hooks in the outbuildings by your parents' cottage. In another shed trout was smoked. The heating range, which was installed by your dad when you were fourteen to

63

run some radiators, was bought from a local farmer, a cut-and-shunt boiler, previously used to incinerate stillborn lambs. Your mother washed all the clothes by hand until that same year, when his paintings started bringing in good money, and a machine was bought and plumbed into the greasy, goose-hung bothy.

And when your best friend Nicki collapsed with an asthma attack on the moor, she was airlifted to Newcastle Infirmary by helicopter, after forty-five minutes of lying under a witch-hazel bush, her brain bluely solidifying. It was January. The black furrows were frozen and an earthy winter scent radiated from the ground. You ran back from the phone box along the road and wrapped Nicki in your coat and held her hand. It was the first and only time you've had to dial the emergency number. You waited for help, so insanely long, it seemed. Then the sky was ripped open by noise. You watched the Sea King buzz down through sleet, and you opened Nicki's mouth because the wind from the propeller blades seemed strong enough to re-inflate her lungs. The witch-hazel carried pale orange flowers on its bare twigs, the blossoms impossibly delicate in the storm of the landing.

And that was that for Nicki. Deep Indefinite Unconsciousness. Technically, she is still alive. Officially, she was lucky. They got to her just in time to scrape up off the hillside the last biological part of her life. It's not hard for you to associate the north with tragedy. Nicki. Danny. There's always half a truth to cliché.

You've been wondering lately when the moment is that somebody is truly lost to you. For example, when will Nicki's family finally give up hope and switch off the machines? She lies there, day after day, as she has for years, living by medical proxy, her hair glossy as conkers, electrically retrograde behind her skull. You still visit her when you are home. You've got used to it – being chatty and fey, nothing but the sound of your voice in the room and the soft flushing of the ventilator. You tell her what is going on in the world, wondering if she has any notion what year it is now. After the nurses leave her room, you ask her to wake up. There is never a response. You whisper down into her ear. It's like making a confession to the oblivious ground, or blowing across the top of an empty bottle.

Her sisters send you Christmas cards each year on her behalf – the secretarial custodians of Nicki's half-life. How could they know if a week after The Decision was made – after they had brushed her hair and changed her nightgown a last time, and told her *goodbye we love you darling girl* – that this was not the week she was due to sit up, finally, and ask what she got for her A level history, say she fancied a Rich Tea biscuit, and wonder if her boyfriend Andy had been in to see her. Only to find out the prick had married her younger cousin, a year after she went under.

The doctors measure her brain activity. From time to time there are electrical spikes, heat blooms. There's no way of knowing how aware she is, what she is hearing, what she is feeling. The doctors say the green flares might be dreams. They say: don't dismiss her existence in case she is trapped within herself. Her spirit rattling around mutely, like a pea in a dead whistle.

On your fifth date you told Nathan about Nicki, about what happened when you were teenagers. You were in a café on Betterton Street. There was a plate of cheese on the table in front of you, a basket of bread, two glasses of red wine. Downstairs there was a reading going on. Every few minutes you could hear thin choppy clapping, like the clapping at a village cricket match. His face fell. *I know it's sudden, but I love you, will you marry me?* It was as if it was you who had survived near-death in the winter snow, as if the true miracle was that you were sitting there eating cheese, and it was vital that he ask you.

He reached over and put his hands behind your neck, and in doing so caught a finger in your hair-band and pulled out your ponytail. It was an awkward moment. Your hair spilled forwards. He kissed you. You said nothing. There was silence for a while, then sporadic clapping. He has never asked again. He was hurt, you're sure. But you kept going out, regardless. You became comfortable, dependent, you enjoyed mutually satisfying sex. You cooked fresh pastas in the evenings, slept against each other's backs, holidayed abroad. Then you moved in together. You upgraded from two shared suburban houses with fox-skunked gardens to one stylish sky-lit conservation-area flat, right by the heath.

Here, you have domestic security. The mortgage goes out by standing order; sensibly you pay more than the interest every month. Laundry collects in a wicker hamper and is regularly washed. The floors are slick, dust-free; in the cupboard is one of those click-together devices to sweep, with detachable cloths that attract cobwebs like magic. Ladles and spoons live in the second down of four fitted pine drawers, below a sophisticated granite counter. Everything in the flat is ordered, utilised, pleasing. The second bedroom, with its expensive pro-photo lighting rig, umbrellas and snoots, serves as a small studio. The bathroom, a makeshift darkroom. You like to develop yourself, check temperatures, make timings; you're old-school. You still work with film whenever you can. You like the bursting shutter, the winding motor, the choice of lens. None of the equipment has recently been used.

There is a roll of film in the bottom-loading rangefinder, your first decent camera, which contains Danny. He is sitting on a bench in the train station, surrounded by pigeons, on his last visit to London.

Over the last few weeks you haven't been spending much time

at home. You've been at Borwood House organising the new exhibition, or out running on the heath. You've been going up north to see your mum and dad, to make sure they are managing OK. A few times you've gone into the city to meet your lover, in the bars in Soho, or by the lock. Once the two of you went to a club down a flight of stairs in Shoreditch with an entry fee and dark letterboxed rooms. Afterwards you fell upon each other in the church grounds nearby. A few times you've used a hotel. You let him undress you, and put pillows beneath your stomach. You watched the local movement of his hips and waist in the mirror opposite the bed. You were hurried and left your phone switched on. The ringing didn't stop you. Afterwards there were messages from Nathan, which you deleted.

In the beginning things were fine with Nathan, and you felt happy. You used him as a muse. You photographed him, exhibited the prints, exposed him to the scrutiny of the public. He was good-humoured, sat for you nude, let you manipulate his poses. His body was interesting; he wore his muscles tautly against his skin. You got right into the polished crevices, the brackish ghylls. He was the subject of your most acclaimed series of compositions, which was short-listed for a major prize, and widely reviewed. The press compared you to your father, talked about geo-portraiture. There was talk of fetishes. Reviewers wondered whether this was a response to the legacy of Peter Caldicutt, whether you were trying to be difficult and controversial.

Once, when you were shooting the series, you put Nathan in your best tie-top stockings. Agent Provocateur. The hairs of his legs broke through the black mesh and his muscles gave the material an interesting look. It excited you both, and you went to bed and didn't speak, but instead took turns doing whatever you wanted, with urgency and experiment. You tried it again a few more times, but the eroticism lessened, then failed, and you stopped.

The two of you are different now, calmer. There is still sex, occasionally, but it is no longer a priority to seduce or be seduced by him. You recognise him more as a housemate, a person who becomes gently furious at the news every night, a decent cook. All the powers you have for capriciousness, all the potency you wield – and you do wield it, with dark sedge eyes, good legs, the ability to turn male heads on entering a room, and talent – seem superfluous to the dynamic of the relationship now. You still bring him tea every morning, and comfort his headaches with paracetamol. You are generous with birthday presents. But there's no entitlement to your body any more, granted through arduous solicitation, an obvious hard-on when you undress. Now you wear your best lingerie to work, the silk dampening, the lace cuffs stiff under your dress. Your mind tracks to someone else when you touch yourself, and you think of that time in the churchyard, his mouth nuzzling against your soaked underwear, the desperate thrusts. At night sometimes the ache becomes unbearable. You leave the room where Nathan is sitting reading or watching television. *You OK, Suze?* he calls. To leave a room abruptly might still mean a sharp descent into sorrow. You say you're fine, just going to the bathroom. You lock the door; lean forward against the cold mirror. You feel down inside your bra, unfasten however many buttons on your jeans you need to.

The first time it happened was at Borwood House. You'd been thinking of Danny. You were downloading the certificates of objects that are being sent to the gallery for the new exhibition – the odd little artefacts that once belonged to the great twentieth-century painters and are somehow relevant to their legacies. Angela had just decided on a title for the show: *In the Artist's Shoes*. She had gone to buy you both coffees from the café on the heath to celebrate, and you were thinking about Danny, about the red trainers he always wore, like a man ten years younger, like a boy. He had multiple pairs. For a moment you thought about crying. You knew it would make you feel better, but the distance to the emotion seemed too far to travel.

Something came over you, a different impulse. You shut the laptop, stood up, and went to the snug room at the back of the gallery where Tom was making notes on the texts. The door was closed. You didn't knock. You opened it, and went inside. He was working as usual with the curtains drawn, in lamplight, bent over the documents on the table. You moved behind him, and stood there. Then you leaned over and kissed the back of his neck, just beneath his dark hairline. He made a soft-throated noise, and turned slightly. Perhaps he didn't see that it was you, perhaps he didn't smell your perfume. Perhaps he knew. But he did not recoil. Instead he reached up and held the back of your head so you wouldn't pull away. Then he stood up and drew you to him. You felt a rush of chemical gold overwhelm you, like something taken intravenously.

There was only the humidity of your mouths as you kissed. The excitement passed between you on your tongues. He put a hand round your neck and pulled back. *Where is she? She's not here?* You looked at his mouth, glazed from your own, his beautiful lips, with the tiny white scar on the membrane. He put a hand underneath your dress. *Non voglio fermarmi.*

You pushed him back on the desk, unzipped his trousers. He was hard, the skin smooth over the tightness. You kept him in your mouth even at the end when he tried to gain polite release before coming. It was easy. It was inexcusable.

Translated from the Bottle Journals

Much has been made of this studio of mine, which is also my bedroom. There is talk of rustication and asceticism, the robes of the profession. Really I am no monk. It is simply that I favour the light and the space in here and I need room to stretch the canvases. If I enjoy the company of a visitor, or Antonio wishes to see the recent productions, they are welcome inside. After all, it is not a closed sanctuary where rare species live, or shrouds are kept. It is simply a room of manufacture and of rest. Theresa is permitted to clean only the sleeping quarter, so a line of dust several decades thick now exists between my bed and the work area. My footprints of dust in the rest of the house are a constant source of irritation to her. But I can always be found for you to scold me, I say to her – you can trap me like a wolf sneaking in from the Balkans. We do not always see eye to eye, but Theresa has never attempted to clean further into the room. She is an honest woman and has a respect for this occupation, and this is all that I require.

Theresa's father, Corrado, was a carpenter and my dear friend for many years. I called him Graffio. He provided wood for the frames and the long trestles in the studio. He was a man always surrounded by shavings and chippings and he was deeply contented in his vocation. Little blond curls were always in his hair and on his clothing. He was also a skilled guitar maker and a very good player. To be in his presence was very fine, like opening a cedar box for a cigar. Often we would take a glass of limoncello into his workshop at the end the day while the resin dried. The fragrance of timber is beautifully stimulating, as if the sanguine humour of nature is released when the cord is cut open. When Graffio died there was no one left of my old friends with whom to listen to the football or sit in the shade of the square. Though the family has often invited me to eat with them during Festa de l'Unità, I have not imposed myself upon them as I did when he was alive.

It still surprises me the attention paid to this bare and simple room. To sleep with one's working medium is not so unusual – the apprentices of the Renaissance often had no choice. But the head of an artist is always occupied by his craft, no matter where he sleeps. There is nothing extraordinary to speak of in here – I am not a collector of the macabre. There are three trestles of varying heights. The objects are kept underneath until called into duty. Sometimes the bottles seem to be huddled, like ceramic flocks sheltering from a storm, and I think of the old shepherds with their herds, moving like the shadows of clouds across the hills. I have not counted them but by now there must be about one hundred. Together they seem plain, like a chorus, but singly they are, of course, unique.

The tables are covered in rolls of brown paper bought from the postal union. I also use an unbleached linen screen behind the tables to mask their physical context. I admire the polished woods of the Dutch but I have no desire to reproduce them. The ceiling light has been here longer than I and I am in no position to remove it, but it is dismal to work with it lit, like being in the interrogation room. Our tremors, which unscrew sconces and ruin walls without discrimination, have not seen fit to remove the old chandelier. Sadly the cracks in the wall do not extend that far. There are some forms of light that do more harm than good. It is of interest, but ultimately of little importance, to know the work shifts of artists. It should simply be said that we are all governed by the sun. The writer might opt to be nocturnal – he with his dark pupils and his head full of owls. It is supposed that the sinister quality of paraffin lamps was reproduced exactly as it was in the old night surgeries, illuminating the grey sinews, but by the application of paint the artist is a magician of light.

The room has gained infamy with very little help from me. It is discussed and photographed. It is given unique status because it contains the future as undoubtedly as it does the past. The bottles are also painted, and into some I have poured coloured pigments. In this way they lose identification and gain a sense of the modern. Dust also dresses them, lying thickly on their rims and shoulders. Over the years they have travelled in many coats.

I am asked so often about them that I forget to be patient. They are an enigma, which lies beyond me, and is used by others to illustrate matters of superior concern: the health of our great arts, the political currents. These bottles are the cast-aways of this world. They have no value or purpose and they have no genre, but are simply the architecture of the visual world, its daily experience. Some see in them cities. Some see icons. They have been recovered from cellars and attics, from refuse sites and the markets of Europe. The tallest blue one was found in the ruined farmhouse at Via Lame, in a cracked sink, and there was no hope for it other than to collect drips. A hornet's nest was woven on to the gable above the sink where my father once leant the handle of a flail and spat out feathers and dirt. Another two, formerly white, are inscribed and originate from Persia. In addition there are decanters and jugs, coffee pots, latte bowls, vases, canisters, Bleriot's oil pitcher, and so forth. Nautili, boxes. But it is the bottles which infuriate; it is the bottles which invite endless speculation. Recently I have felt compelled to give some away as gifts.

Theresa can sometimes be found looking at the studio tables from the room's dusty meridian. After her chores she has been known to loiter. Her stance is the stance of a woman preparing to take the sacrament, rather than a woman standing behind the silk cordon of a museum. What are her thoughts about my bottles? What does she see in them? Though I know she considers herself inferior, I believe her country pragmatism might outweigh the convolutions of the academics. She stands at a distance with her hands clasped. I would like to ask her. Has she ever seen a sarcophagus or the masterpieces? Has she gone into the basilicas of the region without her prayer book, simply to observe the frescoes? Has she taken the bus to Monterchi to pray for the safe births of her grandchildren beneath the partitioned Madonna? And has she realised all the angels of Piero wear his own voluptuous mouth?

There is no embargo, I say to her, please approach further if you wish. Then she is startled and will not discuss her thoughts but retrieves her basket and locates her bicycle, and down the hill she goes.

So it is left to others to conclude that I am relativist, existentialist, totalitist, making of course good titles in the magazines and establishing bold reputations for themselves. The critics insist on labels. They put forward ideas of Fascism and Constructivism and now also ideas of the East. I try not to be impolite, but it is necessary to discredit such notions. There is much false association to overcome. There is still talk of Il Duce and collaboration, regardless of the tragedy, or perhaps because of it.

Wars do not end with flags and liberation, nor does aggrieved blood settle in the generations counted on one hand. Art is not of an administration simply because it is bought and hung in its corridors. The supreme leaders may extol the virtues of nationalism and instruct us in artistic loyalty, but the independence of the imagination prevails. I cannot account for the consciences and proclivities of my old acquaintances. I have no desire to defend my own early affiliation and belief in the system. But I know this: zealots beget zealots. Ultimately Fascism was the enemy of the still-life. It dismissed the grottoes and the dogs and the wild game of xenia, and became the despotic patron of the figurative. The ignorant Cinti would have made Botticelli imitators of us all had we not smuggled into Italy the inferior genre, had not the sympathy of a few brave admirers prevailed.

Once, several years ago, a commission came to me from a wealthy patron. He requested a display of instruments to celebrate his family of musicians. He provided me with an excellent lyre for the composition – its curves were two hundred years old and it was immensely beautiful. He received in return a painting containing a trumpet from the market with an injured bell and missing valve, having fallen from its case before it arrived at the stall. He accepted it graciously and there was no penalty.

I won no public commission early in my career. Then I was not among the favoured. I have worked despite every establishment and have known obstacles and ridicule before any favour. The names of those loyal individuals remain private and I will not exhibit them if they wish to remain so. How easy it would be to show my inquisitors the marked register I have kept all these years when they accuse me of deception, when they accuse me of emerging ennobled from extremis. How easy it would be to say to them: do you see whose name is printed here, do you know who this is, now, please tell me again about Mussolini. Yet so too are there names for whom the heavy boots might still come with papers for arrest. It is a paradox. These young journalists do not understand this country's past. They broker factions, and they stir trouble, when we are already divided enough. Perhaps instead they should be setting Canario dogs in the pits.

They are as eager to mythologise this life. The retention. The reclusion. The obsession with position and form, creating and recreating. I was born in the last century. The days pass by and I am able and I am working – surely this is enough? The Salon of the Refused is long gone, I tell them, now we are all equal in our failures and successes, and without ceremony. They are not practitioners. They do not know the ingredients of tempera, nor the touch of a miniver brush against the finger.

In the pages of the journals I appear as another man, a man of uniforms and suspicions and oblique messages. I do not recognise this creation of theirs. He is not even a distant cousin. Antonio does not censor the clippings, and for this I am grateful, even as I am filled with dread. This week I have read that I am an untrained draughtsman who cannot draw a chair or the levelled horizon. I, who took the Academy medal for *ornato*, with distinction, with excellence!

Such accusations trouble the heart and leave me tired. Let them write what they will. Tomorrow when we wake the sun will amaze us all with its industry. Theresa will beat flat strips of the boar which Giancarlo has shot and hung. She will stir orange flowers into her salad. She will stand before the invisible rope in the studio and wonder which footprints in the dust lead towards the real bottles and which lead towards duplicity. She will come no closer to guessing, and neither will I.

The indifference of dust as it covers each cornice of glass. Yes! Give me the indifference of dust!

The Fool on the Hill

There's nothing he can do about the cows on the road when they're being herded in for milking. Full cows make way for no man. Nor are they bothered by the murderous shrieking of the car, not like the lolling and loping hares, which rise up, indignant for a moment, then catapult off into the ditches. Peter puts the Daf in neutral, winds down the window and inhales the moor. The hares seem bigger this year, bigger every year. Haunches, whiskers, paws: he's sure they're expanding. Maybe it's Sellafield's radiation, reaching inland. Maybe it was that lurid rain drifting over from Chernobyl, incubating the little buggers in their forms with an alarming energy. Come the apocalypse it'll be the super-size hare owning the country, with its lengthening backbone and its shrewd, alien face, of this he is certain. The cows' days are numbered though. They're such antiquated creations, relics of another era. He watches them plodding along, enslaved by their produce and oblivious to what is in front and behind. Their hooves clatter on the concrete as the car shrills.

The afternoon is hotter than it seemed inside the stone of the cottage, and its copper-green light is becoming gold. Perfect for a late series of sketches if he sets up soon, but all he can do is wait, large and tacky behind the steering wheel, and watch the big bovine arses wallowing, hipbones and shoulders hoisted high like masts, sails of flesh billowing out. The farm dogs sool between their legs. 'Come along, ladies.' On the wall top a couple of rooks have the look of factory masters, monitoring their workers, ready to crack the whip.

Rob Robertson nods to Peter as he tromps past the car behind his cattle. 'How-do, Wilse. Bonny afternoon.' His wellies are lathered in wet, mustard-coloured turd, and his wool shirt is buttoned down over his big sprouting chest. 'Mr Robertson, sir.' Peter doffs two fingers off his forehead. 'Isn't it just bloody gorgeous!' 'Aye. Grand day for a drive. Got a picnic?'

Cordial as ever, his neighbour. But implicit in this exchange is the fact that Peter Caldicutt is not out 'working' like the rest of them. He is not fetching his animals from their paddocks to the pump sheds; he is not punching in and out at the biscuit factory; he is not even, frankly, creasing the crotch of a cheap suit in an office in town. He is in fact doing nothing. Well, he's doing something alternative, something un-listable. He is sitting in his runt of a car, in his colourful overalls and gender-neutral smock, with a shoe-caddy of brushes and pencils on the passenger seat. He is somehow playing hooky from the proper daily business.

But that's OK. That's manageable. They like him all the same, this affable eccentric, this entertaining, be-hatted fellow, who is often in the pub of an evening, who helps out come bailing or mending time, who might have negligible income, or might in fact be a millionaire – there's just no telling. 'How's the painting, Wilse? Pretty colour on the fell today. Heard you on the radio. *Cumberland News* says you've gotta picture in The National.' He does know his lifestyle is something of a confusion, with its unusual hours and occasional celebrity. But he's been here long enough to be, almost, just and so, a local. One of them. An acceptable, topographical feature.

And, let's face it, it is exempting – self-employment. Very nice to have time and freedom, and yes, all right, money. Nice to enjoy what you do for a living, and not be dreaming of murder or arson every day in a municipal cubicle. Trips out at milking time on a whim, to an exhibition, to the pipe shop, the matinee, or to see a skull-cluster of stones in a pool at low tide on the coast, are very agreeable. He doesn't have to get a wash until mid-afternoon if he doesn't want to. He can read in bed when he wakes up, or listen to *Woman's Hour*. Bloody hell – he could wear sling-back, leopard-skin stilettos and arse-jewellery in the studio if he so desired!

Not that there isn't any order. It isn't professional anarchy. But from the outside the perks certainly look good – mobility at his own discretion, the absence of a twattish boss, a punch-card, and a starchy uniform. Stovetop espresso five times a day instead of thin metallic tea pissing out of a machine into a plastic cup. Might as well make the most of such privilege. Might as well appreciate it and say he's lucky. 'I'm a lucky man,' he says in interview, 'getting to do what I do. Don't think I don't know that.' No. He doesn't have to rush pell-mell round the supermarket after ten hours in a polystyrene office, or be ruthless towards other drivers in rush-hour queues. There might be unusual exchanges with the taxman, there might be days when the Muse is off banging some other artist, but once you've got the hang of the credit system, once you realise Miss Mnemosyne will come back after her dirty little affair, things do get a lot easier.

Yes. It is a pleasure, putting on a coat, midday, mid-week, and walking to the cairn at the summit of the old corpse road. It's a joy, being in his workable home, with its mismatched, notched crockery and under-door draughts, the brisk accessible kettle and the sagey deodorant of Lydia lingering if she's just passed through the room. But he's earned the bastard lot! He's earned it with dedication, long hours, lost weekends, rejections, ridicule, out-of-voguery, and taking an enormous bloody punt and being nifty with a brush and sticking at it. Dues have been paid. He's risked a risky profession, and it's paid off. And for that he is proud, and for that he doesn't mind Rob Robertson's playful rebuke. It's not like he hasn't worked a million shitty jobs before the only one he ever wanted eventually became his. Barkeep, road sweeper, sausage packer, cleaner, fly and lure seller, bastard rent collector, toyboy. Not like he hasn't been skint as a rag-and-bone man. Not like he isn't intimately acquainted with the fag end of the country's social order – the weak broth, the pneumoconiosis, the booze, the glory-hole of working class solidarity.

But. He's not complaining. Not today anyway. Not with this gilding, long summer light, and the promise of severe, photogenic shadows in the ravine. Sitting behind a sloppy armada of cows is not much to have to contend with really. He is a patient man. He is accustomed. He's groovy.

Fed up with itself, the car stalls. He turns the engine over a couple of times until it fires. A dirty tubercular cough splutters from the exhaust pipe. Rob Robertson looks back over his shoulder and the wall-top rooks swivel their beaky faces to admonish the disgraceful noise. Haughty buggers – they'd have his eyes out too given half a chance! On the moor, foxgloves are rising from the charred ruins of the bushes that have been burnt back, and the whin smells sweet. Cuckoo-pint is growing along the slopes of the vallum. He wonders if the nettles are too tough now to make a pudding – he's had a recipe stuffed in a drawer in the studio for years that he'd like to try. So many things still to do, eh Peter. 'There's no such thing as ennui, except for the lobotomised,' he tells Susan and Danny when they complain about being bored. He's never bored. Although these cows are beginning to test his chipper reserves.

* * *

Lydia's red VW is trundling back over the road in the distance. At a fair old lick is how his wife drives. Round the corner by the farmyard she comes, over the cattle-grid with a loud metal thrum, over that bump where the concrete kinks – the car pitches sharply up, and quickly nods down. 'Oooh, the suspension! Careful, love!' There's the whingeing of brakes, and then she's lost from sight on the other side of the black-and-white herd.

Lydia accompanies him on trips out sometimes, now the kids are self-sufficient and mostly elsewhere. Together they travel light, carrying small rucksacks of equipment instead of papooses. If he's walking up a fell, she'll sometimes join him, or she'll cut down to the nearest waterway in search of rarities, taking her camera with her. Other days he leaves her to her own machinations at home, carried out under the cover of chores, behind the tent of bright cottons on the washing line or in amongst the jams. 'I think I'll mooch about at home today', she'll say, her grey eyes already mulching paper in a bucket or stripping varnish from a salvaged bureau as they look up at him. 'Right-o, cheerio, love, good luck with the japanning,' he'll say, planting a big clumsy kiss on her face that misses her lips and squashes her nose.

When he gets back she'll have developed a roll of photographs in the pantry; they'll be dripping chemicals on to the floor, drumming the wax-paper lids of jars. The vegetable patch will be dark with freshly turned sods, carrots left clarty in the sink for him to scrub. She'll have added denim patchwork pieces to his holey dungarees, or expanded the quilt hanging in the little upstairs room that used to be Susan's, and is Susan's again until she moves, along with prosaically blacking the hearth and splitting kindling. He never knows where she finds the time for everything.

He suspects, no, let's be honest, he knows, that it's not him

Susan gets her organising skills from – her tidiness and productivity – and her natural instinct for dark rooms. He and Danny can't stand that whole thing – the claustrophobia, the shrewy optics, the tortuous pong. But the Caldicutt women seem immune. Already their daughter is attracting attention with her work, has walked straight into the best art school in the country, has received a decent amateur prize with which she has bought a classy camera. Clever lass. She is what her brother calls the brains of the operation. Why is it then he worries most about her? Why doesn't he stress so much about Danny, who is, like his old man, a drop-out, who has been in gentle trouble with the law for possession and distribution of the herb, who is as flaky as chocolate and has decided to steward the summer music festivals and live like a pauper for the rest of the year? She's the one on the fast track, off to Goldsmiths any day now. She's the one with ambition, the gumption, the get-up-and-go. Why then does he worry about the pull of her strings?

Movement. Suddenly the road up ahead is visible. The cows have docked in the corrugated shed. There's Lydia in her scarlet bug, revving it up, spinning grit. He puts the car into sticky forward gear and pulls away with a squeal. The doomsday hares, having returned to the road like the plague, scarper again. His wife, sitting with plenty of air between her spine and the seat, holds her hand up and zips by him. 'How was yoga?' he calls.

Five o'clock at the Gelt ravine. He parks on the verge above, skirts round the edge of the crags and sets his caddy down on a shelf of rock. This time of year the darkness in the crevices has the consistency of creosote as shadows spool into the valley below. The face of the gorge is like a gothic portrait, like the

Sargent painting of Stevenson. It makes him think about Donald, with his long hair worn over his face to cover the scars from the accident on the roof with the bitumen. He's often wondered how it must have felt, to have his skin scalded off like that. Terrible. Medieval. Poor old Donald. It took years for him to start going out in public again, and then he insisted on using his brown locks to mask the damage. Even longer for him to start doing readings again. The burn has healed well over the years; when he tucks his hair behind his ear, Peter can see the slow, yellow recovery. But the damage is vast. Donald doesn't drive, not because he's a woolly poet, but because his right eye is missing, and he has no depth perception.

Maybe he'll phone him later to see if he and Caron want a pint in the Jerry. It'll be a nice night to sit out and get mildly loaded and shoot the breeze. Maybe Lydia and the kids will come too and they can all roll home and have a nightcap. He'll open a new bottle of elderflower. Yeah, he could fancy a pint or two after this. The charcoal's feeling nice in his hand, fast and loose, and it's leaving true lines. The wind along the crag ripples the page, and he reaches for a clip from the caddy to hold it down.

Sing once again with me, our strange duet.

Phantom of the bloody Opera. The funny thing is, Donald's never written about any of it, and this has always surprised Peter. You would expect a writer to draw from such an experience. You'd expect there to be some kind of formal quarrel with what happened, a step into the hazelled ground. At the readings, Peter watches the audience, wonders what they think about that avalanched cheek and inflexible glass orb; whether they have any idea what his scalp looks like under his hair. They never ask. They applaud the ones about snooker and sex. He signs their copies.

* * *

Such stark light. He's caught it on the page – in the slashed fissures and pockmarks, in the crags. Yes. It is a strange profession, the seduction of stone, the attempt to relocate a mountain on to canvas. 'It's all geology, Petie,' is what his old man would probably say. 'It might not be dollying coal up on conveyors, but the principle's the same.' His levelling, lucid father. With the cough that would seem to last for ever, but would cut the man down in a year, halfway through his fifth decade. God bless the black-lunged, shafted miners.

Now the light is tilting. Maybe there's a better angle to be had. He pockets the charcoal stick and slips the sketchpad inside his shirt, snug against his belly. He leaves the caddy tucked into the alcove of the shelf. Down in the crevice might be best, looking up at the giant. He begins to climb down, dropping over the outcrops, his boot tips slotting into the ledges. It's a nice feeling in his muscles – the hold, the stretch – though he can feel the morning's run in his legs. But he could probably make this descent blindfolded, he's done it so many times. Down, down, twenty feet, thirty. Not too taxing a climb. Not really as sheer as it looks. Soon the grade becomes flatter, opening out into a tumbled skirt of scree and big shingle. He jumps from rock to rock in the bottom of the gorge.

Manoeuvres like this would make Lydia twitchy if she found out about them. 'You're not a young buck any more, darling,' she'd say. 'What if you lost your balance? What if you slipped and fell and broke your back?' But heights have never bothered him; if they had, he wouldn't have managed to fashion the extreme landscapes he has. Clambering about on the summits and ridges feels like second nature – you can't explain this to someone for whom it's just plain hairy. He doesn't have the phobic urge to topple over into the rushing chasm. He doesn't get the fear. And if he slipped and fell and broke his back, well, it'd be a damn sight preferable to being rear-ended by cancer, or making that long, map-less walk into dementia. In fact, it's how he'd like to go, given the choice. Not something your cautious wife wants to hear of course. It's better to let her see a safely finished painting rather than reveal exactly where he made the studies from; which heavenly, inaccessible pinnacle; which granite eyrie.

He retrieves the pad from his smock, now a little damp at the edges with perspiration. A few more quick sketches, then that'll be him. A good day's work. The sun sinks on the horizon, crowning the upper striation of the gorge with fierce light.

He removes the clip, flicks back through images. Perfect. Enough. Time to head home now for a nice tea and then a few pints. He stows the pad inside his shirt, makes his way back over the scree. There's nothing like it, this demob pleasure that comes after accomplishing a task. The giddy satisfaction, feelings of affection for the world. Probably just as good as moving the cows, eh, Mr Robertson. Yeah. They can think he's nutty. They can think he's a slacker. This is what it boils down to: knowing you've done something useful. Feeling elated and useful, feeling spritely and sure-footed. Feeling the ground beneath you is just.

Then again, the ground beneath him right now feels quite the opposite. It feels infirm; it feels loose. There is a strange sensation, of movement, of motion. The big, lichen-backed stone under his left foot is shifting, rotating. He can hear it grinding rubble as it rolls, tipping him sideways. Given that no one is around to attend to his reaction, it feels absurdly unnecessary when he hears himself say, 'Woah.' Time seems bizarrely roomy while this stone-back rodeo is in progress. There is time enough to register a few thoughts. The idea of an earthquake.

The striking of flint in the gorge. Lydia, that day she held her finger to her lips and pointed to a stag by the river with bloody velvets. 'Do you see it, Peter?' He tries to jump, but the rock has already moved too far. His boot slips. He feels a grazing sting, hears a crack.

It takes an additional epic second for his mind to process the results.

His left leg has been fed into a slim channel between two boulders. The roller has come to a halt above his ankle, no, against his ankle. He has been cast awkwardly to the side and is half kneeling. There is the painful realisation that the accident is bad, then just pain – not ordinary pain, but something vivid and coruscating, as first his shocked silence, then his nauseous whimper, then his primal bellowing attests to. And though an instinctual physiological directive is telling him to get out of the trench, to extract himself pronto from the bite of the rock jaws, he cannot. Because after another deranged few moments of slapping the leg, and yanking it, and trying to lever the raw shin this way and that, excruciatingly, ball-witheringly, it is apparent these are *objets d'occlusion*, it is apparent that he is, well and truly, trapped. Peter, Peter, Peter.

The Divine Vision of Annette Tambroni

The strongest perfume of all the flowers on the market stall is that of the lilies. The scent has something lush and unsteadying about it. Uncle Marcello prides himself on the successful hot-housing of such flora. He has strains that are very difficult to raise in the soil here. Annette must be careful when handling the lilies – their pollen is worn tremulously and the smallest knock or brush could dislodge it and stain her clothing or the clothing of customers. The strokes of orange and yellow are impossible to remove. When they are in season the lilies have a curious effect. They breathe their scent over everything, their long dusted tongues panting the aroma. The perfume is insistent, a soprano pitch, which lifts above the rest of the bouquets. It tingles the bridge of Annette's nose when she leans close, making her hands and neck feel soft, like the time Uncle Marcello gave her a tumbler of *nocino* to sip.

Those who buy lilies behave in a way that suggests dreaminess. They sigh. They sing and hum under their breath. They make unwitting noises, as if enjoying a delicious plate of food. They flirt. All around them are the notes of a peculiar kind of love. Perhaps, if flowers are blessings of God as her mother suggests, the lily serves a different function to the virtuous rose. White lilies are for annunciation and grace, such as the angel offered to the Madonna. But the stargazers and the tigers are vivid and exotic, their shapes and colours voluptuous, and their fragrances intoxicating.

Her mother does not keep lilies in Castrabecco, as she keeps cuttings of other flowers. She finds them extravagant and inappropriate. She says they are too expensive to waste. The white ones are for church, and the others are suitable only for the bordello. Her mother has opinions about the inappropriateness of many things. She has opinions about Annette's unruly hair braids, about the scandalous price of renting their stall, and the money-raking of the cooperatives, the council and the government. She has things to say about the attire of President Saragat, and the political mistresses. Her firmest opinions are always about what is moral and what is not. And yet she does not often leave the house. She does not investigate for herself the corruptions of Italy, but prefers to read about them at the kitchen table.

Maurizio brings her newspapers and fashion magazines, which she tuts over. Annette will often asks her mother to read to her, but she prefers not to read things out loud, only to comment on the terrible state of things, on the infidelities, the actresses and lipsticks, and the hundreds and thousands of refrigerators leaving the country versus the lack of refrigeration in their own house. 'We are perfectly cool,' Uncle Marcello says. 'The flowers do not suffer, why should we? Wouldn't you rather have a television, Rosaria?'

Uncle Marcello spends approximately three-quarters of his life at the greenhouses and the growing plots, according to Tommaso, who has recently begun to calculate fractions in his schoolbook. Sometimes Uncle Marcello sleeps in the gardens, on a low wooden pallet between trellises, and other times he sleeps at Castrabecco. He arrives at mealtimes with dirty fingernails, which Annette's mother does not like, and shares his ideas for new strains of flowers he hopes to create. Frequently he arrives with sample sketches of cross-pollinations to show them, and Annette wishes she could see the drawings, the lavish hypothetical hybrids that Uncle

Marcello will attempt to engineer with medical depressors and cookery utensils; the colours of the bells and the petals he will try to reverse. 'Can you imagine what would happen,' he asks, 'if the fuchsia was released from its red and purple collar? How beautiful it would be if it were the colour of an English primrose. So light. A little angel or a fairy.'

He owns many books on the subject, and he also owns a scientific microscope, which he keeps in the small brick office of the greenhouses, which Maurizio is not allowed to use, because he is bullish, but Annette may adjust if Uncle Marcello is present to assist. While Mauri shovels clods of earth and prepares troughs, Annette and her uncle sometimes examine the secret infinitesimal beauty of plants, their heads close together over the device, Uncle Marcello's hair resting crisply against Annette's cheek. She cannot see exactly what is clipped to the stage under the objective lenses. The details are too small and precise, and the iris diaphragm arranges the light too intensely for her pupils. But her uncle will describe the specimen, putting his eye to the ocular piece and his warm calloused hand over hers on the coarse focus. His long middle finger gently revolves the fine focus. On the glass plate, he tells her, are delicate filaments and farina, pollens like star clusters and intimate tissues, blushing pigments and freckled crevices. These are descriptions which sound to Annette like the alien creatures in the space films Mauri watches, like those moist, tendrilled, protuberant things, programmed to find humans, breed with them and build new colonies, according to Hollywood.

When they have finished, Uncle Marcello cleans the aperture, the lenses, and the stage, with a special cloth kept in the microscope case. Then the device is lifted away and stowed below the desk.

Uncle Marcello speaks with reverence about the early English gardeners who experimented with reproduction using hazel catkins and cabbages, carnations and tulips. To Annette the English surnames seem as unusual as the experiments conducted two hundred years ago: Fairchild, Dobbs, Wentworth, Miller, Morland. To make her uncle happy, she recites the list and adds 'Marcello Tambroni'. Pinned to the wall of the office are drawings of English garden fairies, and photographs of fairies that are hoaxes. Uncle Marcello tells her he has seen fairies hiding in the grass heaps, but when Mauri sings pop songs loudly they are frightened away.

His hands are precise and slow whenever he fixes the end of Annette's braids with a ribbon. Just as carefully he scrapes powder from the stamen of one varietal and transfers it to the organs of a different species altogether. He re-pots. He waits. He waters. He hopes. In one of the small glass conservatories he has a laboratory of attempted fusions. They are his garden children, he tells Annette, and he loves them as a father. It is very sad when they fail.

Over lunch or dinner, Annette's mother sometimes makes wild breeding suggestions, many of which Marcello declares immediately impossible, like the marriage of marigolds and cyclamen, apples and limes, pumpkins and zucchini. 'Rosaria, if you come to the nursery I will show you the correct proce- dure,' he tells her. 'You have not been for a very long time. Did you not use to visit my brother there every day?' When he says this, the room becomes quiet, except for Tommaso popping his mouth and Mauri scraping up the last of the soup from the tureen. 'You don't understand what it is I am suggest- ing,' she says. 'You are mistaking me for someone else, Marcello.' Then Uncle Marcello says quietly, almost in a whisper, 'Sometimes we must put away our sadness and remember what fortune offers us. You are not a nun.' 'God gives me no options. He is the only choice,' she replies, her voice as bitter as radicchio.

Arguments such as this are difficult for Annette to follow. There seem to be strange currents at work when her mother and her uncle speak. They might be playing chess or a card game. When she asks Mauri why they can never agree, Mauri tells her it is a question of frustration. He says one day it will all explode, then maybe they will have another little brother or sister. 'A half-breed!' he laughs, pleased with his joke. Annette giggles, though she does not know exactly what he means. In her mind's eye she pictures Tommaso as a baby, mixed with a tropical flower. There are green shoots growing underneath his toenails and in his navel. His tongue, when he cries, is a blue spotted tube, sticky with sap.

Rosaria Tambroni prays every day at the foot of her bed, or beneath the coral rosary in the kitchen, which was her grand-mother's. She prays with intensity, forgetting Tommaso's milk, which burns in the pan, and the coffee on the stove, which spits dryly. She prays frequently, but seldom goes to mass. She does not attend the festivals or the parades. She does not help prepare *mosto* under the piazza trees, or join in the October celebrations with the other women. She does not leave the house unless it is for a particular reason – a religious expedition of some kind, a feeling that comes upon her like a fever and will not leave her until she has put on her shawl and prepared herself to face whatever it is that she must face. Then she will march out, her arms swinging, her knuckles swelling and whitening, as if the skin might burst open, to see Father Mencaroni, or to inform the vendor of magazines and books that he must stop selling profane material to her second youngest son, or to the house of her sister, or to stare at the road leading to the cimitero di campagna. Until these purposeful moods arrive, she prepares tall cascading sprays for weddings in the stone room of Castrabecco, cuts silks, which she sells to dressmakers, and weaves funeral wreaths. Sometimes Annette wishes her mother would march to the church of San Lorenzo and, with her extraordinary, livid piety, which withers all its recipients, demand that the Bestia stop leering at her daughter. She imagines her taking an axe to the panel of the Deposition and extracting the evil face, then burning it. But this event is unlikely.

Once her mother was more sociable. There is a photograph in a frame on her dresser, in which she is dancing with Annette's father. She is wearing a bolero jacket and a skirt now out of fashion. Her hair is long and loose. They are linked severely by the hands, their expressions fierce and amorous. There is another photograph beside it, in which she is practising ballet. Behind her is a row of diplomats or honoured guests in dark suits and tall hats. Once, when she was very little, Annette's father said that before their engagement, her mother had been to Austria and Germany and had danced before royalty. Annette wishes she had seen her mother dancing. Often she goes into the bedroom and lifts the photographs and brings each in turn close to her face. From the wardrobe comes the smell of her mother's old clothes and her petticoats, the smell of vinegar and lace. On the table is her gold-edged Bible.

Annette wonders if her mother will ever recover from such loss. She still wears the long black dresses that cover her ankles and fall in a gather, like a curate's hood, at the shoulders. She communicates feverishly with God about her past misfortune, and finds no joy in living. Uncle Marcello says it is a shame for such a young woman to continue to wear such dresses. That she wears them to hide herself.

Annette's mother's eyes are only a little short-sighted. She does not wear glasses, not even on the fine chain around her neck, but she has seen things. She has seen that there are great oceans of darkness in which her daughter might be swept away. There are daily assaults her daughter might encounter. An avalanche of aubergines rolling towards her in the market, or a hole in the pavement with Southerners inside, or a lascivious kiss from a stranger. She will not tolerate her daughter's curiosity about these subjects. 'Enough of this inquisition!' she cries, when Annette asks how the aubergines would get loose, or why the hole has not been filled by street workers, or when she asks whether the Bestia can climb from the heavy gilt frame and move unnoticed through the street, and whether he wears the crimson wattle of a cockerel, or has sallow haunted eyes like the wolf of Saint Francis. 'Just promise me you will be vigilant and good. That is all I ask!'

Annette promises, and tries to do her best. But if she brings home fish with fingermarks on the scales her mother will always notice. 'You should be more careful not to grope at things,' she says. 'It gives you away.' When Mauri dances with Annette in the courtyard holding her hips and swaying her like a bell, she will rap on the window, or fling it open, and say, 'How many more times must I tell you.' When she suffers headaches the whole house must muffle itself, and tiptoe and whisper. Annette must go to the cupboard in the kitchen and find the tin of camomile flowers with which to make an infusion. She must soak a cotton napkin in the grassy tonic while her mother lies on the crocheted cover of her bed. She drapes the towel over her mother's forehead and presses it gently. She hears her mother weeping. 'I am so tired,' she whispers. 'I have been left alone with too many reminders. Other mothers have daughters who are able to help them. Other women have husbands who fell poplars for their daughter's wedding. What hope is there?'

'Let me help more,' Annette suggests, stirring the bowl of dusty yellow flowers and floating stalks. 'I know where the flour is kept, and the eggs.' But her mother continues to weep;

she is inconsolable. 'It's OK. Leave me alone now. Go to mass. Take flowers to Papa's grave and tell him we miss him.'

Before her vision deteriorated completely, Annette would look at her mother sitting at the dresser, anointing herself with oils. She would watch her brushing her hair and smoothing her eyebrows, plucking them in the centre so they became separate, and she would think her most beautiful. Before the final sickness, the blizzard that descended from nowhere and severed the nerves, there were still tunnels of sight. She could move her head around and find the cameo of this sombre, elegant woman. At the table when they sat for meals, if she looked up and to the right, she could see her mother's crucifix, lying in the milky hollow of her breasts. The sunlight would glimmer and flash against it, like a match flaring inside Annette's head. 'It makes you seem simple,' her mother commented, 'when you dip and tip your head like that. Are things getting worse, Annette? Should we go back to the doctor and see if he can provide some dark glasses?' 'Yeah. Then she can sing the Blues,' said Mauri.

When she was ten years old, warm drops were sprinkled into her eyes from a pipette every night. Annette imagined that the solution melted the frost creeping around her pupils, like the ice on the windowpanes of Castrabecco in winter. She would stay very still while her mother held her chin and administered the prescription, trying not to blink just at the moment the splash landed on each eye. She always did blink and her lashes would squeeze out the fluid and it would trickle over her cheeks. And they would try again, Annette looking up, her neck stretched long and her eyes wide, like a baby bird.

Even when she could still see, there were days Annette felt unsure of the things surrounding her. The edges wobbled and warped. Sometimes she could not capture an image by moving her head around and she would require verification. 'Am I wearing a blue coat today?' she would ask her mother. 'Is that a cat sleeping on the roof? Is it Mauri walking across the gardens with Uncle Marcello? Is Tommaso doing a handstand against the wall?' 'Yes, yes, yes!' her mother would snap. Or, if she had a headache and was tired and angry, 'No, Annette,' she would say, 'that is a dead thing, which you should be grateful you cannot see.' Or, 'That is a wicked sinful thing, please look away.' Or, 'That is the Bestia, quickly, walk on.' And Annette would cover her face and mewl like a lost kitten as they hurried down the street.

But at school, when Signor Giorgio came to instruct the class on drafting and colouring, he told her that her paintings of flowers were in fact very good. They were small miracles that contained absolutely the soul of the still-life, he said. He told her that her name was French, and that there was a great French painter who slowly lost his sight, but that because of this he was able to create works of subtlety and innovation. Annette liked that Signor Giorgio wore heavy medical spectacles too, like the spectacles she had been issued by Dottor Florio. Whenever he entered the classroom he would smile at her, and pinch the arms of his spectacles between his fingers, as if he were saying, look, today we are both wearing our ridiculous contraptions. He did not mind if she moved her head around in arcs and circles until she could locate the object they were drawing, or the blue suspenders lying against his shirt, or his white hair. He smelled of smoke, like a bonfire in autumn, and he was wise and kind. 'Remember,' he told her, 'when there is no more hope, we shall each of us see by our mind's eye.'

94

The Mirror Crisis

If you didn't live in London you could probably survive on your income from self-employment alone. Enough projects come your way, you've established yourself as a bright new talent in the field, and there are loyal galleries. But this is a city of financial haemophilia. Rent, mortgages, Oyster cards, gas, electricity, recreation, food; it costs, even to breathe. You know only a few artists who can subsist independently. It is simply the way of it here – writers teach or moonlight as journalists, painters take civic commissions, sound engineers work in advertising, actresses pull pints and make bad receptionists.

You like your other job. You like Borwood House. It's not the best set-up for exhibitions, hasn't the natural light or the dimensions of the Soane or the Tate Modern, but its proportions are decent and it has character – a late-Victorian town house with high ceilings, stained glass, and dado rails intact. You helped set the place up. Angela, your oldest university friend, organised the conversion with an unlikely bank loan and some family money. She wanted you in on it and pitched it in a way that sounded exciting and feasible. *It will be a different kind of production space*, she said. *Imagine it. A little Left Bank. Licensed. Quirky. Eight pounds entry with a glass of wine maybe – it's competitive, it'll work. Come on, Suze*, she said, *we won't have to fanny about with P45s any more. It's stupid not to get a bit of security at our age.* You weren't sure she would be able to pull it off, all the advertising, the security systems, and the introductions into the notoriously elite art circuit. But her powers of facilitation were surprising. The gallery's reputation grew, the number of visitors increasing each year. There has been Arts Council funding. Borwood has recently hosted the drawings of Schiele and Goya. It's the real deal.

The job is interesting enough. You don't have to be at the gallery until midday, and it's a short walk across the heath from the flat. You suppose you qualify as management, though this has never quite been made clear. You were solely responsible for the place while Angela was on maternity leave. You help arrange the collections, write press releases, and dress the rooms. You're usually the last to leave. You check the thermostat, switch off the lights and lock up at 6 p.m. This gives you the champagne-diamond light of London's mornings to be at one of the studios, or to go to the lab for printing, have a run, spread a piece of toast with butter, shower, and then step into a dress or a suit. From bohemian to corporate.

When asked, over canapés and sparkling wine at viewings and parties, what it is that you do, you say you are a curator. You say nothing about photography, the Deutsche Börse, the royal portrait. It's simpler that way. There are days when you feel like a fraud for saying it; it isn't what you really do, it isn't how you see yourself. But there are days you feel like a fraud for signing your work, putting your surname to it. There's no getting away from the man that name belongs to, he who has long been established as one of the country's greatest landscapists, he who is one of his generation's formidable male eccentrics.

Peter Caldicutt: reliably outspoken, dashing and dishevelled, a British Council-hating Communist who is liable to drunkenly piss in nineteenth-century museum fountains after previews, and who is the subject of two short BBC films. Your dad. His paintings were the first thing you understood to be art. You had no true notion of his reputation until you went away to art college and your tutors began asking questions about what your father was really like and whether he taught you what you knew. It was just his job, making pictures. Sometimes there was money. Other times there were spells of relying heavily on the vegetable patch in the garden and on the chicken coop, and a bit of poaching on the estate. Times when your mum worked two or three jobs. Only when you became a teenager did things seem easier, and the newfound security manifested in overseas travels, the conversion of the outbuildings, and an annual young-artist award set up in his name.

You and Danny were neither encouraged into nor intimidated out of the foundation year. Danny dropped out, predictably, and seemed only to want to go because you were going. *I'll enrol if you do, Suze.* You finished with high marks and applied to universities. In the acceptance letter from Goldsmiths they asked for grades much lower than the prospectuses had indicated. If you'd been Susan Smith or Jones, Patel or McMillan, no doubt it would have been different. But you were Susan Caldicutt. You were, after a fashion, a celebrity daughter. Your dad was madly proud, and oblivious to the fact that he might have had, inadvertently, a hand in everything.

But even left to your own devices, there was not much chance you'd have been a brain surgeon or an accountant. Not with this colossal man in the foreground, who smoked dope and rock-climbed with the Earl's sons, who walked around either stark bollock-naked or dressed for the theatre, who bivouacked next to precipitous cairns and had parties wilder than you and Danny. Not with the mysterious, rag-strewn room upstairs in the cottage, intermittently rendered off-limits by this seven-foot, wild-eyed, bereted king, and host to, it seemed when you were young, all the summits of human expression possible. Not with those vertiginous oil paintings hung in every alcove – even over the toilet – which you could stare at for hours and still never be able to say what it was about them you loved.

There was no getting around your father. His vim. His magnetism. The stories he used to tell you, about *The Scenes, Those Days, The Decade.* About Picasso and St Ives and LSD. At your school he was known as *The Beardy Weirdy,* or *Caldicurser* – the dad who swore all the time, regardless of the teachers. *Had a good bloody day, kids? Give the car a shove, the fucking battery's dead again.*

There were times you didn't get on. Times when he infuriated and embarrassed you, was too loud and opinionated, too unmanageable – going on the radio, telling it like he saw it, being controversial, not being sober. *I'm not black and I'm not a lesbian, but I like a drink, and that's what you people find interesting about me. Not the fucking art, you ignorant bastards, looking for your industry darlings and your Oxford crew. Howay, you wouldn't recognise talent if it crawled up inside your arsehole.* The dead airwaves. The apologies. There were times you wanted him to just be normal. To just shut up for a minute. You had your spats, your rows, and your rebellions over the years, though what constituted a rebellion when you had permission to curse, get laid, get high, travel abroad, all before you were sixteen, you never really knew.

You disliked yourself for not liking him. You always wanted to have your mum's stoicism or Danny's attitude of acceptance. It was so admirable, your brother's approach to dealing with him. Do as Dad does. Drink the lethal homebrew. Get loaded. Dance in the supermarket. Read the poetry out loud. Be unabashed, be uninhibited, be free. Join the madness, is what it amounted to. Put on lunatic garb like the Emperor. And Danny never minded; he could always go there. Danny, with his family zest and his eternally game spirit. Danny with his early weakness for booze and weed, and his advocacy of all things liberal and life-affirming.

Even these last few years, the gap was there. *Wilse wants us home for Guy Fawkes*, your brother would inform you over the phone, *he's planning some kind of shindig. He's built the Houses of Parliament up on the moor.* And you'd complain, and he'd say, *Hey, come on, it'll be a laugh. I'm making a mini-Blair for the roof. He's got a rocket in his arse.* You might be the artist, but you're also the impostor. Danny was the true chip off the old block, the apple not far fallen from the crooked tree.

Your commute on foot to the gallery, over the blustery stretch of heath, is almost satisfying enough to make living in the city worthwhile. This is what you tell yourself every day. It's nothing like your formative landscape though, nothing like the wet invigorating ticking in the air up there, the ripe horizons, the freshened skin. But it's the trade-off for demanding something more cosmopolitan out of life, for weighted salaries, opportunity, and being able to get a takeaway at 4 a.m.

You're fond of the heath. While others scream themselves hoarse and escalate their blood pressure on the M25, or sardine it on the tube, you get to stroll across this cultivated wilderness. The stress of the city is temporarily jettisoned here. Kids canter about in pleated school uniforms, launching plastic sandwich boxes on the pond. Cat-hipped mothers push prams and lend lip-gloss to each other while dogs hurtle after balls. This is the meteorological zoo where the city keeps its winds. Up above, kites with streamers pitch and drag in the buffeting air. As you walk your hair straightens, your skirt snaps and flutters. In the summer you watch people wilt on blankets and pet heavily, like the couples on the prohibition signs at swimming pools. In winter, fog and rain obscure the racks of period houses on either side. You squint and step off the tarmac paths bisecting the expanse and lose your co-ordinates momentarily. You pretend it is your home county underfoot, crusty with moor grass and prudishly draped with cloud. Ten minutes after setting off across the heath, you arrive at work.

The current exhibition will be something of a novelty. You still aren't entirely sure about its concept. At first you did not like the idea at all. Being something of a purist, it sounded to you like a gimmick, its focus on personality rather than art. You thought the public wouldn't want to pay to see a collection of memento mori and soiled knick-knacks. But Angela was gung-ho as usual. She secured loans from private museums, archives and well-off families, and the show is going ahead. Currently en route to Borwood House are a number of heavily insured dispatches containing some real anthropological curiosities. There are combs, and surrealist pipes, callipers, brass-handled syringes with needles still bearing addict DNA, tooth-cups and hairbrushes. There's a wicker girdle used by Manet that is currently listing in the Channel, waiting for permission to enter the port of Dover. There are spectacles, monocles, inkwells, and beads. A pair of bed slippers. A lock of hair from Kokoschka's infamous doll. There are handkerchiefs, photographs, letters, and the Italian diary, which Tom is translating.

You thought your father, of all people, would disapprove. You thought he would issue you with one of his standard lectures about idiotic administration, money wasted, *dimwits with purse strings*. But he did not. Instead he seems peculiarly interested in the items of the collection. Last night you rang to see how your parents were, to check in, to tell them what you are doing and to reassure them, as you do most days now, that they still have one of their offspring. His spirits lifted a little when you talked about the exhibition. *Hey, I bet there's some bloody deviant stuff, eh Suze? I bet there's vintage dildos and all sorts of jiggery-pokery. Those randy old sods! When's the opening? You'll get us on the bloody list, eh?*

It was nice to hear his gigantic old voice back again, banging down the phone after weeks of quiet depression, good to imagine him sitting in his usual chair with his foot up, balancing the receiver between his ear and his shoulder, and rolling his tobacco into a black paper while he nattered on with you. His great rimy sole stretched out towards the hearth, toes furling and unfurling. You were midway through a sentence when he clattered the phone to the floor and you heard him yell out *I'll be back in a minute, Sue.* Then squeaking stair boards, and silence except for a faint crackle down the line. After several minutes he picked the receiver up again. *I just needed a pee.* You talked a while longer, then said goodbye.

After you hung up, you thought about the place downstairs in Shoreditch. You'd walked along its corridor with Tom, not touching, but close together. There was the smell of something sweet in the air, like unpasteurised honey, speckled with pollen and lustrous. There were liquorice-black doors with small windows. You'd expected a worse environment, somewhere silty and culpable. You'd expected disturbing scenes inside. Multiples. People being stretched and held down perhaps. Everything done roughly and expressions of distress, breasts being flung and rocked beneath bodies. As you walked down the corridor you wished for a moment you hadn't come here with him, and you weren't sure how it had happened, how it had been agreed. It was only the second time you'd arranged to meet in the city. In the bar you'd had a drink, two drinks. You had both heard of the place, but you don't know which of you suggested it. Because of what you'd begun doing you felt adventurous. You felt upended, sensed the lees of sex drifting in the air around you. The idea seemed un-boundaried and appropriate.

When you looked through the glass pane it was very delicate, exquisite even. A man kneeling in front of a woman, giving her oral sex. A second man came into the room. He entered her by fractions; pain and rapture registered on her face, though she must have been used to it. The glass panel was thin enough to hear their sounds. She was shaved. You couldn't see it all. The act was carried out as if you were not there looking. Watching excited Tom and his reaction excited you. Afterwards, you wanted each other urgently. You tore your dress on the railing of the churchyard. He couldn't stop himself coming inside you.

You could say you didn't mean for it to happen. You could say that it is out of your hands, out of your control. You are simply searching for feeling, for meaning, and it was this that sent you to him the first time, and to the hotels, and to that accommodating place of voyeurs. It is this which made you show him the hidden clasp of your dress under your lifted arm, while your other hand held his wrist, letting go of it as he worked his fingers across your ribcage, to your softly polished nipple. It is a workable defence. These exchanges are simply a confirmation of life to your entropic atoms, an attempt to reverse the exodus of your psyche. You are simply grief fucking. But you are too good at it. This beautiful wet correction, this deep erotic. You are too generous and emotional at his mouth and his prick not to recognise the possibility of something else, something meaningful. You have both become reckless. Once Angela was still in the building, holding their baby on her lap, nursing it. You kissed, only two doors away from her, after he found you sitting in the cloakroom, your mobile pressed against your forehead, having scrolled no further in the index than Danny's undeleted number.

Susan, he whispered. *Conosco questa sensazione. Non ci sono bordi a cui aggrapparsi. È come essere pazzi. Aggrappati a me.* You didn't understand what he was saying, until he kissed you. It was a kiss of such complicity, of such uncomplicated sympathy, that you felt for the first time not alone in your suffering. His hands held the sides of your head while you continued to cry. She could have walked in at any moment. When he drew back and looked at you, you felt certain he had lost someone too. Later, in the emptiness of the gallery after Angela had gone home, with the door locked and the sound of cars on the road outside beginning to thin, you lay back on the floor. You felt yourself tense as he worked himself in. The smell of the day was on your bodies, transferring between your hands and mouths. Both of you struggled to breathe. And it was as if he was staring into the void, making love to those rich and fallow griefs between. Then his eyes closed and he swore and gathered you to him.

Always there are apologies after finishing, as if you have offended each other with such efficient function, such discomposure. You both swear it will not happen gain, and you both know it will continue. It is a good fit, this indiscretion. It has the right scent. There is the match of something disturbed. It is a romance of ill-health. Like hyacinth, like sugar and must, his serum, and you taste him elsewhere. You carry away images of him to use later, his lightly muscled groin, his eyes put into climax as you are.

You know you must be wearing this illicit new history. Soon someone will see it. The smears on your breasts when you undress. His semen dry as lichen on your skin. In the shower, the soap pulps, your hands wearing it down like the two incessant tides of the sea. But you can still feel the sting and tear of that first time, the bruising at the neck of your womb. You can still smell him. You know that soon your raw interior will be revealed, its marks and bacteria, its record of infidelities. And so you flee. You pull on layers of clothing, phone National Rail Enquiries, and leave messages on phones where you know Nathan will not be. You go north, back to the fells, to the cottage with its stained gable and its crow-stepped chimneys. You go back to your beginning, the place where Danny first existed, where he was with you.

No one has questioned your movements. Angela trusts you; she trusts your symptoms. Nathan too knows you are deeply injured. The darkly obvious looms close by, encompassing everything. It is huge, your bereavement. It is consuming, protecting. Loss has cast you utterly into shadow. They all tiptoe around the tragedy. They tiptoe around you. After losing him, so violently and suddenly, your vagary, your absence, must be understandable. You are heart-broken. You are recovering. You are letting go.

Translated from the Bottle Journals

On the days the envelopes arrive from England my spirits are lifted and I am more charmed by the things in my house. Antonio forwards all correspondence and I should like to be dutiful and reply, but still there is no return address. Peter is a transient agent! I am beginning to understand that these letters are simply gifts and I should accept them gratefully and enjoy them. Currently Peter is reading the Irish *Ulysses*. After many attempts he has not read past the first twenty pages. Something in the language has prevented him, he says. But on the last attempt a revelation! The text is a doorway, or a device for transporting the mind. In itself it resists interpretation, but instead affords the opportunity to think in tandem, like a man riding a bicycle while on board a ship. Peter thinks this is what Joyce intended. It will not make him unhappy to be oblivious to the narrative until the book's very end, he writes, for he is sure to enlighten his mind in other ways.

Such interesting philosophy! My advice would be to concentrate. There are ideas in my young friend's head which are perhaps too rapid. He has the energy of immature creativity, of a newly found muscle. And he runs and runs. Yet is he not close to a curious truth? Even as I write this, the breeze through the open kitchen door opens in turn the door of the studio.

To Peter, the efforts of life must seem to be inevitably rewarded; the human system is one of cooperation and opportunity. He searches for satisfaction, and little doubts its existence. This is a quality so precious in the young. He is generous to an old man whom he has not met. After reading his letter I am able to forget the discomfort that has returned to my chest and the rotten taste in my mouth. I am able to forget that the doctor has visited to make an assessment and his suspicions are grave and that I have an appointment at the hospital. I find myself transforming ordinary things into joys; the scent of rosemary in the garden, rosemary baked on to the crust of the bread. I imagine Benicio lying at my feet again, and I am content.

Peter says that he will borrow a camera from a friend and photograph his paintings outside against a wall, which will complement their images, and then he will send them to me. It will be some time before he can afford to develop the photographs. He is no longer cleaning the orchestra pit. He is working in the bar.

I am reminded of my own youth – the sparse possessions, the poverty and hunger, too much acid in the stomach. The priorities of culture and a carafe, access to the museums and churches, and exact-fitting shoes with which to walk their rooms, with which to stand in reverence. I remember passionate conversation, which could not be anything other than profound, because profundity atones for poor revenue. And the arguments of students in the cafés and bars of the red city – the styles and schools, the old and the new; and such were the merits and such were the techniques and such was the integrity. Tradition versus the contemporary manifestos. What fierce advocates we were. How little we knew about war then, and how terribly we would learn. Each night a new argument, books and papers and glasses flung to the tiles with emphasis, accusations of killing the country or laments for a country already lying dead. The conflict of young men! We were as engaged in our battles as the mercenaries of Florence and Milan.

But all of us with the same sickness, the same manipulations and gratitude for Cennini. All learning to mend like tailors, cotton at the elbow and knee; our mothers mixing flour carefully against eggs, counting beans, cutting cheese to see daylight through it, and our sisters taking cherries from the trees by the railway station. In winter, boiling goat's glue or quicklime to make domestic cements or mordants with white lead and verdigris, to earn a small income. And in summer painting the large civic properties until it rained. And working in the fields, and selling olive oil and making soap.

And finding the most unusual strong-boned girl to make love to and use as a model – if she had distinguished flesh between her hip and her navel, if her eyes were like marble and her hair auburn, if she would wear it down across her breasts or up off her neck, if she set jealousy among the young men like a songbird among cats, if she brought her temper or her sexuality to the canvas. Her heels in the summer storms made careful steps across the cobbled stones of each courtyard she visited. She was immortalised by whichever artist she came to with her modern love.

We were all emaciated and our hearts and livers were inflamed. We measured our passions like weights on empty scales. And the only cure, for conventionalists and Futurists alike, was the fresh colour squeezed on to the palette. And then another, compatible, deposited by its side.

I remember the Café Bassano with its Romany music and heavy corrugated awning. The weeping accordion café we called it. I went there first as a student and then many years later as a tutor, after touring Italy to study the masters. The bread was so stale it was hard enough to break a tooth, and the stale bread soup had too much garlic. This did not change in a decade! But it was a venue close to the studios of the

Accademia – convenient – and we were creatures of habit. I was in love with the woman who brought trays of hazelnuts to the tables. Once the other students and teachers had departed I watched her folding linens and removing ash, sometimes tying her coat at the waist to go to deposit money in the bank. To make one glass of wine last so long in order to gaze – this was my talent! And ordering a second glass I could ill afford, in case she might return for the evening menu.

How my heart lifted when she did step back into Bassano, with her hair pinned up so chicly, a discreet garnet within the soft black. I imagined that jewel lost in my glass; I pleaded with it to fall. I was a middle-aged man, lecturing every day, and yet I was mute. So many times I tried to speak her name and could not, until finally she sat with me and spoke it: Dina. My voice is lost again today and every day when they ask me about her, whenever they talk of the camps.

In the valley I can hear the barking of dogs. Giancarlo and his brothers have found another boar. Soon the hunting dogs that have failed will be beaten and released into the woods. Two white dogs have already passed the house this morning. They were hungry and their ribs stuck out and their bells were ringing so pitifully. They become the ghosts of the forests, these dogs. They join the outlawed trespass of the wolf. I confess that I do not like such a penalty – it is an unnecessary thing. The men of the town would consider me sentimental for thinking it, of course.

I found my dog Benicio at the end of the season also. He was under a bridge in the long grass with injured back legs, as if the boar had trampled him. He was the last of an abandoned pack, trying to bark, but with a tongue so dry it sounded like sticks snapping. The bodies of the others were not even warm. They had been shot and they were bloody. I put him in my tobacco coat and took him to the stream and fed him water from my palm until he could be held from underneath to lap at the water's edge. Then he began to shake furiously and then he slept. I made splints for his legs.

There was a Spanish poet who wrote that thirst is humanity turned brittle; it is the desiccation of faith itself. And so I named the dog after the poet. For a month the dog slept on my overcoat and nowhere else. It could never be put away into the cupboard because he would whine for it. Gradually he stood up and walked again, but throughout his life he limped. He loved to drink from the rivers and the lake and the fountain in the square, and he would drink without his thirst ever being slaked, until dragged away by the collar. They say that animals are not rational, but it is we who are most dangerous in our rationality. How else can the cruelty of this century be explained?

The girl in the Café Bassano already knew my name. My colleagues at the Accademia talked loudly of my peculiar paintings, and my love for Holland and the folk art of Czechoslovakia, calling me *der hohe maler* or *festo*. I was considered a native foreigner. Because of my timidity and inexperience they would tease me, instructing me to go to each attractive lady with protestations and flowers. They would straighten my collar and replace my hat like so many fussing mothers. And I would be pushed forward having prepared no romantic statement. Only when they were gone from the café would I look openly at Dina in the smoke between the tables.

I have never drunk wine quickly, not even on our wedding day.

Even after many years her name is still a thing of rawness for me. Her name cannot be left sacred – cannot be left in the black documents with so many others. They would make a saint of her now though perhaps their fathers and uncles were the ones who failed her. With continual naivety I face their questions about my life. With tired duty. An interview might turn to ash at any moment if Dina is mentioned. First they will always talk of business. To what extent do I adhere to historic privation and self-sufficiency, for no other painter of the century is so contained in subject matter and execution? Why do I only paint bottles? What is the reason? My replies are invariable. I am not the rogue of such imagining. The continuity of art is unquestionable. How can I abdicate the influence of Giotto? How am I unlike Uccello – meticulous and mathematical with his pavements, but stripping armour from the warhorse that its form be better seen? How can I say of Cézanne he is my opposite in visual organisation? How, in fact, might I be devoid of any of these great influences? I am incremental. I am a fraction of change only. The seashell bathed by its own interior light, the balustrade of shadow around the rim of the bottle, the plane through the glass gathered on the table, the objective of my whole life's work – it is all inherited. It is a house of immortal fathers in which I work, and their discipline finds consequence in the rooms of my expression. But just as I am a good and faithful son, so too must I become disobedient, and rise up against them. This is my responsibility. For how else is art?

Yes, yes, they say, and they turn to personal matters. What then of the Madonna and her tradition? The holy mother of us all, with a dead child in her arms? What of your wife?

They expect confession. They sense the frailty of old age. What might I say in the end that they do not already know? That no one believed the race manifesto. That Colonel Segre shot himself with his service pistol. That Dina sang 'Giovinezza' and gave away her wedding ring. That she donated once to the Zionist cause, and was born in the Jewish ghetto. That she had no baptismal certificate but was a patriot, loving Italy as I loved Italy. That I returned one day to find her missing, and neither the popular rejection nor the fifty kilograms of gold could save her. That our trains used to travel slowly north, and at the junctions they altered their courses.

In *Il Libro dell'Arte*, Cennini teaches us how to paint wounds, using unalloyed vermilion as the base, and lac resin applied sparingly, so the blood continues to shine. To look inside those red windows at the Uffizi today is to witness five-hundred-year-old pain as if it were a harm committed today. In these preparatory passages there is also a section on how to paint a dead man. I have often wondered if the condition of death is perhaps less grave to the human anatomy than physical injuries. For in death there is release from suffering. Sadly, the master craftsman is unable to instruct us in the healing of wounds.

The Fool on the Hill

Here it comes again. The fire in his calf muscle, the hot instrument being pushed up his femur, through the sinew, up into his scrotum, up into his abdomen. The searing makes him clench and unclench his fists, clutch the boulders and lean away from the vice of stone as if away from the pain itself. He grinds his teeth, counts through it. One, two. Threefourfive. Six. Seven. Breathe. Breathe, Peter. Come on, get the air down. Eight, nine. Breathe, you fucker. Pant as if in childbirth, lion-inhale like Lydia does in yoga. It'll pass. It'll pass as it did before, a minute ago.

Already it's going, see, already those burning lances are being withdrawn slowly down the leg, retracted back into the ankle. The pain is going, and with it the internal wildness, the violent mania, the desire to demonically vomit. OK, then. Good. Good. Calm. Better. Now he can think again. Now he can focus.

How long has he been here, pinned like this? Maybe forty-five minutes now? An hour? It's hard to say. It feels like longer, though the lurid intensity hasn't waned. Maybe less time then – twenty minutes? The light has gone from the top of the ravine wall and the floor of the gulley is in shadow. The blue of the sky has graduated from navy at its highest point to palest blue on the horizon. If he twists round to face the flatter side of the cutting – not too far round or the leg will start up again – he can see one or two stars, just the faintest glimmer. One is moving – a comet, or a plane perhaps – and beyond it, acres of freedom.

It's difficult to get comfortable. The stuck leg has thrown him into an awkward angle. The foot's not quite down on the ground, at least he doesn't think it's touching, but he doesn't want to try moving it again: it's too fragile. The other leg is having to compensate, bent up on the boulder or set down in the trench behind the other, though neither position is helpful. At best he can only lean against the rocks, taking his weight on to one buttock. He can't sit properly or alter the bend of the trapped knee. And he can't get a clear view of the point of imprisonment; he can't really assess the damage. The withers of the boulders are in the way, the light is fading quickly and it's too dark down there.

Not that he really wants to see the injury – the thought of it is enough to make him feel queasy, and make his mind start running crazy. Is it a break? Crush injury or open fracture? Oh Christ, is it a partial fucking amputation? Is the foot dangling loose on just a thread or two of skin, like an uncooked sausage, the tendon severed and recoiling up the back of his leg? Oh fuck! Is he going to lose it and be a cripple? He'll have to get a prosthetic for the stump. He'll have to use a wheelchair. No more running. No more climbing, or even bloody walking properly. How many operations? He hates hospitals. All that suffering and hopelessness. His mum in her incontinent dementia. His dad coughing up black chunks into a kidney dish, rotting inside like an old log.

Knock it off, Peter! Don't think like that. Don't rush to the worst conclusion. Be sensible. It'll be a broken bone, clean and simple. Well, maybe not clean, but mendable. It'll be ten weeks in plaster with a pair of nifty crutches and a bolted joint, and a very good excuse to drink shinny by the fire all day. Soon he'll be telling war stories in the pub, and showing off a magnificent, grinning scar. He'll be embellishing the tale for Susan and Danny – how he hopped all the way round the gorge to the car (a good mile), how it was very lucky the car only had one forward gear so he didn't have to keep using the clutch, destiny some might say, blah blah. Now. He's got to think. He should try shouting again. 'Helllooooo? Heeellllllllooooo?' His voice booms and echoes in the ravine. Someone will hear that, they're bound to. This isn't the Langdales or the Scottish Highlands. It's not Snow-bloody-donia. He isn't miles from civilisation, even though the population round here is sparse. Kids out roaming about. A man walking his dog before bed. A farmer on a quad bike. Someone will hear.

The wind lilts softly between the walls. It is cool down in the dark cleft of the gorge. A lapwing calls from its nest on the moorland beyond. Peter concentrates, collects himself. He turns his upper body clockwise and puts his palms against the boulder that originally moved, the smaller of the two collaborators. He braces the free leg on the ground and bends. The sketchpad under his shirt sticks into his ribs, so he retrieves it, places it to the side, and sets himself up again. He heaves. He gives it everything he's got. The veins on his forehead begin to bulge. Then, half a roar, the involuntary product of his vocal cords. Come on. Move. Roll. Roll it over, Sisyphus.

But it's useless. The rock will not shift. He can't get a good enough position to throw his full weight into the move. He relaxes, breathes out, looks down at the grey, lumpen back. It's big. Must weigh two hundred pounds at least? OK. OK then. Lateral thinking, inverse physics. He will have to try pulling.

He looks at his palms, anaemic from the pressure of pushing, and flaps blood back into his hands. He turns his body anticlockwise, redistributes his free leg, and slips his fingers into the depressions of the rock. He gathers his energy. But then, oh hell, it's starting up again – that gory pain. He straightens, stays still, swallows a mouthful of bile. His ankle is on fire. Some fucker is scraping a knife up the bone, beginning to drive it higher into the kneecap. Please, he whispers, please, no. No! It's much worse this time. Like gunpowder lit in a wound. Like electricity passing through a bullet hole. Oh God. Please make it stop. It is appalling. Sorry, sorry, sorry. Why is he apologising?

He feels suddenly a desperate urge to piss. He scrambles a hand to his fly but it meets with thick, impenetrable material. No way in, he's in his overalls. He will have to unclip the fastening on his shoulders, and quickly. The clasps jam. He tugs them open, shrugs the denim down around his hips. He grasps his cock, and aims away over the litter of stones. Thank God. Better. The leg begins to fade. It feels like he's pissing out the pain. The stream of warm urine splatters on the top of the rocks. He hoses them down. Fuck you, you bastards.

Pulling won't work either. Even though it feels like the power in his arms and back is greater, still he can't throw himself into it. The thing won't budge. Each time he has tried the pain has returned, more and more inflamed. He will have to get comfortable, keep yelling, and hope someone comes. Darkness is flushing into the sky, like ink into water. What time is it? Time for everyone to be inside. The chances of discovery are slim really. A more susceptible mind might panic now. A weaker disposition might turn hysterical. He will have to centre himself, be Zen. He will have to meditate, or attempt to – he's never actually tried before – and let his purified mind manage the situation. Lydia has described this state to him, and he has paid attention, sort of. A releasing of anxiety, a whitening, she says, then answers and forbearance arrive. How hard can it be?

So. Empty, empty, empty. What can he think about?

* * *

Such a bloody shame! The day started so well, what with the run, and the pretty light, and the feeling of contentment, and the kids both being home. And a good day's work too, which is not always the case. He's not always so ethical. Even removed from the conventional systems, he knows he must turn his hand to something useful, but too often does not. Often he is lazy. Often he procrastinates, distracts himself, and fiddles on, while a voice in his head tells him he is wasteful, he is wretched. Then he becomes desultory. He becomes blacker than obsidian – consumed by guilt and worthlessness. 'Men should set to, as soon as they've digested their food' was one of his father's old adages. And 'A good plumb line is the working mind', whatever that one meant.

But there are days in the studio when he drinks nothing but homebrew and smokes too much pinch and can't hold down a conversation about anything with his wife, and he is, well, the foulest git. She's thrown him out before, and thrown a heel of bread into the lane after him, slamming the door like she wants the house to come down around her. It takes a lot, but lovely placid Lydia can be riled. Her inner banshee can be summoned. And then she is quite simply terrifying, and must be left alone to re-metamorphose. So he'll spend the night on the fells. It isn't purely punishment for the domestic malady. Lydia knows what will jolt him out of a filthy mood. She knows the tonic properties of spry grass under his backside and hedgerow foraging, the peating back over of campfires at sun-up. She knows him.

After the off-the-Richter-scale booming of the front door, he'll rove about, huffing and coughing like a disgruntled ram, then he will light out into the hills. He'll walk for hours, tossing away the bread in fury, and picking it up again. He'll aim to get some height, altitudinally if not morally, then he'll select a divot between granite slabs and chuck himself down.

Once settled, his mental torments are indulged fully. He will ruminate, tracking back through the years, revisiting other women, bad events, and disappointments, old arguments, while the sky passes grey-white overhead, and buzzards drift upwards on the aerial thermals. He will lament his lost talent, his pathetic life, and his unbearable lot. He will wonder why he should go on living. He will know, balls to bone, that a more miserable bastard than he there never was.

And then he'll remember that he likes looking up. It reminds him of Lydia, when they first met, on her back in the fields of Lanercost Priory, facing an enormous teal dusk and the endlessness of space with such amity. She was clicking the number of bats departing the ruins with a thumb-counter. How lovely she was, with her halo of brown hair on the ground. How inspiring was her calmness.

Peter was aggravated that day. He was explosively angry, possibly only a few ventricle pumps away from premature coronary. A public arts meeting in the North-East he'd attended had dissolved into ridiculous back-tracking, funding had been pulled, his preliminary work for the project rendered useless. Doomed from the start, of course – art to fix a fucked-up town. A civic car-park mural – what a joke. He was offered his petrol money back, though he'd stormed out before recouping it. The commission was his first British endeavour after leaving America, and on top of all the other recent galactic failures it was simply too much.

The arterial route home was heaving with traffic, so he'd got off on to the old military road and gone into Roman ruin country. By Birdoswald his car was juddering, and at Banks the shredded tyre had started to slap the ground like a bested wrestler. When he got out to inspect it, he'd found the wheel rim stripped. He'd hoofed the car door, and begun to march ahead, furiously, hoping to hitch somewhere down the line, or catch the last train at Brampton, then stop over in Carlisle with a friend. But, given the supreme arsery of the day, he suspected he'd have to walk all the way.

It always surprised him whenever he saw the priory's gothic frame, ruined and grizzled at one end, robust and functioning at the other, like a living thing that refused to die, even though its back end was already decomposing. The apple trees in the old quarter-garden were laden with big crisp globes – their branches were bowed over with fruit – and unholy fury had given him an appetite. There were a couple of cars parked outside by the massive stud door, the chance of a ride maybe, so he'd decided to investigate.

She was in a group of six voluntary bat watchers stationed around the monastery. She was lying not far away from the river and the heavy Cumbrian evening was balanced on the tip of her nose. Her brow was rippled, her eyes rolled up to the heavens. 'Lie down,' she'd suggested, and he'd dropped down next to her. 'Two hundred and nineteen, or eighteen,' she said. 'They're quick. Don't confuse them with swifts. Here.' She passed him the counter and let her elbow rest on his arm. Above – an incalculable, endless space, under which he'd felt microbial and strangely calm. He could smell the wild rhubarb down by the river, its red-and-green leaves tart and starchy, and the river itself. Click. 'Two-twenty.'

Lydia. His marrow. His marra.

Is she starting to worry now, he wonders? Is this later than he usually gets home? Usual. But there is no usual. Unusual is usual where Peter Caldicutt is concerned. If he stays out all night, it isn't a novelty; it doesn't signify crisis or calamity, infidelity or abduction. He could be walking Helvellyn by moonlight with the Patterdale walking group. He could be sleeping it off on Donald's couch, or hunting rabbits on the estate. She will simply expect to see him the next day, smoked and sooty from his bonfire, crow's-feet stark white from squinting into the flames. She will expect to have to trim his beard where he has singed it by blowing too close to the embers, and they will laugh about the terrible smell – that awful tannic fume – which will remind them of the lacquered bouffants of the girls in school going up when they leant too close to the Bunsen flames. Remember those days?

Suddenly he can't help thinking about the abattoirs. He worked there for a few months, ten years ago, when the outbreak happened. He never got used to watching the creatures react to the smell of their own kind being burned. The bulging of panicked eyes in the fleecy trailers. The plaintive bleating. The sudden mayhem that ensued, legs and horns breaking as the poor creatures tried to jump through the gaps in the trailer bars. He can't help thinking about it now, here, with his leg held fast, and the incendiary pain licking up the muscle again.

When the light turns negative he can still see, but only in a loose, nocturnal way. The air around thickens. He is certain no one will hear him now when he shouts. 'Heelloooo. Down heeeere. I'm huuurt,' his voice booming in the stadium of the ravine. All the dogs are walked. Children are watching telly in bed, or sleeping. Someone might be out for a late-night romp in their car, but with the heavy breathing and the clambering between seats it is doubtful they will be paying attention to what's outside in the dark. He will have to work himself free somehow, or be patient, stay put until dawn, and hope he is found. The madman's curse, sleeping out under the stars – that's what they used to say about the navvies – and though he has always loved it, he does not tonight. Tonight everything is wrong. The scree is silent, but within the silence the ground crackles and chimes, skitters and ticks. In the ravine, the wind is hawing between the channels of boulders, and there is the eerie percussion of little stones rolling over in supplication, like stag beetles under the moon. And he does not like this lonely quarry sonata at all.

No, she will not worry yet. His absence is not alarming, and is never held against him. Those nights he stays out, if Lydia is gone the next morning about her business or to the Mill café with a friend, there's always a new loaf of bread set out on the table for the prodigal husband.

The Divine Vision of Annette Tambroni

The church of San Lorenzo smells of cherry wood and juniper smoke. In the cool solemnity is the ancient mortuary perfume of old women and the dripping baptismal tears of little babies. As Annette approaches the altar she feels the evil gaze upon her, compelling her face to tilt upwards, instead of down into the position of sacramental humility. The priest clears his throat. He administers the body of Christ, which tastes of bulrushes. The host dissolves on her tongue, cobwebs between her teeth, vanishing as if it were never there. She prays for her mother, for Uncle Marcello and her brothers, including Vincenzo, who has emigrated to South America, and Andrea in Turin.

Father Mencaroni speaks of the fasting of Saint Catherine. How she took slow joy in the peeling of the orange, how she rubbed one segment of its flesh against her gums and teeth. How this simple ritual was enough for her. God's devotion sustained her, he says, not mortal appetites. Mauri shuffles in the pew and sighs. He unwraps chewing gum inside his pocket and Annette hears the wet popping of his jaw as he begins to work it. He reaches over and tickles Annette's arm, then pinches it. 'Quick, Tarantella, dance, dance!' he whispers. Tommaso is kicking his shoes together and giggling. Somebody in the pew behind shushes them.

Though her brothers are light-hearted, there is an ill force in the air. Annette feels it against her face, a sensation like pushing into the damp, heavy wool hanging in the courtyard when the bedding is washed. From the gilt cage above the altar rail he is still watching her. He is watching her through her clothing, and his tongue is flicking at the buttons on the hem of her dress.

After mass, Annette greets those who call to her and ask about her mother. 'Not with you again today?' 'Mamma is sick,' she explains. 'Ah, yes, of course.' On the stone steps of San Lorenzo, as they wait for Father Mencaroni to press their hands, she hears snippets of conversation not intended for her ears. 'Keep her uneducated . . . very pretty if you don't consider . . . surely a brassiere now . . . yes, yes . . . beautiful arrangements . . . such humiliation . . . the mistress . . . in prison.' Tommaso holds her skirt and winds round and round her, twisting the material into a tight tourniquet. Then he swaps hands and winds round the other way. Maurizio says he is tired of waiting and is going to swim in the lake with friends. 'Netta, I'm going to take off all my clothes and lie flat on a rock,' he whispers. 'What do you think about that piece of information?' Then he makes a fist with a hand and rests it on the crown of Annette's head. With the other hand he taps it, as if breaking an egg, and gently his hand opens and his palm slithers through her scarf and her hair. She pulls his elbows down to his sides. 'Stop. It's disgusting.' Mauri puts his hands into his pockets and she hears him slouch off down the steps.

When it is hot Maurizio swims in the lake or lies in the tall grass with his shirt off, turning dark brown. When he comes home his skin smells of chaff and lake water and the musk of the sun. Sometimes he walks to the viaduct and smokes cigarettes and then chews mint. He and the other boys hold on to the lower beams and wait for a train to pass overhead and shake their bones, seeing who will be the last to drop. They look at magazines that stay hidden between the girders. At these meetings they discuss important things, he tells Annette, like measurements and speed and strikers. They go to watch films like the *Torn Curtain* and *The Dreamers*. The girl who works at the cinema selling tickets is very pretty. Maurizio says she is in love with him, and that she has offered to show him her secret garden.

Meanwhile Annette must look after Tommaso, taking him to the greenhouses or to the cimitero di campagna where they pay respects to their father. This is their duty and their responsibility. Their oldest brother, Andrea, is married and has children of his own. In Turin he works at the Fiat factory. Before that he worked at the Coca-Cola factory. Before that, a precision-tool factory. Vincenzo has been in Argentina for several years: 'the land of forgetting' their mother calls it, sniffing loudly, whenever she talks about his desertion.

It is pointless, her mother says, for Annette to go to the cinema and pay money for a film she can't watch but can only hear. She may as well listen to the radio, which is free. And the mezzanine is too dangerous, and such a suggestive venue is not a suitable environment for an innocent girl. Italian films now contain lewdness and violence, and American films are filled with prostitutes and criminals with guns. 'I cannot be sure what influence they will have on you,' she says. Then she sighs. 'Joseph used to take me to watch Garbo, but that's finished now.' When Annette asks why Mauri is allowed to see prostitutes on the screen her mother says he may watch them because he knows how to confess and cleanse his conscience. God knows to forgive men for their primitive urges, she says. He has been doing this for centuries.

More importantly, Annette is forbidden to swim in the lake. She is to keep her legs covered and to wear a headscarf if she ever goes near the water. There are giant eels that can smell the scent of girls from the depths and will slither out from under the rocks to attack them. 'No one has ever been attacked by a giant eel, Rosaria!' Uncle Marcello protests when Annette's mother begins with her underwater fable. 'At least not in a lake. What kind of nonsense is this for the girl to believe in!' But her mother is resolute. There is to be no swimming.

Instead, Annette and Tommaso visit the cimitero di campagna. Their father has been dead a long time, long enough for their mother to put away her cowled dress were she to choose to. Annette remembers only his neat moustache, trimmed down exactly from his nose so that it formed a thin orderly hedge on his lip. His work boots were heavily soiled. His street shoes were always polished. His eyes were as green as river algae and he was handsome. Uncle Marcello has the same green eyes, but he has a weaker chin, according to her mother. Her father was Marcello's older brother but, her mother says, in spirit he was much younger.

Tommaso remembers nothing of their father. He was just a baby when he died. He likes visiting the old walled enclosure at the top of the flight of steps on the outskirts of the town, in the same way he likes bicycling, football, learning new songs at the Montessori and writing stories.

He takes off his shoes and they walk up the steep, foot-polished steps together. The heat collects in the wings and wells of stone; Tommaso says he can feel it on his bare toes. He counts the steps. Forty-six, forty-seven, forty-eight. He must place both feet on every step or it does not count, he tells Annette. At the top, sixty-two, he has an announcement to make. He would like to race in the Tour de France. He is going to begin training tomorrow. He will eat only raw eggs to prepare. He will drink only goat's milk. He will require a striped, tight-fitting jersey with the number 6 stitched to the back. This is how old he is, and it is also his lucky number.

Around the shady grove, the trees hiss and rustle. Annette

opens the gate with a creak, and they enter the small city of the dead, with its roofs and chambers, its walls of remembrance and its fenced tombs. She gathers the dried flowers from the niche where her father's handsome, moustachioed photograph resides. The blooms crumble and disintegrate like ash. She puts new cuttings into the little tin canister. The last of the white roses, and white cultivated cyclamens whose hearts are bigger than the cyclamens under the olive trees in the hills. 'Why doesn't he wash off in the rain?' Tommaso asks.

'He's waterproof. He'll always be here.'

Beside the other photographs are jugs of wine and oil. Brooms of sage have been burned, and incense cones. Someone has left a candle flickering, its waxy taper studded with cloves. There is a Polaroid picture of a new baby, Tommaso reports, after his customary detective tour of the cimitero; its tiny feet and hands, he says, are bumpy and curled like cabbage leaves. Annette runs her fingers around the stonework. She pulls small weeds and mosses from the crevices. Tommaso has begun building a pyramid with pebbles on the flat rim of the monument. 'You're giving Papa a shave,' he says. There is a small china statue of the Madonna, which has fallen over on to its face. 'She's looking pale,' says Tommaso. 'Has she seen a ghost?' The sun has bleached the Madonna's robes to ivory, like an old wedding-cake ornament. Annette blows the dust and dirt from the creases, rubs her clean with a wetted finger, and stands her upright again.

She wonders if her father misses them. She wonders if he misses the flowers he used to grow and the rooms of Castrabecco. She chats to him as she administers to the niche. 'Uncle Marcello says business is reasonable. Poppies should come up next week in the fields. Uncle Marcello says some people believe if you look at a poppy without making the sign of the cross it will make you go blind. Do you believe it, Papa?'

Tommaso drops the last pebble, his arm at full stretch, and the little pyramid collapses. 'Is that what you did, Annette?' She shakes her head. 'I can still see some things.'

'But you can't find the edges,' he says.

She smiles. 'Yes. I can. I can find yours,' and she tickles him until he squeals.

It is true that she does not often take anyone's arm. She can remember all the routes to and from the familiar places; they exist as remembered geometries, blue lines in her mind. She can still see light, sometimes colour, sometimes movement. It is like occasional weather inside her head. 'Uncle Marcello is having trouble with the greenfly again,' she tells the photograph. 'He wishes you were here to consult. He doesn't want to use chemicals. He says chemicals are barbaric. But the vinegar isn't working any more. He says they even seem to like it. He says he's going to cause a drought in Modena.'

Tommaso has wandered back out of the enclosure. He is looking for small wildflowers with which to make a necklace. His school teacher has shown him how to split the stems in the middle to make an eyelet, through which another stalk can be fed, and then another, and another, until the chain is long enough to pass over his head, and he can crown himself prince of the forest. It must be placed tenderly around the neck without breaking any of the frail clasps.

After attending to her father, Annette crosses the cimitero to visit the chamber of Signor Giorgio. She empties the tall bottle on the carved shelf and into it she slips two stems. There are seldom other offerings left for him, no candles, no wines, though once Tommaso said he saw an old woman weeping as she left the crypt. There is a plaque on the wall that commemorates him as an artist of great importance.

When the artist first came to the school, Signora Russo told them that he was very respected, and they were fortunate to be able to share his generosity and his intellect. Their parents would of course know of him and his famous still-life paintings. She said that he was not an advocate of brutality, as some newspapers had suggested, and they were not to talk about the rumours in his presence. In the classroom the other children would bend over their drawings and constantly ask him questions, inviting him to look at what they had produced. 'Signor Giorgio, how do I clean the brushes? Tipped down or tipped up, which way is correct? Signor Giorgio, look at my work. I have copied this stone to make a mountain like Cennino Cennini instructs us. Signor Giorgio, how old you are! How white your hair is! Are you as old as Michelangelo? We can hear you breathing like a winter sheep!' And with his good humour and patience their tutor would laugh, a broken coughing laugh, and he would answer their questions and instruct them again how to make solidifying dots or modelling gesso, how to animate limbs and how to dry brushes. Annette did not solicit his attention but instead waited for him to make his way around the room to her. If the weather was good, he took them on field trips, where they would search for useful tools and find shapes to study. Sometimes he held her hand.

Every week he told them secrets about the glorious nature of art; then he said these were not secrets after all because everyone with an inquiring disposition and a desire to be an artist was entitled to know them. And he set them a task with the pencils, and a task with the ink, and he went to each child and watched them work and asked questions about the picture they were making. He listened very carefully as they answered. When he arrived at Annette's station, she would put her brush aside and turn towards him, giving him her full attention. He was very tall. His trousers rode up above his ankles. There was often a rushing sound in his chest, like the sea in a shell, and his breath was gamey, like lamb fat. She didn't mind because he was very encouraging. His compliments made heat spill into her cheeks and rash her neck.

He told Annette he liked her paintings of the flowers she had brought from Castrabecco best of all. He told her the flowers in her paintings contained exactly the purple substance of the flowers on the desk in front of her. He said he could even detect the fragrance of the paintings from the other side of the room. 'Such a remarkable waft of begonias,' he would say, 'I felt we must have been overtaken by them while my back was turned talking to Sandro. Let us open the window and see if your painting can entice the butterflies.'

Once he asked if her eye condition brought any discomfort. She told him her eyes felt quite comfortable ordinarily. They were snowy and sore from time to time, and her back hurt when she had to bend over the page to concentrate on joining her letters together properly. It was almost no longer possible for her to read the books given to them for recitation, she said, and her recitation was slower than everyone else's and sometimes she did not recite at all. One day in the future she would be blind, she told him. Her family had been forewarned, it was expected. Signor Giorgio sighed deeply, and gently put a hand on her shoulder. 'You are an illumination,' he said. It was then that he told her about the mind's eye. He said that between the articles of reality and their depiction lay an invisible place, which was filled with as many things as could be seen in the visual world and more. This was the place to which Annette could go when her sight eventually failed her. She could go there to see her beautiful flowers. He said that, in the history of art, painted flowers were treasures that defied time.

He sat with her a long time that afternoon. He told her about the artists of Holland who had created fanciful bouquets from their imaginations, with pineapples and quinces, the bounty of the different seasons combined together. In these paintings there would often be something sinister and cautionary in the corner, a little unpleasant danger, like a fly walking towards an apple, a snail on the lip of a jug, or some mould or blemish on the rind of a clementine. This was called symbolism. 'It is like life,' he said. 'All things desist. All things are temporary.' The Dutch artists were conveying the truth about nature, and reminding everyone that life was short, even while their paintings were impossibly artificial.

The next week he brought a large picture book with a canvas cover, full of the impossible paintings. He also brought a magnifying glass with a horn handle, which expanded the image beneath and lifted it from the page. She studied the images carefully. On one page there was a still-life picture with a bird about to peck at a fig. Signor Giorgio told her that such works contained many messages. Though everything seemed captured and held in a single chosen moment, the world beyond could be seen, endlessly. For example – he turned the page – there, could she see it? In the glass vase holding the pale pink rose was reflected the artist's window, which was a window showing what was outside his studio. 'Can you see?' he asked, and Annette bent close until she could make out the four squares of light in the perfect glass.

For two weeks there were no lessons, but when he returned he brought a gift for her and said that she might take it home. It was a bottle. He said it had been one of his favourite tools and in it was all his life's work. He said he was very glad to have met her, even so late in his life. She did not know why he had given her the gift or what he meant. It was an old bottle, with flakes of paint on it, but she cherished it. He came to the school only once more, and for that lesson he had to remain seated while the children carried their work over to his chair.

Until then Annette brought flowers into school for the drawing classes, which she stole from the stone storage room of Castrabecco. She would wait until her mother was talking with Mauri beside the van, then take a cutting. She would shake beads of dew from the stems, place them down inside her pinafore and button up her cardigan. If Uncle Marcello saw her hiding the blooms he would tiptoe over to her and hold his finger to his lips. 'Shh. I will keep your secret. Don't get pollen on your dress.'

Whichever the stolen item, Annette would tell Signor Giorgio about its folk history. 'The first bell in Nola was made because a bishop saw these growing in a clearing nearby,' she would say, pointing to the peal of campanulas on the table. Then she would gently tap the stem to make the flowers sway. 'See.' She would offer any such note of plant trivia her uncle had told her, and her tutor would clap his hands together and say, 'Marvellous!' When he died she felt as if she had lost someone very special, like a grandfather. She returned the bottle to him, placing it on his tomb in the cimitero di campagna, and continued to bring him flowers.

The Mirror Crisis

The worst part was having no idea – not an inkling, not the faintest glimmer of sadness, like dew in the corner of your dreams. You had no clue that Danny had veered his bike on to the motorway, that he was swerving cheerfully from the hard shoulder to the third lane and back again, like the apparition of an Edwardian soak, a century late for a midnight appointment. Danny, on top of that brilliant contraption, perfectly balanced, bare-chested and wearing moleskin trousers, making one of his impromptu nocturnal runs to the farm. Danny, high as a kite, kept warm by the ardent adventure that was his life and by the bowl of dope he'd smoked, the empty road before him, the winter frost and icy moonlight.

Now it's clear. Now you can see it all. A man and a bike on the carriageway at night, like a silent-picture routine. The starry darkness. The lisping wheels of that revolutionary machine going, for fifteen immortal minutes, the perfect speed. Danny with the world to himself. Danny weaving, standing up on the seat. Danny steering hands-free. Danny flying. How close it must have been to rapture. Now you can see it all.

But that night you slept right through as he pedalled on. You barely turned beneath the covers or altered position. There were no terrors, no anxieties nesting in your brain; there was no unconscious euphoria as your brother freewheeled. You found out by the trilling of the telephone the next morning what had happened. Peter Caldicutt told you the news and he was gutted, hollowed out of himself. There was not a trace of the Geordie, no hint of the decades in Cumbria. All that came from him was that awful empty voice, immaculately reproduced down the wires, and caught in the same quiet loop, whispering over and over. *He's gone. He's gone. He's gone.* Then you heard gentle words and your mum took the receiver from him. *No lights. Danny had no lights on the bike*, she explained. *The wagon driver didn't see him until it was too late. You didn't know. We thought . . . we thought maybe . . .*

They must have imagined that, subconsciously, something bad would have registered. That by the powers of gestational unity and the currents in your cerebella, you would already have known. But no. You didn't know. All night your ear had been folded over like a clamshell on the pillow. You were switched off. Severed. Independent. Healthy. You didn't sit bolt upright in bed, fumbling for the lamp and screaming. You didn't even reach for the glass of water on the bed-stand as you usually do midway through the night, and feel, for one brief moment before falling away again, an inexplicable sadness, or phantom pain.

You were standing naked and damp from the shower, holding the phone. You'd slipped on the bath mat in an effort to get to it before it rang off. You thought it might have been work-related. In the stillness after you hung up, you felt a bead of water trickle across your stomach and down your hip, and then you felt that dissolving feeling you have had ever since.

Nathan had already left for work. You could have called his mobile and had him come home, but you didn't. You stood dripping on the hall floor. You could feel your cells trickling away. Everything began to rush past. You put your hands on the phone table and the wood clucked under your grip, and you had to kneel.

When it passed you went to the bedroom and got dressed. You put on your best dress in fact, the one with the empire waist and the red silk panelling. You pulled on your brown leather coat and your sopping hair began to make dark stains on it. The closest bag to hand was an old satchel destined for the charity shop, propped by the front door. You put a few random things inside – underwear, jewellery, and your passport, inexplicably. You left your Leica in the studio, then, changing your mind, you packed it. You closed the door to the flat, locked it. You told yourself you were standing on the outside. You told yourself to move.

You have a car. It's not often used in London, but it's reliable. You could have driven, but you didn't trust yourself to make the drive up country. Your hands were not working. You didn't want to negotiate difficult traffic. You didn't want to sit for hours on the carriageway in among the queues. And no, no, no, you did not want to pass the slip road on the motorway where Danny had begun his boyish joyride, which had led him, four miles later, to the axles of a lorry coming the other way.

You did not want to see a shrine. Radio Cumbria was broadcasting the news at ten now that you had all been notified. Across the county people would hear the announcement and pause, hands to their mouths. They would shake their heads, and they would say, *Ah no, not Danny Caldicutt, not dippy Danny, not Dan the Man. Not the crazy fella from the scrapyard. Not the bass player from Dogtale. Not him*. There would be flowers laid at the spot, you knew it, because Danny was known and was enjoyed by all; he was one of Cumbria's favourite sons. Danny with his manic street introductions, his talkative pub personality, and his unsolicited lectures on ufology. Danny with his hemp bags and colourful shoes, the rounds-on-him and the experimental lentils, his given-away savings. Danny with his vast, reasonless smile. And one or two people would surely have clambered over the motorway embankment, slipped across the lanes between thundering commuters, and left a simple bunch of flowers on the median.

You made your way to Euston, stunned and silent, your body horribly disintegrating, but still cooperative. You found a discreet single seat on the Virgin main-liner, so that you wouldn't have to face anyone. At Preston you were taken off by the train manager, then put back on the next one heading north, thirty-five minutes and one donated sedative later. You had cried so dangerously that all the other passengers had emptied from your carriage, as if they were afraid you were about to break the news, whispered in your ear by God himself, that the world was finishing, now, now, now.

No. This wasn't the worst part. The worst part was not your inability to predict events, your failure to receive that dark neural information. It was not the five-hour locomoting asylum that passed through Wigan, Warrington Bank Quay, Lancaster, Oxenholme. It was not finding your dad up in the lime quarry, later that day, with a pick axe, exhausted, his hands pulped and bloody from hours of breaking stone, or seeing your mum, his mother, your mother, for once in her steady, meditative life turned inside out by grief, totally overcome. Even the funeral, which Nathan drove up for, was not as bad as you'd expected. The arrangements for Danny's interment were fuelled by the adrenalin of having to do what needed to be done. With familial cohesion and endless pots of tea you bore the awfulness together.

It was going through Danny's things in his flat in town that finally broke you. It was doing the job that people always say is the most difficult duty of bereavement. It was smelling him on his clothing, his signature odour: sweat, Obsession and pheromones. It was seeing his last cup of tea with its thick mouldering meniscus sitting next to the sink, half drunk – evidence of a man once thirsty, once living. It was dismantling the proof of Danny that hurt the most, pouring out the tea, washing the cup, packing his stuff up. You had, via the clearing of daily instruments and ordinary items, like his keys and his harmonica, his badly rinsed contact lenses and his strange vintage medical kit with its lint and gammy tube of silver cream, decreed that all the accoutrements of his existence were now meaningless, redundant. Not knowing his location, not knowing where to look, or how to find him, even though proof of his being lay all around, even though it seemed at any moment he might stumble home and be, as he always was, so pleased to see you: this is what put you face down on the floor, crying until you retched, crying until the corners of your mouth tore and bled, holding his old red trainers to your chest, and calling for him and calling for him. Some kind, internal mechanism saved you, provided anaesthetic. A switch flicked, your eyes closed, and your head went dark.

Personal effects: how irrelevant they are, how sad, how lost, how vagrant, without the force that gives them purpose.

He didn't have much in the flat of course. He wasn't one for hoarding junk, not domestically anyway. There was no extensive CD collection, no Dungeons & Dragons figures in their original boxes, no cufflinks belted down in their cases by elastic loops. His money went on other things: beer, dope, a pouch of Kendal Twist every week – like father, like son – buses to London, copper flex, a blacksmith course, and any piece of architectural salvage that spoke to him, demanding rescue. Chimney pots, stained glass, iron. Leaning against the walls of his yard were old gateposts and banisters, weather vanes and barbers' poles. Stacked in neat piles under the washing line were painted Victorian tiles, enamelled cabinets and zinc watering cans.

The wheel of a gypsy caravan.

A brass pump-hose.

Danny the barrow-man. Danny the champion of bespoke and bygone things.

As you stood in the crowded yard you thought about that sixth-form trip to the V&A, when you and he had walked along the corridor of metalwork, under wrought black roses and ornate tulip brackets. Suddenly your dopey brother had woken up to the possibilities of art and craft. *Look, Suze. Look, it's so beautiful. How do they do that?*, his pond-brown eyes wide open, pushing his dark carpet fringe to one side. He had sat down right there and written something in his dog-eared, doodled-over notebook, his legs sprawling out, getting in the way of tourists. Danny with his pubescent masculinity, who had only just grown into his chest and his height, whom the girls at school had only just begun to notice.

He'd stood up, put his hands either side of a great Meccano angel, and pushed gently. You don't know why. Maybe because he always had to put his hands on things. The sculpture rocked back and the tip of one wing hit the arbour at its side. It clanged like a dropped bell. *Boooooong.* The muse had spoken. The look on his face. Stupefaction. Pure joy. Cue the guards, and the pair of you were chucked out of the museum, to the mortification of your teacher, who *thought better of you at least, Susan*. A typically Caldicutt disgrace of course. Your dad thought it was brilliant when you told him, one for the proles, and he kept the letter the school sent home, sticking it up on the studio wall.

Danny had a little yellow book – *Wrought Ironwork: A Manual of Instruction for Craftsmen* – that he carried every-where he went. He would quote bits of it like philosophy, in situations where he considered it pertinent. *Metal worked on the anvil has grace which belies its strength,* he'd say on someone's birthday, as if providing the answer to the universe. You found it on his living-room shelf next to the bong. You kept it – it was one of the only things you did keep. The rest – the bedcover smelling of incense, the farmboy overalls, the rusty saucepan and wok – you boxed up for Oxfam. Danny's old boss at the scrappy had agreed to empty the yard. He'd offered you money but you said no.

Both Danny's girlfriends had called round while you were packing things away, within fifteen minutes of each other, as if they'd coordinated their movements, and they probably had. Heather and Terry. Terry and Heather. At the funeral they had stood together, holding hands, giving each other tissues.

When she arrived at the flat, Terry had a piece of paper with her, on which Danny had constructed a ridiculous pissed-up last will and testament. He'd done it one night when they'd gone dam-diving at Thirlmere, she said. She thought it should be handed over, given to a solicitor, to see if it was valid. It was sealed, folded in half, and cruttered. She didn't know what was in it, she said she hadn't looked; she wasn't that sort of person. You told her it probably wouldn't be applicable if it wasn't officially notarised, but you thanked her anyway.

You'd met her once before at the flat, her composure soft-soaked on Danny's couch, smoke curling from the sides of her mouth as she let go of the pipe. She was pretty, wide-eyed, blonde. *Wow, you two look dead similar,* she'd said. *It's a bit spooky.* Then she'd giggled. *I've never been with a woman.* Now she was looking at you soberly through strands of corn-yellow fringe, and again must have been seeing a lot of him in you. Your facial slopes and tones were always just about the same, give or take his square chin, your refined brows. You both wore a red blush just above your jaw-line in cold weather. You still do.

Terry wondered if she could take one of his photographs of the two of them together, to remember him by. She knew where there was one tucked in a dresser drawer, and it was a bit rude anyway. You didn't tell her you'd already found it, under the ragged chaos of his T-shirts, that you'd seen the two of them, naked, in front of a Lakeland river, a place you recognised because you had swum there every summer of childhood with him. It was a place where the golden mouths of fish blew upwards in the brackish water while you sprawled on your stomachs on the bank and flicked them bread. The reeds grew long beards in the shallows, and you and he would wade through them in your plastic sandals. When you came out your legs would be covered in tiny green worms. You used to pick them off each other, as slowly as you could, seeing who could stand to wear the tickling creatures longest. It was in this place, aged eleven, you'd discovered how you were different, putting a hand there carefully, and describing what you felt. *Like a Chinese finger trap. Like gone-down balloons.*

In the photograph they were wet-skinned after swimming and pink-shouldered from the sun, her with extraordinary chestnut nipples, his genitals like catkins. You'd put it back in the bureau face down, embarrassed, disarmed by its erotic quality. You'd wondered who had taken it, or whether it had been timed.

As Terry was leaving, she'd hugged you and said that Danny had gotten her off junk, and away from a man who used to clobber her senseless in Harraby. She said he was a darling to her; he made her think about being OK and being free. And as far as she knew he was always a darling to Heather too.

That was the thing. Danny never went in for monogamy. He

138

never chose. *I can't do conventional,* he used to say. *They're all so nice. And I'm way too weak with the booze in me.* He told them all very early on that his love was a shared commodity, and went with the ones who didn't mind. The liberals, the hippies, the partygoers, and those girls for whom casual consensual sex was a step up in a relationship. There was something about it you took comfort in: his refusal to prioritise, his being un-winnable. Sometimes you felt guilty, for the connection between the two of you, for having had an unfair advantage all those years – as if, after you, none of them could stack up. True enough, they were all variably inferior. You knew it when he said things like, *She's a babe but she's just not on my wavelength, Suze. She doesn't totally get what's in my head.*

There was never any damage done in the end. He was considerate. He talked them through it, said goodbye in bed and out of it, let them stay an extra day or two. He remained in contact, a semi-reliable friend, an occasional subsidiser of rent. He was simply Danny, a joker, a drinker, the sweet-hearted, sensitive, un-marrying man. Shallow, but for his depth.

Your parents grew used to meeting one pretty fool-stung girlfriend after another. They got good at temporary welcomes, the remembering of names for bumpings-into at the supermarket and the bank. It was very amicable. Hello, love. Hello, Shelley. Hello, Caroline. Kat. Della. Pamela. Amanda. Clare. Alison. Gillian. Rachel. Freya. Fiona. Lorraine. Rosie. Sharon.

At the flat you waited for Terry to go, then you opened the envelope and unfolded the paper. His handwriting was as bad as ever, made worse by the influence of whatever they had taken, and the idiotic anticipation of tombstoning thirty feet down into pitch-black water. There wasn't much to read – just three lines. You'd expected a thicker tome, reams of loopy, mushroomy crap scrawled across the page, because it usually took Danny a good few goes to find the meaning in what he was trying to say. Danny had never quite arrived at maturity. You'd assumed that he'd be eternally juvenile and hare-brained, and you'd always have the task of dismissing his crackpot notions or humouring him. Danny never quite got to grips with the real world. He always thought things could be knocked together somehow, towed or balanced, spun or floated or flown, when it was obvious to any halfwit that they could not.

Like the time, aged fourteen, he decided to paraglide off Skiddaw using an old sailcloth tied to his belt, and they had to pin his leg in two places at the local infirmary.

Like last year, when he entered the river Eden paddle race, with an oil-drum yacht – *The Dirty Sanchez*. You and Nathan had tracked his progress from the bank, cheering him on as the kayaks made off downstream. You'd watched him float along at a glacial pace, the various agricultural inflatables bulging below the planking. *She'll pick up speed,* he'd reassured you, grinning, *she just needs to build up a head of steam*. He was wearing flip-flops, a Hawaiian shirt, and blow-up armbands. He'd roped a four-pack of beer to the deck and he pulled it up from the water and opened a can. When the raft ground to a halt in the rapids, Danny had leapt into the water, splashing around and drenching himself, and he'd managing to tug the rusty hull free. The other supporters had laughed and cheered as your brother gave the thumbs-up. Two hundred yards further on the vessel had begun listing badly. People yelled at Danny to abandon ship. In the end it was Nathan who had intervened, heroically jumping off the sandstone bluffs into the water, and helping your brother to tow the sinking *Sanchez* into an inlet, where she was hastily dismantled. The two of them had swum to the finish line with a tractor tyre floating between them. Then Danny had chased you down, picked you up, and thrown you in the river, as if you were eleven years old again.

You loved this quality about him. His yaw. His silliness. His lovely, lofty profundity. He was a boy with a brain full of gorgeous, ludicrous thoughts, even at the age of thirty-five. He didn't understand doom. And you so badly wanted him to succeed. Just once. To build his machine, ride the rapids, fly. In Danny you could see a wonkier version of your dad, the progeny of those adventure-inventor Caldicutt chromosomes. When Terry handed you the will, this is what you expected – more of the same. Obscure quotes and hip musical instructions, the desire for sloe poteen to be passed round in some nude forest ceremony. You'd have put good money on it. But you were wrong.

Don't stick me in the ground. I want Suze to make a big bonfire. Toss me on.

You read it and you felt your heart drop inside its bone cavity. All he wanted in the end was you. It was extraordinary to be reminded in that single moment of who he was and who you were. Compatible birth mates, biological repeaters. Closer than anyone else could ever be to you, and you to he.

You sat on the floor of his flat, now empty and smelling of mildew, and folded and unfolded the note. You read it again. You thought about Dr Dixon and the insects in his aquarium trees, their bodies damp with mucus after crawling from their skins. *Say I do, Sue. Say I do.* You remembered how as a child you had gradually lost a sense of what Danny was doing in the next-door room – pulling off his socks, watching a spider scuttle, picking his nose. You retuned the channel, started broadcasting on another frequency, clean and static-less and one-way. *I, I, I,* you repeated, *me, me, me.*

And you thought about the time Danny had run away. It was at the end of that six-month period of treatment at the clinic. He had slipped out of the cottage and on to the moors one afternoon, and had hidden under a thorn tree. He was upset because you weren't playing head-talk any more, and he thought you were angry with him. When it became apparent he was missing, you went out with your parents to try to find him. You called his name. You tried to think where he would be – you tried to know where he would be – on the huge brown expanse of the moor. You had never felt so lonely. You had never been so sorry. After what seemed like hours, your dad found him curled under a blackthorn, his arms scratched and bleeding. He was sound asleep. When he was lifted out he woke up. He took your hand. You were forgiven.

Occasionally there were reminders, a residue of some kind. He'd laugh out loud if you were thinking something funny, and say he wanted tuna mayonnaise for his lunch if you had planned on having it. The day you got your first period he seemed aware, if not of the uterine aches, then of some kind of general malaise, because during your next lesson together he handed you a Disprin tablet from the chalky stash of pills he kept in his pencil tin.

You were still siblings, still the Caldicutt twins. But cognitively you went your separate ways. At school you accelerated through academic disciplines while Danny tooled around, arranged local haunted-house tours, scoured the fields and marshes for mushrooms, got into Ecstasy and speed. He formed discordant bands, cycled the Roman roads. After his foundation year, there was never an attempt to make it past amateur artist. He was a craftsman of the ordinary, he said, a plain old smithy. *I'm a lesser-bearded Ruskin, a salon-less Courbet.* Not a Peter. Not a Suzie. He was happy for you and your dad, proud of the acclaim, the attention, proud too of everything your mum did, her loaves, her scrapbooks, the haircuts she gave him. He was humble, and deeply pleased.

Your silly, soulful brother. The one on the right side of the womb, the one, it turns out, earmarked for extinction. Cut short in his prime, they said at the funeral. *Poor Danny,* people said, *why did it have to be him? Life is so cruel. He got such a raw deal.*

But that's not true. Danny was blessed. He was touched by the hand of a benign deity. He was living the dream, seizing the day. Somehow your brother avoided the solemnity and dross of the modern world. A tap dripped happiness into his temperamental reservoir. There was no lust for money or new things, no lamenting the terrible state of the world and the depravity of humankind. Instead he tracked comet showers, had skinny-dipping parties, read Walt Whitman. He shared flats above chippies and launderettes with old friends from school, worked for minimum wages, saved up to go to Greece and Glastonbury and to get ferries to Man for the races. Then he always came back again. *I'm all right here, Suze,* he would say to you when you offered to help set him up in the city. *This is home. I like it here.* Danny with his flat of so few items and his slack wallet. But almost five hundred people turned up to his funeral, from Carlisle, Bowness, and Scotland, from Hexham and London. And didn't they sing for him.

No. Danny wasn't unlucky to be killed. The world was unlucky to lose him.

Don't stick me in the ground. I want Suze to make a big bonfire. Toss me on.

You pocketed the note, took the boxes out to the car. You locked up the flat, and dropped the keys down to the po-faced landlady in the shop below. She said something to you about having him as a tenant. You didn't hear and you didn't care. You were thinking about Halloween, when you were teenagers, running crazy between the burning whin bushes. All across the common land in the darkness, the wagging yellow cones of gorse that you had fired. Danny would yell at you to light another one and you'd hold the lighter to the green spines and hear them rat-tat-tat-tatting as they caught. Then you'd take turns to jump across the flames, from blackness into blackness. When you ran and launched yourself Danny would be so afraid and full of laughter. He'd wait on the other side and grab you.

You drove out of town and turned on to the military road towards your parents' cottage. As you drove into the hills, you had a strange fantasy, about making his pyre, like he had asked you to. You imagined laying his body on a mound of hawthorn and sitting with it as the sun went down and then lighting the fire. The wind would bellow it fierce, until the red embers were hot enough to leave no trace of hair or bone or molar, not even the pins screwed into his leg. His essence would billow across the valley. And when the fire burnt down, the soft tresses of ash would blow away, and nothing would remain above the ruined black cot of stone.

You were thinking of this as you drove back to the cottage, and it was so very comforting, and for the first time in days you felt he was close.

Translated from the Bottle Journals

I fear we are beginning to lose our oldest skills. The repair of mosaics and frescoes is a delicate matter and one that is currently providing much consternation. The younger generations do not understand the manufacturing processes and the raw materials with which we have produced great works. These lessons are still relevant – there is much the medievalists can teach us about quality and application. During class on Thursday I asked the children to tell me about paint, about how it is made and where it comes from. To children, paint is a miracle produced alchemically within the tube. Suppose the shops were shut, I proposed, and the materials not available to us. Suppose the factories stopped making these miraculous tubes. There would be no violet, no orange, or green, or indigo. Is it not a predicament in which we find ourselves? But what solution might there be?

Next I produced quills of goose feather and showed them how to split the shaft and insert and bind the brush and trim the tip, and I gave them a rudimentary lesson on the manufacture of yellow. We walked to the mountainside and took ochre out of its seams with palette knives and the children were obliged to grind the earth with pestles and bind the substance and strain it, which they did with great enthusiasm. Suddenly they were the busy apprentices of the fifteenth century. Now you can see, I said to them, that as artists you are free to paint whenever you choose. The use of such methods is a long and trusted endeavour. It is not naïve. It is not quaint. You can wear the leather apron of the journeyman with pride. You are enabled always by the grace of the land.

Signora Russo permits the children to leave the establishment if they hold a knotted rope, which I must lead. It is knotted to indicate the number of children; each child holds a knot when we walk. I do not know if this is the typical method for transporting her assembly or whether she is worried that I will lose some of them down the burrows and into the lake. I have no trouble remembering where I have placed my shoes each morning, I tell her. I am reminded of the Eastern fairytales my mother told me as a boy. And with our childish knots, safely through the woods we go.

My cough has become less offensive. I have felt well all week and so have postponed the appointment at the hospital. I know I am old and susceptible: I do not need a medical diagnosis stating this. I only need to look up from the page to see that my garden has become a province of tangled grass. The garlic thrives, as do the small fruits and herbs, but much else is running away. We have had heavy rain and the banks have begun to erode. Theresa cannot attend to these tasks, though she has sympathy for the garden and my affection for it and my increasing inability to care for it. Giancarlo has helped with repairs in the past. I have no wish to employ a gardener. It would be to admit defeat.

Theresa is filling her big pan with the last tomatoes as I write. Later she will prick their skins and remove their seeds. She will take the sauce home balanced on her bicycle seat. Today we have not been getting along. Theresa is vexed by the library of books in the house – that is to say my collection of books, catalogues, and pamphlets. The piles are impossible to clean round, she says. Ants nest between them and then march into the kitchen, into the pot of honey and the pot of sweet dates. But ants are marvellous creatures, I tell her. Do you know they have a private stomach for themselves and a public stomach for the good of the colony? If an ant could read a newspaper surely it would choose *L'Unità*?

She does not wish to be told jokes or teased about her proclivities. She wishes to re-order the books and put them on the shelves. By this she means she wishes to dispose of them. All the shelves at Serra Partucci already contain books. I suspect that she believes books to be unimportant. She is a provincial woman who cannot tolerate literature. Her opinions are intractable and she will not be enlightened. If I contradict her she becomes sullen and puts too much salt into her dishes to dry up my mouth. In the past I have accused her of attempting to poison her employer. We can pass hours in silence if the mood of the day is one of bitter disagreement. The books will leave this residence only after I do and much less quickly than Theresa if an ultimatum is issued. I informed her of this quite plainly this morning. No doubt I have become abrupt over the years. This afternoon, by way of a truce, I found a poem in the collection of Giacomo Leopardi and read it to her. 'And as I hear the wind rustling among these plants, I go on and compare this voice to that infinite silence.' He is the most crystalline of writers. She left the room halfway through the recitation. She is often an intolerable creature.

Once I made for Theresa a little straw model to show the frame of a lizard. One long piece and two shorter horizontal pieces twisted to it. It looked, in fact, like her double crucifix. I have also shown the children in the school this replica. This is how the lizard moves, I said, and I bent the front and back legs together on the left, and then I bent the front and back legs together on the right. This is how they can climb to such great height, I said. This gives them great speed and great stability. Do you see? Theresa retrieved her dustpan from the cupboard and swept the model into it and deposited it outside, and then she collected her bicycle and went home.

The slow rusted bicycle of Theresa, its wheels pleading for oil with each rotation as she pushes the contraption down the hill.

There has been no letter from Peter this week. I have been spoiled to receive so many. I think of him often. I wonder how he progresses with his studies and his painting. What are his current philosophies? Which sculptors and colourists does he admire, and how will he begin to articulate these influences? How will this Peter of the Rocks found his church? He should heed the words of Cennini, who writes so intelligently on the subject.

> *You, therefore, who with lofty spirit are fired with this ambition, and are about to enter the profession, begin by decking yourself with this attire: Enthusiasm, Reverence, Obedience and Constancy. And begin to submit yourself to the direction of a master for instruction as early as you can; and do not leave the master until you have to.*

For three years I studied in the red city. It was a different age of learning then. The gates of Accademia di belle Arti were decorative iron. But as immovable as this firmament were the teachings within the establishment. All affiliation and experimentation with the modern was quickly denounced. In my youth, I burned pictures related to Braque and the fragmentalists. The scholars at the Academy would tolerate no such curiosity or experimentation – they believed in paralysis and perfection. All attempts at the primitivist styles were accused of impatriotism and, if found guilty, we were made to study the great pieces again, and in some cases retake *corso comune* as humiliation. These teachers could, with one stroke, intervene and impose upon any painting that offended them. I have never felt such frustration as when watching a canvas dividing its wooden brace as the flames consume it. I have never once touched a brush to the paintings of my students.

In these times, poetry was the only salvation, and we were, all of us, poets and hungry for what the true poets were saying. It was they who collated our passion and our insult. It was they who reminded us to breathe when we held our breath, and taught us courage.

I have prepared a canvas for the new painting but I have altered the position of the bottles again – something was not quite right. I have written to inform Antonio. Each time I begin a painting I think I know everything, I believe myself fully equipped to work, but in truth I am starting with nothing and I know nothing. It can be a desolate thing. I am unable to convince myself of success. When I turn to look in the studio mirror I see a man of superficial health who reads poetry to his housekeeper instead of going to the hospital. I watch him. His hair is shockingly white. He smokes until the cigarette scalds his fingers. He smokes another. He waits for something – a bird, perhaps – to flit across the window, or for an announcement from the wind at the door of the house. He waits for permission from the objects on the table. He considers the spaces between. He rearranges by a fraction.

Peter must visit the National Gallery in London. He must see the glazed earthenware and the pewter, the wet fish-scales and gold-ringed eyes in the marine studies of Velázquez. He must see the liquid pooled in the sockets. He must see these paintings and not try to interpret utensils or religion or any such thing, nor should he try to unravel the symbolism of Vanitas or the elegant paradox of each title. Peter must feel the temperature of the bream, the death-shroud of seas over it, and the crackling of garlic skin as it is peeled. He must hear the sound of grinding in the kitchen mortar. And he must see the dragonfly of van Os – arrested – its transparent wings, its essence of flight. In America he must see Cotán's quince and cabbage, suspended, tied delicately with string. The melon's seeds slipping from the orange flesh.

I would present him with the timeless gifts of the *nature morte*. Still-life with citrons and walnuts. Still-life with lobster, the serration of claws. Still-life with parrot, and fruits out of season. Still-life with cloves, chilli, eggs, hare, dead birds, dewdrops, and rose. With asparagus, coins, straw skull, wicker, terracotta vase. Still-life with drinking horn.

Only then will he begin to understand living art.

The Fool on the Hill

The temperature is dropping, and the night is beginning to get uncomfortable. After all, he has on only the flowery cotton undershirt and the overalls, and wasn't expecting to have to use a coat – typical northerner, coming out unprepared. The chill breath in the gorge circles his shoulders, stealing the heat from his body. There is less pain in his leg now though, or perhaps he is getting used to it. For an hour he has been fighting the cold, blowing into his cupped hands, flapping his arms and going nowhere, like a clipped bird. He has been throwing punches out into the darkness, boxing to keep his blood warm. A song is lodged in his head, something the kids have been listening to over and over on the stereo – some Manchester band, something about wanting to be a dog. Not a bad tune compared to the other crap on the radio these days. For some reason it's stuck on repeat, is going round and round, and he's been humming it, nodding his head to its melody. It's keeping his spirits up at least, giving him something to think about. He's even caught himself laughing a few times at the idiocy of his predicament, and that's made him feel better too.

It's apparent tonight that this is the changeover season. He can feel summer's end. There's the memory of frost down in the earth's membranes. The northern rivers are carrying a message to the Solway that winter is coming. It's nippiest on his arse, where he's leaning against the stone. Things are getting particularly numb down there. The rocks seem to have their own gelid circulation; they seem reptilian that way. But that's rocks for you, Peter – creatures with a system all their own. Hasn't he said it many times, in interviews, and to visiting collectors? 'The rocks, the rocks are alive . . .'

Hoist by your own petard, daft bugger. The irony is not lost on him. To have wound up here, stuck fast in this landscape, pincered between two apparently sentient, apparently wilful obelisks. To have been caught out by this densest of environments, which he has spent a lifetime rendering. Yes. It's just perfect. And if he doesn't get out of here, if he gets hypothermia, starves, dehydrates, and carks it; if the rooks start pecking out his eyes and have away with his nose; if no one in fact finds him down in this semi-remote gulley for years, until he resembles an odd, upright bouquet of bones, they will all say it: what an ironic way to go. How fitting. How right, how totally bloody *meaningful!*

He is not going to get hypothermia. This isn't Everest. He is not icebound. Yes, he is thirsty. Yes, the injury is probably not very pretty; it may even be severe – a bloody bundle of skin and splinters down there, impacted, mashed, beyond repair. But this is a minor inconvenience in the scheme of all mountain disasters. Unlikely it will become legend. Unlikely he will have to eat himself to survive. It probably won't make it past *Border News*. Yeah. He can see the smirking presenter now, turning the page for this last somewhat entertaining item. 'Yesterday a local artist discovered there's more to his landscapes than meets the eye.' Oh Christ! How will he live it down? Maybe he can keep it quiet. If the Mountain Rescue aren't involved. If there's no filmed helicopter drama, no Ian Lumb or Adrian Bodger being winched down in a fluorescent helmet. 'Oh, it's you, Peter. How're you doing, lad?'

I wanna, I wanna, I wanna be a dog.

On the other hand, if he's honest, Mountain Rescue would be welcome right about now. His position is, in actual fact, intractable. It is fairly bloody miserable. And the leg is really sore. It isn't the wild, contractive pain of a few hours ago; now it's levelled off, and is just very tender. But a needle full of anaesthetic would be really good. And maybe this won't hurt his profile at all. He could give an exclusive account to one of the art supplements. The mountain versus me! Maybe it'll give him some kudos, it'll be something to rival the urban set, always banging on about how dangerous and radical and cutting-edge they are.

Oh come on. Here he is, wedged under a lump of fell, and he's being competitive with his peers. Don't be so ridiculous, Peter, don't be a clod. He's got to put the testosterone to better use. He's got to concentrate on getting free. 'Bastard! Bastaaaards!' Yes, that's more like it. Diabolical, unhinged ranting. Very helpful, very gainful. Numpty. Dimwit. Bozo.

Right. No. He's got to think positive. Got to gather himself. These stones are not his enemies. They are not vengeful organisms with creepy arctic blood and carnivorous appetites. They are his lifelong friends. He respects them. He must put the wounded, and frankly a little hysterical, side of his imagination away. This is not comeuppance. It is not self-prophesying fate. This place might presently be fucking him up quite savagely but he must remember he loves it. He has always loved it.

Beaches, mountains, rivers. These have all been his working provinces. Places where the weather intensifies. Places where the rock is clean – polished by water or rough air, with a texture older than dinosaur skeleton, so old it has moved beyond history. Corrie. Tarn. Glacier-run. Causeway. Craters. Ghylls. Sea runes. The Cumbrian hills. The coastlines. He has chosen places of rock over all else, rock in the majority

– towering, teetering magma – or rock in paucity – sediments, submerged in sand and fluid. Stone is as honest as landscape gets. It is this that has governed his career, made him antiquated, then avant-garde, then antiquated again.

He still doesn't know why, though he's come up with plenty of interesting explanations over the years, some nonsensical, some verging on the supernatural. In his own head he has always struggled to define this obsession with substance, this sensibility. Ever since his father walked up the return, sooty-faced, with that marine fossil he had tapped out of the lime-stone above the coal seam, coming in and placing it on the table in front of his son, Peter has been held. The boyhood interest in cave art, hieroglyphics, the collecting of petrified roots and heathers, arrowheads, dobbies. The brickworks, the amphitheatres, the Greek marbles. Caspar David Friedrich, Brancusi. He can hear himself wittering on about muses, call-ings, proclivities; he can see himself drawing figure-eight infinities in the air with his smoking hand while the camera records him; and simultaneously that pedantic voice is saying, no, that's not it, you're talking rubbish. Never stopped him trying.

He is a bit dippy on the subject, admittedly. He is a bit evan-gelical, a bit happy-clappy. But there are the facts of the matter – the geomagnetics. Geiger readings tell strange stories in these parts of the British Isles; they are often high, very high. Their stoddering needles lend authenticity to theories of nuclear infection, blast-off sites or alien visitation, the hum of an energy not kinetic, not electric, not periodic either, but energy nevertheless, stoked into the earth's layers. There is some undiscovered life-force, he is sure of it. Something living. Something assayable. The rocks really are alive.

He can't tell people this of course, this nuttiness, this flap-doodle, science bastardised into conspiracy theory. Though he often does tell people, or tries to. Over the sticky bar in the Queen's Head. Into the fuzzy microphone and the amused face of the journalist. It's what he says and is known to say – eccentric, florid things. This is who he is – England's traditional modern landscapist, full of brio and home-cooked whisky, working three thousand feet up and pretty close to the edge of entertaining psychosis.

Ivan Dyas understood it of course. Good old Ivan. A giant in his field and Peter's only amenable tutor at the Liverpool art school. The prescient, sweaty man slapped him hard on the back when Peter revealed his peculiar fascination. 'Excellent. Many would kill for such an infatuation, laddo. It'll be this that does the business for you, if you let it.' They were such good pals. All those trips to exhibitions. The hours spent in the pubs – The Throstle's Nest, The Why Not, and Doctor Duncan's. The debates and discussions, the drinking competitions, looking at the wannabes in Kavanagh's. It all seems such a long time ago now. Ivan Dyas. What a man. Council park sculptor, glassblower, bronze-scale northern Casanova. He remembers him manifesting in college one day like a lusty fawn god before the class, in a long leather coat and a porno moustache. Combining Mersey Beat style with tradesman's knowledge. Espousing wisdoms on a come-and-see-me-after basis, theoretical and metric, practical and prophylactic.

Peter can still see him, sitting on the studio table, one knee flung wide, bollocks straining against the trouser plaid. He knew about rock all right – both kinds. 'You can bang at flint and quartz all you want,' he would say, 'with your big wild swings. But it'll never let you in. It'll not undress for you. You'll break a wrist first, and blunt your instruments, and the Chancellor'll have a fit, but you'll not make a single clean cut. Now. Watch this.' And he would gently tap and pull the hammer and the chisel, as if he was stroking himself off. First Lesson: brute force is more likely to shatter a thumb than damage an igneous block. Not until they understood the grain, the compound, curve, and tensile strength, not until they understood the inherent direction of matter itself, would they progress any further in sculpture (and life, boys and girls, and life!). Sculpture was about respect and intuition, collaboration. Sculpture was seduction, like sex with a young lady (plenty of which was had by the man, much to his wife's dismay).

Peter's time there would have been a waste were it not for him. He'd arrived in Liverpool with scholarship grades and a second-hand donkey jacket, proud son of a miner. He was now, officially, an academic and a painter, two anomalies in the Caldicutt family and proof of the new social mobility. His was a conventional grammar education; he respected the canon and the system that had enabled him, and he would become something of a formalist behind the walls of the studio. But he felt guilty: guilty for his library card, guilty for wanting to read and for his admiration of classical things. He was fashionably working-class, fashionable according to those who weren't. Another form of pity, his old man would have said, another way of telling you what you are, and aren't.

People expected him to be radical, representative, a spokesperson. People ennobled his upbringing, thought his duty was anti-establishmentarianism – popular word back then: they all had to know how to spell it. Never mind his interests. Never mind his freedom. The tutors wanted him to paint in black. They wanted Lowry, they wanted grit. He was back to the mines, back to square one. All he wanted was to smell those heavy, stitched-leaf books and paint the sea. Some bloody revolutionary.

But Dyas was something of an atavist too, for all his current record collection, his praise of contraceptives and new European architecture. There was room for all creeds in his philosophy – Baroque to Bauhaus, Mondrian to Mitchell. Didn't matter, so long as it had integrity, something poignant to say. He'd stride into class, dirty blond curls bouncing round his head, cunny-lip goatee suggesting nothing less than the female labia, and the lecture would begin. The kicking shut of the door – *boom*. A fist pounding the table – *bang*. His releasing of the projector roll – *wham, chugger-chugger-chugger*. 'So. You think Picasso didn't have a clue about proportion then? Right. Put that pencil between your lips, Yvonne,' he'd yell to the black-lashed kitten on the back row. 'Go on, love, and give us a nice pout if you like. There you go. Lovely. Now the rest of you, the measurement from spirit level to eye . . .'

First on the dance floor, last man standing at the bar. An intemperate lover, except when he had loved Raymie. At the funeral four years later, divorced and wrung out from amphetamines, and from worrying about his wife's casual, suicidal joyrides, Peter had missed the reconciliation he so badly desired. He had arrived at the cathedral half cut, and had spewed forth a beery eulogy, to the disgust of the family. 'To my hero, to my bloody hero,' and then he'd put his face on the dead man's lapel and cried like a Spanish widow.

Dyas would get a kick out of this now, surely. *Seduce your way out of this one, Petie*, he would bellow, spreadeagling himself on a nearby boulder, and knocking the top off a bottle of stout. 'Something of a predicament, eh. Something of a rum position, kiddo. Whatever shall we do?' If he could decant the man from his memory into the world again, he would, no matter the bad history. The clouds have moved over and the darkness is intensifying. His mood of levity has left him and he is inalienably alone. Even the company of ghosts would do. Even if it meant standing trial, digging over the offences committed and hearing the charges read. Usurper. Bad friend. Thief. But the chance to apologise to Ivan – wouldn't that be a fine thing, wouldn't he risk unholy resurrection for it? The chance to say he was sorry, that he was cuntstruck, that he was too young to know better. Yes, he would raise corpses for it, Ivan's at least, though maybe not the other one.

Maybe it'd all be water under the bridge anyway – so much time has passed. Maybe they'd just have a good old natter about the state of things. They could opine on various interesting developments. The *Piss Christ*. Mandela. Dubrovnik. Betting odds. Or they could reminisce like two old codgers. Remember the marble pissers in the Philharmonic? You could whizz like a king. Remember Dolores McArthur's splendid tits? Oh yes. Epic. Maybe they would shake hands like decent friends, sit in the cold together and wait for the re-emergence of the stars. Dyas would be incisive, as always. 'Hate to say it, Peter old son, but that sounds like rain.'

And true enough, there is an aspirin flavour to the air, an impending fizz. He can feel the first few drops arriving on his forehead, and then a steady patter begins. Peter looks up. There is just blackness and water. A few minutes, and he is soaked through. The wound begins to nip and sting, and he knows then that the flesh is open. He tears a wet strip from the hem of his shirt and ties a tourniquet at the top of his calf. He doesn't know how much he is bleeding. He doesn't know if he is scratched, or if his life is draining away. He can smell minerals being released from the stones all around, the perfume of the mountain.

The Divine Vision of Annette Tambroni

When the blindness came it was not unexpected. Dottor Florio had outlined the disease. Also there had been a series of unfortunate events and Annette felt she was simply the next in line, like a domino toppling over because the one before it had toppled. First Signor Giorgio had died. He had not come to the school for many weeks. Signora Russo had told them that he was in grave health, and that they should pray for him to recover. They were to continue sketching, of course, and improving their skills. She herself would take the lessons, she said. She placed apples in front of them, and pieces of earthenware. They were to attempt to replicate the sheen and the depth. Once she sat in a chair at the front of the classroom and invited them to attempt a portrait, but there was too much laughter and nonsense, and after ten minutes Signora Russo stood up and invited them to paint their own hands instead.

Not long afterwards she announced at the end of class one day that Signor Giorgio had passed away. She took a handkerchief from her sleeve and pressed at the corners of her eyes and then she sneezed. 'Children,' she said, 'we should not ever forget we were lucky to have received his wisdom. The rest of Italy has not understood Signor Giorgio well. Here, we might have turned our back on such a man. But he was, nevertheless, our comrade. Let us all remember how he graciously shared with us his time and his knowledge. Let us not be too sad.' She blew her nose loudly. When she had recovered she folded her handkerchief into her blouse sleeve, and said there would soon be a museum dedicated to him in the city of Bologna, where he had once studied. When they were older they might like to visit it and admire some of his paintings and read about his life. He had survived very turbulent times, she said. She said those who thought he should not have received the Grand Prize were foolish. She drew out her handkerchief and blew her nose again. Then they sang the anthem, with Signora Russo conducting, and class was dismissed.

As Annette walked home an odd thought occurred to her. She wondered what had happened to Signor Giorgio's big spectacles. Perhaps he'd had them on when he died, because sometimes death came right in the middle of what a person was doing, as it had come to her papa. Perhaps Signor Giorgio had died without his spectacles. Perhaps he had taken them off before he slept and he had died in his sleep. Annette often forgot to take off her glasses when she climbed into bed, and then she would wake up and the frames would have slipped and gored into her nose. If he had died without his spectacles, would he be able to see in heaven? Perhaps in heaven his eyesight would be perfect. She also wondered what he had heard and what he had seen when he died. A red field or the citrine wolf's eye? Bluebottles buzzing? The keys of an old Olivetti striking against its ribbon? Perhaps a firework wailing? She wondered if in any way the Bestia had been involved.

Next there was a disaster at the greenhouses. A mysterious blight had arrived in one of the beds and quickly spread to others. Textbooks were consulted. Vincenzo, Maurizio and Uncle Marcello raked and pruned, uprooted bulbs, and burned piles of leaves. Dark grey, musty-smelling smoke rose from the gardens. The panes of the glasshouses were disinfected with vinegar and newspaper. But the blight continued. In the evenings Uncle Marcello would place a black-spotted leaf next to him on the table and he would study it while eating, sometimes turning it over by its stem, as if it might reveal to him its sinister properties and its transmission code. He telephoned the London botanical gardens and had a difficult conversation in broken English. Afterwards he looked at them and shrugged. After three weeks, he said there would be no profit that year. They would have to rely on the lavenders, the olive oil and the vegetables. Annette's mother said it was a bad omen.

Perhaps it was, because then Vincenzo announced that he was going to South America. Their mother cried for a week, and said she had suffered enough humiliation and desertion already. She accused her son of keeping a whore, of stealing money from the family, of corruption and the abandonment of Italy. But the ticket was already bought and the suitcase packed. He shook hands with his brothers, kissed Annette and baby Tommaso, and unhooked Rosaria Tambroni's clawed fingers from his wrists. 'I will write,' he said. He picked up his suitcase, put on his hat, and walked to the station.

Castrabecco fell into despair afterwards. For days nobody spoke. Nobody dared to sit at Vincenzo's place – a black shawl was folded neatly on his chair, and the chair was turned to face away from the table. Even Mauri's teasing and tickling and playfulness was suspended. Their mother lay in her room with the door locked. Twice there was the sound of violent weeping and something smashing. The family waited in abeyance. Finally it was Tommaso who broke the spell. He pulled himself up off the floor while no one was watching and pushed the mourning chair like a barrow around the room, making the noise of a purring, spluttering engine. He pushed it down the steps and out the door of Castrabecco into the courtyard, where it was left overnight in the rain. Annette retrieved the damp shawl and Uncle Marcello broke up the chair legs and tossed the pieces on to the smouldering bonfires of blighted leaves.

* * *

Then it was Annette's turn. It began as a tickle at the back of her throat, as if a tiny funnel spider were spinning a web between her tonsils. When she swallowed, she could not get rid of the spider or its weaving. Other children were sick at the school. There was talk on the radio of a pandemic in the region, and the school was swiftly closed. It was too late. Annette's temperature rose. Dottor Florio was called and he confirmed that a virus was in her system. 'It's in the glands, so we must watch her closely,' he told her mother. 'This could trigger the degeneration. I think you'd better prepare yourself, Rosaria.'

Annette was sent to bed to rest. It was hard to sleep, and then it was too easy to sleep and she slept for hours and hours. Once she woke and thought it was the middle of the night, but outside the shutters the sun was very bright. She got up confused. Her face, when she located it in the mirror of the bathroom, was strung with pink and white blotches. She looked like a wedding garland. Her hair was wet, as if she had just washed her face, and she felt very cold. The spider had completed its work. Her throat was closed up, full of silk threads, and she had to suck hard at the air. There was a deep tenderness under her arms, as if she had been rubbed with a leather shaving-strop right down to her ribcage.

She went to the kitchen. She wanted to sit by the warm fire, and explain about the spider living in her mouth. Her mother was speaking with Uncle Marcello, who was scrubbing his nails in the sink with a stiff brush. Tommaso was sitting on the floor at their feet. 'She's the only one in the family to be born with such a weakness,' her mother was saying. 'I don't know where it comes from. Perhaps she remained in the womb too long. I don't like to speculate, but you see pictures of those little animals from the forest with eyes like moons that only come out at night and cannot bear the daylight. Who do they remind you of?' Uncle Marcello scrubbed harder at the dark red clay lodged under his nails. 'Yes, she might be from another world, I suppose.' Her mother sighed and then leant out of the shutters and shouted to Mauri to come in and eat. 'Do I see cigarette smoke! Do I smell cigarette smoke? Come in immediately!'

Annette sat beside Tommaso. She was feeling very unwell. Her head ached and shivers kept flurrying through her heart. The floor was unsteady beneath her, as if it contained many new slopes and rises, as if all the tiles were tilting and tipping. 'I see you are up, Netta. We should probably have kept you and Tommaso separate, but now it's too late. Will you try to eat something with us?'

Over dinner there was a discussion about transplanting specimens. Uncle Marcello was convinced his plan to bring in new varieties would be a success. 'If the Duke of Tuscany can collect jasmine from China, then I am certain Marcello Tambroni can grow the plain English daffodil for Easter and encourage a few orchids next to the oven.' His voice rose over the clinking of spoons in the tureen. Annette's mother disagreed. 'How are you going to pay for these imports? It's a ridiculous plan – nobody will buy such a thing. Besides, the soil is too bitter here. They'll die. We'll go broke. This is a traditional business. Joseph would never have attempted something so risky.' 'But Joseph is not here, much as we all wish he still were.' There was a pause. Her mother changed the subject. 'This is not the issue. The issue is that the van will not start, again. We need to buy a reliable one. Andrea could order it from the factory – at trade price.' Uncle Marcello made a snorting noise through his nose. 'And we'll pay for it with what? There is only blight in the bank account!' Tommaso was stirring the sauce on his plate with a finger, and Mauri was catapulting pellets of cheese rind out of the window with a fork. There was a ping every time the metal handle recoiled.

Annette did not feel like eating. Very quietly, very softly, snow was beginning to fall in front of her eyes. She was sure it was only spring, but snowflakes were spiralling down. The green of her vest began to blanch. The golden spools of the lustreware began to fade. In her uncle's wiry hair and along her mother's cowled neckline delicate bolsters were forming, and on the table around the oil and the pepper pot white drifts were beginning to collect. 'Is it wintertime already?' she asked. Her voice sounded very far away. They all turned to her. 'Annette looks like an icicle,' said Mauri. 'Oh, God! The child looks appalling!' exclaimed Uncle Marcello. 'Shall we call the doctor again?' Annette did not hear anyone reply yes or no. The whiteness was now blowing fast and swirling around her. She was freezing one second, and too hot the next. Suddenly she slid sideways from her chair on to Mauri's lap.

That night she dreamt vivid, elaborate dreams. She was searching the Alpine glaciers for cups and saucers. Then white petals were falling from the sky. So many came down that she had to climb through them and lift her face upwards to find air to breathe. She was running. She was standing still. She was surrounded by huge flowers with long, curving thorns. They moved in towards her. Their spurs were pressed into her as if someone were wrapping her tightly into a bouquet. Thorns cut into her ribs, into her face and legs. The dreams went on, delirious and exhausting.

For three days Annette did not get out of bed. The optical snowstorm continued. She trembled under the covers and the covers slipped to the floor. Saint Catherine of Sienna visited her, and Saint Cosmos with his stethoscope. They conferred in Latin. They tangoed, like her parents in the photograph. Her mother brought up broth and held her upright and tried to encourage her to drink. 'I am in your arrangements, Mamma,' she muttered, 'with the roses. Don't sell me at the market. Signor Giorgio can see.' Her mother's voice was perplexed. 'What is this gibberish? Oh! This is an outrage. When will they decide to vaccinate! Please, Annette. Please try not to dribble. You've got to eat.'

Uncle Marcello brought in a bough of honeysuckle and draped it along the low beam above her bed. Its pale yellow sweetness filled the room and her sleep became more settled. He sat with her and took hold of her arm. He kissed the inside of her wrist. When she stretched out her other hand to him, she felt Mauri's sleek hair resting on the bed and the plump lobe of his ear.

On the morning of the fourth day, Annette woke up. Her nightgown was rumpled and damp about her stomach, but the squall inside her head had ended. The room was beautifully still. She reached for her glasses and put them on. She blinked, and blinked again. She rubbed her eyes. But there was nothing to see at all.

Dottor Florio confirmed the damage. He sat on the edge of Annette's bed and shone red lights down the tunnels of her eyes and blew puffs of air on to the corneas with a pair of clinical bellows. He pushed gently at the opaque surfaces with a fingertip. 'I am sorry,' he said. 'The nerves are dead.' She heard her mother choke. 'You've been a very brave girl, Annette,' said the doctor, 'very brave. And we knew, didn't we, what to expect? We were all prepared.' Her mother began to weep. 'But can't she have an operation to restore things? What kind of life is this going to be?' There was fear in her voice, the same high note of fear that sounded whenever she spoke of the tragic incident at the gardens.

Annette reached out and found the ripple of her mother's long mourning dress. She held it to her face and smelled her mother's scent, the scent of heavy nylon and rose. 'It will be an adjusted life,' said the doctor, 'but still a life worth living.' His tone was not sharp but his tongue sounded uncomfortable, as if it had too little space between his teeth to move. 'It's not the Middle Ages. There's Braille. There is a facility in the city – very respected – a special school. I can give you the name. But my recommendation is to keep things normal, keep them the same. Annette will cope better in a place of familiarity. I will speak to Signora Russo. After all, there is no reason why this development cannot be accommodated. We will persevere, will we not?'

If she had imagined a pitch-black terror, like being lost in the mines of Massa, or trapped in the excavated tunnels of the Metropolitana, if she had thought her blindness would be like living in the dark, cracked varnish of the Deposition in the church of San Lorenzo, it was not so. After they had gone, Annette got out of bed and wobbled for a moment, then found her balance. She stood upright and held her arms out. There was still a little weakness from her fever and a salty taste in her mouth, but her head felt clear. She was neither too hot, nor too cold, just hungry. She knelt down on the floor. She said a small prayer to St Francis. Though her eyes were blind, inside a compartment of her head she could still see. She could imagine the room exactly as it had been before the sickness; her dresser with its beaded cloth, the washstand, and the low beam in the ceiling from which Uncle Marcello had strung the honeysuckle. She could imagine her shoes arranged neatly, side by side, their laces tucked inside the leather openings, and, on the window seat, the pot of marigolds peeking out from their green hoods.

She explored the bedroom with her hands. Everything felt as it had before – the cool terracotta tiles, the vertical grain of the table legs. She could smell the last of her illness on the sheets, the wool of her coat in the closet, and the baked clay of the plant holder. She patted a hand underneath the bed and the slapping made a cave-like sound and a shape grew out of it, which was the shape of the space below the bed. She thought of the pulsing and pipping bats at night when they left the chimneys. This was how they mapped the dusk sky, and the tiled roofs of the town, and the trees along the avenues, she thought. The familiar room rose before her out of nothingness, made of textures and fragrances, echoes and holes. Its components began to reintroduce themselves. 'Hello, I am the chair on which you sit your bottom – watch out for that splinter on the left-hand side.' 'Good morning, we are the little pine granules in the wash dish. Don't use too many of us at once or we'll foam uncontrollably.' The two bells of San Lorenzo rang out across the town, saying 'Ave, Annette, Ave.' She pictured Father Mencaroni swinging from the tasselled cords in the bottom of the tower, puffing hard and curtseying, strung between two flat notes.

Over the next few days she made her way around Castrabecco. Her feet were automatic on the stairs – they already knew the distance and the dogleg midway and the gradient from their many previous journeys up and down. It was only when she thought too hard about the position of the bathtub in relation to the sink that she knocked her kneecap hard against the porcelain. Uncle Marcello simmered a pan of buttercups with Vaseline and applied the balm to her bruise. 'Just a period of adjustment,' he said. In the cool back room of the house she put a peg on her nose and ran an inventory, gently tracing the calyxes and sepals of the flowers that Uncle Marcello had brought from the gardens, until they were all identified. Inside them, the tight corrugated knots of unopened petals. Mauri decided it would be helpful if he gave her things to hold, and he delighted in her squeals and guesses.

A pocket of sand. A lump of hairy clay. A soap bubble blown from a pipe, which popped on her jutting finger and splashed against her neck. A tiny frog caught in the courtyard, which pinged and tickled in her closed hand. A dead bird, bald on one side. A raw sausage, cold. A half-cooked sausage, warm. His tongue instead of a slug.

Soon after it was decided that she should no longer attend the school. It was decided in the kitchen between her mother and Uncle Marcello late one evening over a bottle of vin santo and some salty cheese. For two weeks Annette had been taken to school and collected by her mother, which was not their usual custom, but pleased Annette. She had been grazing her legs and dirtying her pinafore. In a letter home Signora Russo had explained that twice there had been a little commotion in class – no genuine cause for alarm, but Annette had disrupted the lesson through no fault of her own. It was innocent, wrote Signora Russo, and she felt confident that everything would settle down. Under the school's policy, however, she was obliged to make a parental report.

That afternoon Annette had also developed a small stomach ache, and then discovered wetness in her underwear. Upon confiding to her mother that she thought she might once again be falling sick, she was questioned at length on the nature of the bloodstain. That it was blood shocked Annette; she had not hurt herself intimately. 'How has this happened?' her mother snapped. 'What have you allowed to happen?' She gripped her daughter's shoulders tightly. 'Tell me!' Annette was at a loss. The day had been ordinary; no crime had been perpetrated either by her or against her as far as she could remember. After the initial panic, the task of explaining that all girls become the monthly brides of Christ fell to Rosaria Tambroni. Women must be adept, she said, at memorising the calendar and preparing themselves. Annette was given a belt and cottons, and her mother, rapidly, and with no small excruciation, explained how to use them.

And that night, in the kitchen, there was a difficult conference. 'Florio is wrong,' her mother said to her uncle. 'It's going to be too much for us to go on as before. There is no dignity in it. Everything is so public.' 'Is it the others?' asked Marcello. 'Are they asking personal questions? It's gossip. They probably want you to talk about you-know-who. They want you to cry on their shoulders.' There was a long pause in the conversation. 'No. But things have become complicated. Annette has developed.' There was another pause, and then a cry of exasperation. 'Oh how ridiculous this is! She is of an age! Do you understand, Marcello?' Uncle Marcello chuckled. 'Ah, such a blessing visits her early.' He refilled their glasses while Rosaria regained her composure. 'Anyway, it is my opinion that a frame should be placed around her life so that everything is contained and manageable. She is at risk. She is vulnerable. I think it is our duty. A mother knows what is best for her children.'

Marcello sighed. 'OK. If it's what you want, then she will be cultivated no further.' There was the chink of wine glasses as the agreement was made. 'Perhaps you are right, Rosa. She is the perfect age. We should arrest her vitality before it has a chance to wilt.'

The Mirror Crisis

After you'd taken care of Danny's flat, and overseen the clearing of salvage from his back yard, you'd spent a few days with your parents. It was March. There was a late fall of snow, and in the fields the first of the lambs rocked against their mothers, red cords trailing from their underbellies. You'd walked over the scratched white moors, raising the peat where you trod. In the farm cottage the three of you had eaten soup for lunch and for dinner. Your mum cut vegetables, skimmed stock, kept busy. At night your father drank steadily, and cried in her arms.

The following week, you went back to the city. Nathan was careful around you, keeping the volume of the television low, speaking softly, standing up and sitting down with a dancer's grace. It felt as if he had lined the walls of the house with insulation. On the fridge you noticed he had tacked a card with the number of a local support group, as if he imagined you might meet with them on Tuesday and Saturday evenings, and cry it out, then drink thin social tea. At night you dreamt circus dreams, of a man on fire cycling along a dark road. There was a voice, *Wave to Danny, sweetheart, he's waving back.* When you woke you felt unawake, as if you were simply in another dream.

You tried to return to normal, to some semblance at least of normality. You tried to fight your way back into life. You swam hard against the strong current that wanted to take you the other way. You got up, got dressed, and went to work. You ate, you spoke, you participated, but part of you was gone. The hands pouring milk from the bottle were no longer yours. They felt numb, and when the bottle slipped from your grasp, smashed on the kitchen floor and cut your legs, the red drip-drip seemed inconsequential. That feeling of daily animus, that life-gust, which you had always taken for granted, was simply not there. Your body went about its business, but you were not the driving force. You were still alive. Danny wasn't. It made no sense.

You had known to expect darkness, of course – the bleak aftermath, the dimming of the world's light and colour and music. You had known that in the wake of tragedy comes sadness, spiritual adjustment. You'd seen it in Nicki's family, in their sallowness, their troubled pronouncements, the way they never quite managed to let her go, or find anything else of commensurate importance. They were caught in a long elegy.

The current was so strong. You wanted to go with it. You wanted not to fight against it. Danny had left you behind. He'd gone somewhere deep, where air and sustenance were irrelevant. His corpse was in the fresh, yew-shadowed earth of the cemetery, but you knew this was not his locus. He was out there somewhere, somewhere thick and quiet; you could sense it. The pull, his note, your body's dissolution: they were all inviting you to follow. And because you loved him, because you had always loved him, you went. You fell into a steep dive. You held your breath, stretched out your arms, and kicked hard after your brother.

You lay in bed with your back to Nathan and your head turned towards the heath, and you thought of that imaginary pyre. Danny, with his river-skin evaporating and his head of smoke. Danny with his mouth and eyes like chimney holes, hot coals packed around his ribs. You wondered what the smell of his burning flesh would be like. Like a slaughterhouse perhaps, with notes of fur and bowel, and intestinal cud, but not frightening, not sickening. There was almost peace in it. Nathan put his hand on your shoulder and turned you gently to him. *Hey, can't sleep? Do you want me to read to you? Come on, love.* After he had drifted off, you left the bed and switched on the television. You flicked between channels, looking for scenes of violence and trauma and late-night horror.

At the gallery Angela and Tom were thoughtful. They gave you space to mourn, space to dwell in this strange, removed state. When they spoke to you, asking if you would like a coffee or a sandwich, the words arrived muted and echoing, as if spoken underwater. You responded with minimal gestures. A shaken head. A nod. The workload was light. A display of modern folk art was in its last few weeks at the gallery – a series of fairground etchings, barge-ware, treen, and decorated eggs. You sat at the heavy leathered desk, preparing paperwork for the forthcoming European exhibition, mapping the rooms, and drafting text for the labels. *The doll, a life-sized replica of his lover, Alma, was destroyed by the artist after it proved to be a disappointing substitute. The lock of hair, allegedly rescued by . . .* You typed the words, but your mind was on other things.

When the gallery quietened, you took the phone book out of the drawer and leafed through its membranous pages. Seventeen funeral directors were listed locally. One by one, you dialled their numbers, told them about Danny, and asked for help. In each voice was cool, elegant sympathy. You imagined Restoration blue walls, like the walls of the parlour where you and your parents had made the arrangements for Danny's burial two weeks earlier. They asked about preferences – cremation, burial, home rest – and were met with your silence. The questions were gently repeated. They offered to take your number and call back later, at an appropriate time, when you were feeling better. Still you did not reply. They could not give you what you wanted. You wanted to know his state, how it felt and tasted, how it was to be lost. You could not explain to them that in knowing was companionship. In knowing was finding Danny, somewhere in the brown vastness, asleep. When you gave no suitable answers, they politely hung up. You turned instead to the place where all depraved civilian requests are made and met: the internet.

You waited until Angela and Tom had gone home. *You really don't mind locking up?* Angela had asked. *Please don't feel you have to work late. We're on top of everything.* You told her it was OK. She smiled, pulled on her coat. *Well, we'd better pick up the baby.* Tom lingered for a moment by the front door. *I liked him very much,* he said. The door of Borwood House closed and you locked it behind them. You opened your laptop, went to a search engine and typed in a few choice words. Thousands of links came up. You clicked on one at random, not knowing what to expect. Within seconds the Underworld had opened, and you had crossed the river Styx.

The entries were awful and mesmerising. Behind the densely pixellated doors was every facet of loss and longing, every mortal imagining. There were testimonies about what it was like to die and be brought back again, about sex with angels. *First he fucked me with the spur of his wing. When they come their eyes are like black fire.* There were holocaust museums, skull catacombs, funeral tailors, and fetishes. There were collectors of Nazi death certificates and exhumation jewellery auctions. Graveyard doggers. Cancer insurers. Psychics. Necrophiliacs, who only wanted one last embrace, the kiss of glued-shut lips, a lifted dress. There was autopsy pornography. Auto-strangulation pornography. Transplant donor pornography. There were joint-suicide stories, love murders, re-enactments. You watched a video of someone's mother dying, and a grainy clip of a man climbing on to a pale, still body on a mortuary table. When his pelvis began moving whoever was videoing said, *Yeah, yeah like that.* There was no way of knowing if it was staged. The film paused a second later, and a window appeared asking you for payment details. With each click, there was death and sex, sex and death, hand in hand, over and over, in beautiful, appalling congress.

You could not stop. You stayed late into the evening, not moving from your seat and ignoring the buzz of your phone, the screen in front of you radiant.

When you left the gallery it was 2 a.m. You set the alarm and locked the door. The heath was dark, but for the row of orange streetlights along the central path. The battery on your phone had died, so you could not return Nathan's calls, or ask him to meet you. You didn't want to go back into the gallery to call a taxi. It was cold – the front that had left snow in the north had moved south – and your breath smoked in the night air. By the triangle of shops, a car door slammed, and someone shouted. There was the low rumble of the city in the distance; traffic moving elsewhere, jets up above.

You crossed the road and began walking home. Everything you had seen online began to flicker in your mind – the images, the accounts. The death masks. Live beheading of pris-oners. The Victorian portraits of loved ones laced tightly into boots, their hair combed flat, tiny buttons fastened up their necks. The Ripper's victims: black slashes across their throats, black stitching down their torsos, black cavities in their abdomens. *More the work of a devil than of a man.* You began to walk across the heath. You knew it was stupid and unsafe, but it didn't matter, it wasn't important. After a few hundred yards the orange pools of light seemed smaller and more contained within the dark expanse. You stepped off the path and walked across the grass. The ground shone with frost. You were not wearing tights and your legs tingled. You heard yourself breathing, heard the scuff of your shoes. When the illumination of the city began to fade either side, you stopped walking and stood still. It was damp and cold, but you stood there for a long time, until you realised what it was you wanted to see, what it was you had not yet seen.

Danny. Danny's long, symmetrical form could not be displayed after he had died. It could not be handsomely arranged on the boughs of a bonfire, under the bitter glow of Orion. He could not be exhibited ever again. You would never see a last physical reflection of yourself in him, never take his hand, never kiss his forehead. The familiar markings – scar on his chin, scar on his leg, moles, bitten fingernails – were gone, skimmed off by tyre tread, diced between the axles. He was his remains. He was bits and pieces. He was annihilated, and there was no option available except the gathering up of his body parts by police officers from among the bicycle spokes, the slipping of red lumps into sealed bags – his hand, his scalp – and the hosing down of the tarmac. Your father was informed that body identification was inadvisable, no, it was impossible, so it was done from a neck chain and a ring, his back molars and his ever-empty wallet. Danny's coffin was closed; it was roomy, providing a sympathetic optical illusion, though it was nowhere near to being filled.

Translated from the Bottle Journals

It is time to be honest. My lungs are beginning to fail. They work only to half their capacity and they commit me to the house much of the time. I have missed two weeks of teaching. Walking the hill has become difficult, and breathing monumental, as if I am indisposed to the air itself. The cypresses at the end of the road seem further away than ever. I shall be sad not to be able to visit them. I like to see them become luminous in the late evening, as if full of green elixir, or watch their branches shuddering in a downpour, their leaves at a furious boil in the wind. All I can do now is salute them from my window.

Though I have days of high energy and optimism, the reverse is often true. It is unfortunate to be an intermittent tutor at the school, and unfair to the children, but if I cannot speak for the rust blowing loose around my heart, what use is my presence among them? If I continue to be absent no doubt the mistress will march the children up here in a prim line, like goats with bells, such is her fanaticism.

The prohibition of ageing! Even bending to retrieve the key from the floor where Theresa has dropped it now requires a Spartan's stamina! Recovering the leather suitcase of mementos and photographs beneath the valance is almost impossible. There is a great pressure in my chest when I stand, as if I were being trampled at the bottom of the old grape vats. Often Theresa will find me, winded in my armchair after returning from a short walk, and then there will be a lecture. She has taken to clipping out these new health warnings from the cigarette packets after they have been thrown out and putting them like coupons in a little pile. What does she hope to exchange them for?

I have had discussions with the doctor about my immodest use of cigarettes. He knows I have a high tolerance for them. But he is a man who favours the pipe, and cannot be too strict on such matters for fear of decommissioning his own habit. Besides, we have both breathed in the debris of our destroyed cities. He too, in his quiet green surgery, habitually clears his throat and recalls the dark dust of towers and loggias. We are old emphysemics, and when we talk we breathe out the past. It is history that makes mortals of us. Florio is concerned. We await the results of the X-ray and I have made a promise to rest. I have mounted my brass pocket watch on the studio wall and I will try to smoke less often, especially at night.

I am intrigued by the business of the X-raying cathode. It appears there is no limit to human inquisitiveness. The procedure is so strange: I did not feel it, but the nurses were instructed to leave the room and the technician wore a heavy lead-lined tabard to avoid radiation. Such a thing is an intrusion of the boldest kind; it is a miracle of science. Or perhaps it is simply a miracle, whereby our divine structures are revealed. The device is being used now to investigate paintings as well as we humans. To expose what was broken and re-cast in a composition is to reveal the fallibility of an artist. The spilled varnish and the misaligned hand, the lost saint and the irregular ghost pavement. All those errors and adjustments in the studios of the past. And in us – the chips and fractures and tumours, the flaws in our exceptional design. Truth has become a hunted thing, but it is eternally insubstantial. The philosophers have always known this.

I am compelled by the possibility of such revelation for the sake of teaching, yet I confess to be horrified by the scrutiny of my own interior and afraid of the evidence. What secrets will they find beside these tarred lungs? A heart full of historic sadnesses perhaps. The soft blue face of Dina, like a cyanotype; the many layers of guilt and the badly repaired peace.

During the allied bombing, we watched our industrial architecture become shingle and relic. The Pope negotiated on behalf of the city of St Francis and others, where it was considered the wealth of Italy lay, but the city of Bologna was unlucky. All the cities of the north came under fire. At that time I felt I could not record any item manufactured by human hand. Instead I turned to the objects of the sea. The paintings of this era were small in scale. All around was devastation, and I painted the shells I had owned as a boy. In the still-lifes they are blushing, as if more than calcium, as if more than invertebrate, and closer in texture perhaps to human ears. There were bodies in the rubble. Sometimes it was possible to hold a mother and daughter, the priest, and the church in which they had all prayed, together in one hand. Many felt this intimate travesty during the rescue operations.

After the war, and the loss of Dina, I moved south to the old region of my family. 'Take me home,' the Spanish poet cried to the ocean. 'Take me home, for I am weary of wars.'

The shell paintings ran for one series. They were not removed from my studio by the Germans, who looted our homes as they withdrew to the north, though several landscapes and still-lives were taken and have never been recovered. They are in locations unknown; even Antonio cannot seem to trace them. The war paintings are owned by the Vatican and a collector in New York. They are known as *The Fighting Shells*.

* * *

Antonio has sent me a good selection of newspapers and catalogues this week. We also spoke on the hospital telephone after my appointment, and he is keen to visit me as soon as we know more. I know he is worried. In his note he inquires after my health, as ever, and asks if there is anything I wish for to make life more comfortable. He comments on some of the articles – the commercial forces of Europe are shifting, he notes. I could have hoped for no more considerate son, were I to have had one. Often Antonio's parcels threaten to spill open, they are so full of cuttings and columns that he thinks will be of interest. He sends copies of the *Paris Review* and *The Nation*. Also the London periodicals and the strip cartoons, which I enjoy.

The news from abroad is intriguing. Krauss and Hughes have taken up the arguments of Rosenberg and Canaday. Abstract Expressionism remains deeply divisive. I do not agree with the theory that in these vast dragged canvases chaos and arrogance are the central motives. The idea of subconscious production is intriguing to me. Intuition remains such a mystery. The objections, however, seem more about notoriety, the fashion of the artists, which restaurants they eat in and with whom they socialise. From obscurity to notoriety in less than a year – it is the era of celebrity. The artist is as the movie star.

There is a new exhibition in London. A painting I donated a few years ago has temporarily been placed amid the opposing forces of North America. It is creating a stir. It has been done deliberately to polarise, but I do not mind this. In fact, I believe it is often necessary for the curators to provoke such discussions. Naturally, there are two opinions of my painting. The first: it is a fierce little thing, all the more worth attending to because it is dwarfed by hysterical compositions. It is contemporary Italy. The second: though it is formally competent, it is a defunct painting. Like Cepheus – the dead constellation – it contains no bright star. Italy is represented by the nostalgic, a redundant cosmos.

And so it continues.

In his letter, Antonio insists I install a telephone at Serra Partucci so that he might speak with me more readily. He has insisted this before many times. You are welcome to speak personally with the municipal engineers, I have told him, and ask if their scaffolds will extend up to the house. And while they are there, they might as well fill the pockets of their overalls with stones from the surface of the moon.

Thinking about it, I would like to smoke very much. It has been my habit for fifty years to smoke outside after dinner and look at the landscape. I am attempting to keep my hand busy by writing, but I desire tobacco. The pocket watch is ticking on the wall and it is making everything worse. I find myself in the end writing nothing of importance. But I must try to keep my word. When she comes tomorrow, Theresa will notice the discarded cigarettes and report them to Florio. I am too old to begin to hide things in poke holes like a schoolboy!

At night the mountainside belongs to others. I feel like an honoured guest. The trees are full of noise and movement, insects shuffling, the slow transit of sap in the bark. Benicio would always try to broker our status at this hour, patrolling the hill in the twilight and scratching at the bottom of trunks and digging between roots. Dogs have a simpler claim to the land than we do. Occasionally his barking woke me in the reading chair, but with no great alarm, and I would sleep again and dream of cats in the alleys and upon the walls of our ruined monuments. Benicio was a nocturnal emissary of unimportant messages. Other times he lay at my feet and the unrest of the night was settled. I had to be careful when I stretched not to knock his back legs, which he always guarded carefully. Theresa does not come after dusk. Her bicycle has no handlebar lantern.

The Fool on the Hill

They will have had their supper by now. They will be sitting by the fire talking about what he could be doing, speculating on his unreliability. Susan, tutting – 'He'll just be in the pub.' Danny – 'Maybe aliens have abducted him. De-de-de-de.' Lydia – quiet and smiling. Or they will be in bed, warm, snug, and he will simply be a vacancy, a hole in the cottage fabric. Meanwhile here he is, wringing wet, unfed, unhappy as hell. His stomach gurgles, and a sour belch makes its way up his pipes. Hungry. They will have had their supper. What was on tonight's menu? Did Lydia mention it this morning? Fish pie. Oh yeah, fish pie. With buttery carrots and peas. He could murder a great enormous dollop of that. With crispy brown potato topping, dill sauce, and salmon and mackerel filling. He'd even eat it off that rock he pissed on a few hours ago, bent over the mound, grunting and snorking like an animal in its byre.

Though the rain must have washed the surface clean by now.

It has stopped falling, more or less. The floor of the ravine is splashing and trickling, like the bed of a river, far below him. He can hear nature getting along just fine, going about its business, regardless of his pitiful arrest. He is hungry and thirsty – the rain he sucked from his palms was only enough to dampen his throat, and the slugs that he can feel sliming up the sides of the rock are not appealing enough to consider eating. Not yet anyway. His clothes are sticking to him: when he pulls his shirt it slurps off his skin. He's wrapped himself up as best he can, arms tucked inside against his sides, but heat is still escaping into the vast draw of night. He can feel the chill making its way into the meat of him. And the foot. Well, that's the most disturbing thing. He can't really feel it any more – not even when he concentrates on that spot, trying to locate the injury. There's nothing. Not a stinging lesion or a swollen outline. Not even a final protesting nerve. There is no pain.

This is not a good sign. Surely it indicates some hideous and irreversible medical condition, which can't be fixed by vascular surgery, grafts, or wires and pins. Fantastic blood loss, necrosis, gangrene. Bye-bye useful, well-loved appendage – and off to the glue factory with you. What if rats have smelled the wound and crept along the gulleys to the ripe offering? They could be starting in on his toes with their rotten yellow teeth, infecting him with disease, and he wouldn't even know. Here's the ridiculous thing: after all the begging, the litigating with God (no longer is he agnostic, no longer atheist), and the mortgaging of years from his old age in exchange for the stopping of the pain, now that it's gone he wants it back, absurdly. Fuck morphine. Fuck blissful analgesics. Fuck compassionate relief. He wants the registry of suffering again. He wants a good old belt of it, a reiteration of his vital signs, even if it means biting off his own tongue and roaring again at the horizon. At least he could call that an affirmation. At least then he could say: I am this war.

Because, what if this is it? What if everything unravels now? What if it is all about to be taken away from him?

It's a terrible thought, the thought of erasure, of hopelessness, the thought of losing himself, his family, his tomorrow. He feels like he is falling though the massive blackness above, spinning and spinning away, even while he is caught in this precise spot, pinned like a fragile butterfly, staked like a stupid scarecrow among the potatoes. It feels like there will be no end to the cold, the wet, the weightless rushing air, this stone crucifixion. Fate it's called. He begins to breathe shallowly and urgently. Ah, the dark epiphany has arrived. He absolutely does not want to be here, here in this rigid, unfair place, in this awful, invalid body, in this bastard providence. He does not want to be this man trapped in the wilderness. He does not want to be Peter. Peter. The name is awful. The name is prison. He doesn't want to be here. 'I don't want to be here!'

He puts his head in his hands. This is it. This is despair. This is the bitter, unalterable heart of the situation. There's nothing he can do. There's no way out. He is choiceless. He is condemned.

The ravine continues to trickle. There is scuttling, like the scuttling of rats. He yells down at the ground. 'Get away!' He peers hard, but there is nothing to see in the blackness. His eyes can't pull out the shapes of the boulders or the top of the cliff. They can't detect any little movements through the tunnels of rock, as if scavengers are gathering. He can't discern his own hands or his body or his damned limb. Perhaps he is no longer there. Peter. Where are you, Peter?

Home. In another dimension, if he had never come here today, if he had not decided to climb down into the bottom of the deep Gelt gorge, or he had taken a different route back across the boulders, he would be home now. He would be where he should be. With them.

There's comfort in thinking about that. The cottage, with its hewn walls full of mice and straw, its warm fireplaces. His brood, his clan. What will they have been up to in his absence?

The usual antics. Danny will have arrived home covered in grass stains and mud, saying he rolled all the way from town and can he have another bath. He's home because she's home. Susan will have thrown buckets of water over him outside while Lydia cheered, and he'll have loved the attention. What a plonker. That pie will have been a beauty, as always. There'll be a portion of it saved, tucked into a compartment in the kitchen range, just in case. They'll have sat at the table after dinner and spoken to each other, in a lower tone than when he's there, naturally. Mr Volume; Mr Have-Another-Glass-of-Homebrew. They've always managed conversation, his family. They've never been stuck over a stuffy platter of English beef, while the mantle clock ticked and the fire crackled. It is not a house of excruciation and repression, where the scrape of cutlery on plates and the dreadful chomping of jaws are the only sounds during meals. There's always something interesting to talk about, a book, a meeting, the news. And they can always fall back on their common currency. 'F'art', the kids call it, doing their buck-toothed posh impression.

There are almost as many of their pictures about the place as his these days. Susan's photographs. A few of her early studies, which she tried to throw out but he 'rescued' from the bin. Danny's benders – those weird snares of junk he's concocted with a welder between one of his many bases, which will find a place on a chest or table, or be strung up from the curtain rails on fishing line by his ma, so the bright blades rotate like a turbine after an apocalypse.

Lydia will have taken a bath, her hair piled up on top of her head in that mad-dame coiffure. He always finds a reason to go into the bathroom while she's in there. 'Oh, I'm just looking for that thing I left, love . . . Oh, I just need a whizz . . .' The transparency. The lovesick folly. She's aged, through motherhood, northern weather, the menopause. Her hair has begun to lose a little of its chestnut gleam, her waist's a little thicker, and there are little blue knots on her outer thighs, which she points out to him occasionally, with a frown. He doesn't mind, doesn't see gun-flaws in her the way he does in canvas. Parts of her still find their way into his compositions. Maybe a rock in a sea pool will be modelled on that beautiful bottom. She is Lydia, the woman who can balance the whole sky on her nose. She is the calm, the anti-cyclone, the eye of his storm. Where would he be without her?

He'll catch her watching the twins sometimes, when they're bickering or play-fighting (in their twenties now, but the same games and provocations still apply), prodding each other with the little mackerel bones from the pie and yelling, 'Wilse, tell him,' 'Wilse, tell her.' A soft, intrigued look on her face. He wonders what she's thinking, what her take on these two pod-dwellers is. She's so good at being internal, his wife. She will not often issue judgement, nor will she declaim. Not like him; Mr Big-Mouth, Mr Well-Here's-What-I-Bloody-Think!

What she likes about his work he's gleaned from the paintings she has chosen to hang in the cottage, and her few light observations about clarity and prophecy, landscapes stripped of former inhabitants, the next Mesolithic age. She likes his human figures frilled and sutured, like ammonites. She hung the paintings the day they moved into the ramshackle Border cottage, while the roof gaped open at one end, and the crows dropped cobs of mud in like a dirty hex upon the new occupants.

There are none of the severe mountain ridges in the house, though. Those are the ones that have fetched big money in America and Canada, that have complicated tax years for them, while enabling the underpinning of the house at its north-west corner. Those are the paintings that have provided funds to travel, to visit collections in the national galleries of the world and spend six months in Italy, finally. That was a good trip – they pulled the kids out of school, much to the disapproval of Headmaster Pokerarse – and spent the time visiting museums like Victorian gentry. Rome: shabby and vandalised, but extraordinary, busted seat of the colossal empire. Green-lipped Venice. Florence, where they couldn't turn around without tripping over a masterpiece. Perseus with the head of the Medusa. The church in Umbria, hung with a thousand tiles depicting a thousand local tragedies. He made those little pilgrimages he had wanted to make for years. Picked up some great souvenirs (and one particularly meaningful 'find', undeclared at customs, naturally). They made a fuss of him at the British Academy; he was on the radar by then, beginning to command respect, beginning to sell expensively.

Now wealthy climbers collect his mountains faithfully – the Rolex-Gore-tex brigade, Lydia calls them. They'll travel up-country when over on business, not only to scale famous peaks in the Lakeland, but to locate his little hub of industry and tell him under his front-door lintel that if it weren't for the detail on the side of such and such a composition, grandly positioned in their study, office or corporate lobby, they never would have found a new route up the crags to the summit. 'Super, I can charge you double for cartography then,' he'll say.

Never mind that fish pie; he could murder a toke. That would take the edge off all this madness. That would give him some reprieve from the existential mind-fuck. Except the pouch is in the bloody car. Why is it never to hand when he needs it? Why does he always have to go and fetch it from the glove box, the kitchen table, the bottom of the laundry hamper? Senility, probably. Welcome to your dotty dotage, laddo. If he could just have a smoke he could clear the cobwebs from his brain and he'd be able to sort this mess out. Come up with a plan to save the perishing foot, and get home, or to the hospital. Instead he's sitting here under the rain clouds, dreaming of a tobacco miracle. He's exhausting himself with nihilism, and expending his energy on imaginary rodents.

What time is it now? Must be late. After midnight. After heart attacks and cancers. After love and lost lovers, after he's been born. Neville Caldicutt will be getting up in a few hours, throwing leaves into the tin teapot, squeaking his bedsprings. 'Mind you keep reading books, Petie. Mind you work hard. There's a whole world out there.' There is a world. But he is tired. He is spent. And the dark is as dark as it is behind his eyes, when he closes them, just for a second.

The Divine Vision of Annette Tambroni

In four years Annette has learned many things. She has learned that customers are more likely to buy flowers on a day of clear skies and moderate wind, rather than of fog or thunderstorms. She has learned to navigate the invisible pathways of the town, and to trust her noisy, vigorous brothers. She has learned to listen with her head cocked, like an owl, and to predict her body's cycles. She has learned that the items of the world have various definitions, and if one is hidden, others will manifest with greater strength. A fire is its warmth on her skin and its spitting, clapping dance. The birds are their different songs in the morning in the courtyard. She has learned that people in the market give the correct change whenever they can, that Elemme is kind and lonely, even though she is married. All people smell differently, like the cardamoms, and nutmegs, and Spanish chillies in the spice jars at the market. Tommaso smells of burnt milk and hyacinths. Maurizio like candle wax, chicken skin, and sometimes cologne from the pharmacy where he has flirted with the girl behind the counter. Her mother's voice always has an undercurrent of dark blue, like the night sky of the Nativity.

She has learned how to find the juiciest fruits in the market's woven punnets. She has memorised the sufferings of the saints – the agonies and banishments and poverty. And, if someone is looking at her, her head will automatically turn towards the gaze like the magnetic needle of a compass. She has learned to live carefully inside the rooms of Castrabecco, in the alleys of the summer theatre and between the hot panes of the green-houses; to walk carefully along the streets to the church of San Lorenzo and up the steps to the cimitero di campagna. She knows not to dress and undress at certain areas of her bedroom with the shutters open, or to invite trouble from boys and demons. She knows there are rules. But she knows also that life is more complicated, that the dimensions of her mind are endless.

On Sundays she continues to tell her papa the small domestic news of Castrabecco and recounts the affairs of the town. This week, Mauri has learned to do one hundred and fifty keep-ups with the football; she counted them for him, listening to his left foot twisting on the ground as he hopped round and the leather slapped against his thigh. At one hundred and eight he went skittering across the courtyard and skilfully recovered the wildly spinning ball. Afterwards, he told her what the shepherds used to do to their goats in the building in which they live, before it was a house, and that night she had a terrible dream in which the men of her family were lined up, in front of the castration blades. Tommaso has been training for the bike races, wearing a rubber swimming-cap, donated to him by his teacher, and with Vaseline on his legs and chest. He is as slippery as a fish and cannot be caught by their mother when it is time to eat. Uncle Marcello has found him a little odometer for the bicycle spokes so that he can know the distances pedalled. For two days the training has been suspended due to a head-cold. Uncle Marcello has prepared a mallow infusion for his sore throat. Another contagion brought from the South on the *treno del sole*, her mother declared when Tommaso began to sniff and cough.

The tourists have arrived again, asking where the best restaurants are, and the pharmacists, the museums and shrines and the sites of the miracles, the stigmata and the bleeding hearts. They wear inappropriate attire to enter San Lorenzo and Father Mencaroni spends much of an afternoon removing baseball hats and asking ladies to cover their legs and heads. The visitors spoon gelato from little cups and look for sweet bunches of fragola to adorn their rented tables. 'How preferable life is here,' they say. In the market on Wednesday a cheer suddenly went up and Elemme told Annette that the railway workers were going to strike for better pay. Uncle Marcello is still battling with the invasion of greenfly. He suspects these to be of foreign origin, having come in with the shipments of orchid bulbs sent by Vincenzo from South America. They are making Chantilly patterns out of all the leaves. In defeat, he has ordered chloroform to clean the bottoms of the trays. She feels the minuscule legs creeping on her neck and ears when she goes to the greenhouses, or, if it is not the flies, it is Mauri.

Such are their lives.

The cimitero di campagna is deserted. Overhead swallows flit and flurry, going to and from their nests under the tiled roofs of the ruins. The sky is busy with feathers. It is a hot day. Annette takes off her scarf and puts it into her pocket. Also in the pocket is a wooden rosary, given to her by the nuns at her confirmation ceremony when she was twelve. It is cheap. Its beads pinch the skin of her neck, and she does not like to wear it. The sun begins to melt like warm caramel through her hair. She wonders again exactly what colour her hair is, whether it has lightened or darkened over the years. Her mother will not confirm whether it is corn-yellow, or flax, or the auburn of summer wheat. It is a vanity to ask such things, her mother says, and what does it matter if she can't see it? But there are so many subtle colours in Annette's head. They span like rainbows across her mind.

Annette can hear the fizzle and tock of fireworks, and the minute laughter of the boys down at the lake. Mauri will be with them. Perhaps he will be diving down through the cool water in search of lost jewellery. Or he will be lying, naked as Adam, on a green rock. After her report, she says a prayer for her father and crosses the cemetery to visit Signor Giorgio.

She still does not know if Signor Giorgio has a family to care for his niche. In the classroom he never mentioned a daughter or a granddaughter, living close by, or in the north. The sole evidence is that Tommaso has seen a weeping woman leaving the tomb. Annette has only ever heard someone taking a photograph close by – the pop of a shutter, the clicking of winding gear. Perhaps an admirer of his paintings. She wonders if the other children remember the artist as she does. She does not often see her old friends to ask. When they rush past her in the market on their way to school or on the way to mass they call to her, 'Hello Netta, goodbye Netta.' That is all. Perhaps they have forgotten the lessons, on how to copy a figure, how to paint the foam of the breaking sea. She sometimes pictures the Dutch still-lifes. She imagines elaborate bouquets, containing cherries and nesting parrots and English willow, all of this held in a large transparent urn, like a world made of glass. She can recall her tutor's gentle instructions. 'Do not be afraid to paint the reverse side of the sunflower,' he once said. 'It is just as worthy of your attention. You will already know the strength of its neck, how it keeps turning to face the sun wherever the sun is in the sky.'

His shadowy tomb is like the third season, even though it is summer. Dry leaves have blown inside, and crisp and curl on the floor, and the place smells smoky, like the smoke of Signor Giorgio's clothes. The rustling of the beech trees by the cimitero gate is hushed. She has already told Signor Giorgio that in previous times beech leaves were used to stuff mattresses, and that the voices of lovers who once whispered under the trees can sometimes be heard whispering inside the bolsters. The sepulchre is a good place to come. It feels restful. His bones must have settled, she thinks. Into the bottle, which he gave her and she has given back, she places a single chrysanthemum, the first of the season. They will continue to flourish through to All Souls' Day. 'You are already dead,' she says. 'I do not wish it.'

As she leaves the tomb she can hear that she is not alone after all. Someone is whistling nearby. The tune has no melody, and the scale slides randomly up and down. It is a strange sound for the cimitero. She is used to the recital of elegies, to crying or prayers. She has heard singing from the old women who come to sweep the pathways, but only hymns. The whistling is too bold. Perhaps there will soon be an interment, she thinks. Perhaps the peck-deads are working in the corner, preparing a new chamber. It is hard to know from which corner the whistling is coming. She turns and tries to place it. After a moment it stops. Perhaps the peck-deads have seen her. But there is nothing, no footsteps, no respectful salutation to indicate neighbourly proximity. She wonders, was it only the warbling and trilling of a bird in the tall beeches beyond the little city of the dead? Perhaps.

She puts on her headscarf and ties it under her chin. She should not have taken it off; it is an informality of which her mother would not approve. She calls good day and takes a step towards the gate. The whistling begins again, closer this time, directly behind her. Or no, directly in front of her. She stands still. How strange. The notes are so agile and light; they skim round the marble sculptures and commemorative pictures like something winged and flying. If Tommaso were not sick, if he were here, he could be playing a trick. But he has never really been able to approach her stealthily, even with bare feet. She can always hear the scrape of his heels, his rustling T-shirt, his excited breath. She is sure he is in bed, reading a comic, or writing a story about bicycle races.

Again, the whistling stops. The warm air drifts. She can smell an extinguished candlewick, or the tannin of the leather factory in the next valley, a brief bitter scent. A cloud sails overhead on a high, rapid current. The sun disappears and returns to its full heat. Someone is here. She can feel it. Someone is here in the cimitero but will not speak or be polite. There is another shadow. She feels pressure, a pressure no greater than the shadow cast by one of the angels on the marble plinths. But this is a shadow coming from beneath, or within. Though the sun blazes hot on her head, she feels the shadow creeping up her legs. It cools her insides. She catches her breath and tries to divine a presence. But there's no ache in the air of someone following a lover. There is no mood of ill will, as when a pickpocket works the market. There is no gesture of friendship, like that of the accordion player from Toulouse, who sang 'Remember Me' to her after she had given him a coin.

The shadow has no mood or purpose. No one is advancing to rest a hand on her shoulder. No one is preparing to greet her or say, yes, the day is fine. No one is slipping shyly away through the rusty gates, leaving the hinges creaking softly behind them. The shadow has not moved – it is simply attending to her, chilling her warm skin, spreading into her core.

Her heart begins to shrink. Perhaps. Perhaps it is Him. But he has never come so far. He has never followed her further than the market, which is close to San Lorenzo, close to his slippery lair in the oil paint. If her little brother were here, he could hold her hand and tell her what he sees. He could even calculate the distance of the cimitero from the church, saying it is approximately a kilometre, or it is five furlongs, having copied the charts on the walls of the Montessori, and she might take comfort in this. How far can the Bestia walk when he stirs within the old varnish and releases himself from the tarnished cage? To the greenhouse garden where her father was killed? To the edge of the summer theatre where he watches Annette on her stool? Here?

If she were to reach down now would there be a trail of saliva on the dusty path, drooled from the gaping hole of his mouth? If she reached out a hand would she find the face with its contortion of muscle and its rasping thorns? Would there be the bloody stump of castration between his goat-hair legs? She listens to the almost silent, heat-slow day. She listens to the swallows overhead and a hawk crying over a warren on the hillside, to the droning of a long-legged insect between patches of ragwort and to the far-off detonation of fireworks. She puts a hand to her throat, but the rosemary spirit-stopper Uncle Marcello made for her is at home, lying safe in the drawer of her dresser. She would like it now, around her neck, or in her pocket, instead of the wooden rosary.

She holds her breath and steps forward. And then she steps again. 'Is it you?' she whispers. 'Where are you? What do you want with me?'

There is no reply.

The Mirror Crisis

Last time you were up north, you went to see Nicki in the hospital. The truth is, you'd been avoiding it. You didn't think you could face it, not with everything else that had happened, another dark chore amid so many. With Nicki you have always felt the urge to confess, to verbalise your troubles. She lies benignly in the starched bed, as if ready with atonement, and it's easy to talk to her, easy to unload. Over the years you've confided lots of things. The rejected marriage proposal. Your feelings of fraudulency. How you might have been instrumental in the dissolution of a couple of Danny's relationships. There's no come-back. You are never judged. You aren't even issued with penitentiaries.

But this recent corruption of life. Your brother's accident. The fatalism. The infidelity. Where would you begin?

Anyway, you felt duty bound to visit her. You felt guilty. You'd just been to the cemetery with your mum and dad. It was a beautiful late spring day, warm by mid-morning. A few stray pieces of blossom were drifting from the trees alongside the crematorium. In the grounds of the cemetery, everything was shooting and budding, and the new lushness was like a country garden. There was a disturbing firmness to the headstones. The dead were staked down. Danny had been gone for seventeen weeks.

Your dad was limping around with his hands rammed into the front pouch of his denims, not really settling or saying anything, occasionally clearing his throat. You watched him pace a taut circumference around the grave, coming no closer than a few feet. There were patches of white in his sandy hair, nicotine stains on his beard. It suddenly occurred to you that your dad was old. He was heading toward seventy. You saw him reach into his pocket, take out a flask, and have a nip, and then another. He was blinking, as if he had grit in his eyes. Your mum set a jar of damson jam down next to Danny's monument. She kissed her hand and touched the stone. Then she went to your father, took his hand, and brought his arm around her shoulders. They held on to each other. *We'll see you back here in an hour,* your mum called to you. *Take your time.*

You stood for a while, looking at the sprigs of grass trying to seed on the bald mound. There were cards and gifts, newly deposited. An unopened beer can. A takeaway fork speared into the earth. A ridiculous plastic toy with green troll hair. Debris left after a festival. There were messages too, like the notes that used to get pinned to the door of his flat at weekends – whimsical and un-profound. *Great shakes, Danny Boy, you wazzock. Hope you're good and wasted now. Mackie. Still owe you a pint of Best, Daz.*

After a few minutes you turned and walked out of the cemetery, through the park to the back of the hospital.

Nicki was in the same room that she has been in for years. She was surrounded, as ever, by photographs, teddy bears and flowers. On the table next to the bed was her CD player and the stack of albums she had listened to as a teenager. You inserted one and pressed play. You wondered how sick she was of hearing Joy Division. You sat down, picked up the hairbrush from the bed-stand, and ran it once through a lock of her hair. It was still beautiful.

An intense nausea flushed through you. You felt your face tingle and your mouth water. You fought against the sensation. The discomfort passed. You were surprised, the feeling was unusual – your stomach is strong and you are almost never sick. You pulled the brush through Nicki's shiny hair once more, working a tangle loose. You looked at her, lying there. Her thin golden eyebrows, her snub nose, the skin smooth around her eyes. She is your age, but she looked like a girl, the muscles of her face blissful and unused. Again you felt like throwing up. You put the brush down and cupped your hands over your mouth, looked towards the door.

It came out of nowhere, the rage. Suddenly you wanted to slap her so hard. You felt such anger towards her. Her apathy, her indecision, her refusal to wake, get up and reclaim her life, or once and for all shut off. Surely there was some choice she could make, you thought, some flickering pilot light in her brain, that could be turned up, that could take charge, rousing her wasted limbs? All the years of stand-by, her visitors held like hostages in this room, ransomed by the slimmest of hopes, and equal to her in their impotency. All the years of dependency and money, waiting for her second coming.

Looking down at her, you couldn't remember her at all, only that sharp feeling of terror as she struggled for air on the moor, as she buckled to her knees, her chest rising and falling massively, her trachea hissing, the snow blowing upwards around her. You couldn't remember what her voice sounded like, only the words, when she called, *To you, Suze,* and passed the netball into the semicircle of the court so you could shoot at goal. You couldn't remember her laughter in the toilets when you had to borrow tampons.

But you could remember Danny. You could remember counting all of Danny's milk teeth with a finger, and wobbling the front ones loose, and how those pink dental tablets you were given to chew at school showed where he was missing plaque after he brushed. You could remember how he turned the pages of a book, pinching the paper together in the middle, and bunching each leaf over, and how his eyes seemed to bruise in their sockets after he'd been on a massive bender, and the way he would sneeze three times, always three, never just once or twice. You could remember a million tiny indelible details about his life, and all of this was useless, an encyclopedia of the redundant, because he was gone.

But there she was, on her back, blushing prettily, her hair growing longer every day. Nicki, still connected to life by some stubborn filament, holding the gift of the present with the loosest grip.

While you were sitting there, trying not to be sick, wanting to strike her, one of the nurses came in to rub her legs and drop saline into her eyes. She recognised you, asked how you were, thanked you for still coming all these years later. She chatted to you indiscreetly. She said Nicki had stopped getting periods now. They had done tests but there was nothing conclusive. It could be early menopause. It could be loss of bone marrow. She began to clean around the hole her food tube slotted into with a cotton swab. *Look. Your friend has brushed your hair, Nicki*, she said. *Isn't that nice of her? I think it's just like being Sleeping Beauty.*

You wondered if that's how the nurse really saw it: a coma like a fairytale curse. Meanwhile Nicki would be helped to eat and piss and cry. Her sores would be irrigated, her densities measured. Her family would bring her birthday cake and tell her the news and pretend she wasn't catatonic. Inside the husk, she might be conscious of everything, the voices, the bathing, those morose repetitious lyrics. Her mind might be shrilling out its state of emergency in a pitch too high for the human ear to register. *Get me out. Get me out of here.* Or she might know nothing at all.

Next to her bed, as the nurse swabbed the distended ring of flesh, you bit your lip and hated her. You wanted to shout in her face, stick pins in her forehead, anything to get a response. You wanted to scream at her for not being Danny, stand up, and walk out. Of that day's visits, you didn't know which was worse – the flowering, planted graveyard to which you had just been, or this vacant form in the bed. Life is a joke, you thought. It is worthless. And there is no point. There is no point.

Your mum made a pot of herbal tea when you got back to the cottage and you sat with her at the kitchen table. The house was cold, the windows trickling with condensation. Neither of them ever notice the chill in the house the way you do now. The south is making you soft. Upstairs you could hear your dad clomping and banging in the studio, the deep drawers of his apothecary chest being jerked open and slammed shut. *Looking for something that probably never existed,* your mum said and smiled, all the tiny lines around her eyes creasing. She was tired, you could see that; her skin was unusually dry and her hair was greyer. Losing a son had altered her vitality; it had leached her lustre. But she was sitting erect in her usual chair by the range, her woollen jumper brightly flecked with blue and yellow, and she seemed to fit the room so well.

When you were a kid it was the same: she always matched the surroundings perfectly, wherever she was, in the garden, by the river, being blown about town when she was shopping. Sometimes she would seem almost to disappear, and then she would move, to fetch something or make something, and you would catch sight of her again, and you would be amazed by her camouflage. You always wanted to ask her how she could accept everything so gracefully, how she could belong?

She was your father's exact opposite. Where he was extraordinarily plumed and song-filled, your mother was quiet and ordinary. They were like finches, the pair of them.

You watched her stirring the pot of tea, holding a strainer

over the cup, the stream of yellow liquid directed perfectly, without a drop being spilled. *Do you want honey, poppet?* She asked as if giving you the option, knowing you take it, and already passing you the jar.

When you were younger she had experimented with Buddhism and had gone on a few retreats, leaving your dad to manage the household. You would hear nothing from her for three weeks. Sometimes you had imagined she'd left you all. No – left him, because he was so often overwhelming. The chaos was always restored within a few hours of her getting home; the beds straightened, the bread bin filled. She would talk about containers and cleansing, the way to breathe. Your dad joked that she was hinting about his homebrew and his rollies, but you could tell he was pleased. She was home and he was over the moon. Often you would see her meditating by the elm tree in the garth, cross-legged, in her moccasins.

She went with you every week to see Dr Dixon at the health clinic. She never went into town to kill the hour, was always there reading *Digest* magazines or bracken-control leaflets when you came back out into the waiting room. Or she'd be gazing at the stick insects twitching on their leaves, fascinated. You knew it bothered her, that she was not really convinced about the need for treatment. She was not one for interference. Later, she apologised for making you go. *We should have trusted you were going to be OK. I hope it wasn't too awful. We weren't trying to hurt you.*

She handed you the cup of tea and the wooden honey pestle. *Darling*, she said, *my darling*, and for a moment the maternal guard slipped, and you saw the rawness behind, as if half of her had been cut away. You stood up, walked round the table and hugged her. You were still hugging her when your dad came in. *Aha! Here you are, pet. In the artist's fucking shoes, eh!* In his hand was a lumpy object wrapped in a piece of chamois leather. He stood in the middle of the room, shrugged his shoulders a couple of times like a magician preparing for a trick. Then he slowly turned back the corners of the wrapping, being a total ham. You were braced, as ever, for proportionate disappointment, for having to put up with some elaborate act, the gold-spun-from-straw routine. Inside the rag was a bottle. You looked at him blankly, waited for him to make his inevitable declaration, which of course he did. *It's for the exhibition. I've hunted it out to loan it to you. Go on. Here.* He waved the bottle at you. After a moment's hesitation you took it. It was a familiar item, the patchy glaze, the old-fashioned proportions. It had been in his studio for years, moving to various new locations around the messy, tobacco-stained room. For a while it had stood on the windowsill, then on the desk. It had been in the alcove next to the fireplace, holding his longest brushes and a dry teasel, part of the clutter, one of your dad's many inexplicable collectables. *That old thing, Peter,* your mum said.

You heard yourself tut in that petulant way, and tried to explain the concept of the exhibition again. You tried to keep a pleasant tone, not turn into the sulky teenager you so often do when he makes a song and dance about something. You explained you couldn't just put any old thing in the show. It had to have associative significance, and where possible, a certificate of authenticity. Van Gogh plus hanky. Magritte plus pipe. An instantly recognisable motif. The words came out wrong, sounded too harsh.

Silence. The usual, awkward interstices between you. You knew it could grow wider or it could come together, one of you had to make a move. Then your dad laughed a high-pitched, boomerang laugh that bounced off the ceiling and the walls and landed back inside him. *It's not mine, Fanny Ann.* He tapped his head. *There is still a bit of computing left up there, you know. It's Giorgio's.* He rested a big paw on your shoulder, leant downwards conspiratorially and whispered. *Right though, you best say it's from an anonymous donator, cause there was a bit of unofficial liberating* en Italia, *if you get my bloody drift.* He made a whistling sound. You heard yourself sigh.

You'd been there before, in this theatre of operations, a hundred times and more. Rationally, you knew what to do. Usually, it was not what you would do. What you would do was refuse to believe his yarn, his hokum, his stupendous bullshit. You'd tell him you weren't seven years old any more, when your dad would go overboard trying to convince you he had known Wallis, Hughes, Warhol, all of them old pals, chums, brothers in arms. You would spit, and shout, and be irrationally annoyed. And this, in the fourth decade of your life, was still the usual drill.

But out of the corner of your eye you saw there were still a few old scabs on his knuckles from breaking stone in the quarry the day that Danny died. They were brown and cracked and dry, and it looked as if he had been worrying them. He had broken one of his own beloved rules – *An artist must always protect his hands* – and so you surprised yourself. You agreed. You said you'd check with Angela and if she had no objection, it could go into the show.

He almost burst with joy. Literally. You could see him inflating, through his shoulders, through his cheeks, as if he was attached to a pneumatic pump. *Brilliant, Suze, just bloody brilliant. I must have found it for a reason. I mean, these things don't just happen . . .*

On the train back to London you opened your bag and took the thing out. It certainly looked the part. He might have got it from a flea market, or a junk shop, or a dead relative; you would probably never know. Or maybe your old man's great-uncle twice removed was the cousin of the reclusive Italian. It was simply a bottle, a bottle by name and description, with no pedigree but for the word of your dad.

The electric doors of the train beeped and closed. People made their way along the aisles looking for reservations, bumping luggage against the armrests, hauling it into seat wells and the overhead racks. You put a hand out to steady the bottle as it rocked on the table. Yeah, you thought, gold star from the Caldicutt school of flimflam, fable and fabrication.

You did swallow his stories once. When you were a kid you bought the whole lot, every last word. Flying in Leonardo's helicopter. Marching with Martin Luther King. Singing with the Beatles. The heroes, the nutcases, the flophouses. And later, the parties, the busts and arrests, those big-haired, Afghaned comrades of a bygone era.

The big man. He was so full of vim, so experienced, so full of life's banquet. To you it seemed he had tasted the wares of the world. You knew you could never live like him, even if you tried. He was too potent, too hungry. No wonder your mother had to be sage. It was probably a reactionary measure, designed to give you and Dan balance. Where your dad was as effervescent as his berry hock, which often exploded on the pantry shelves, she was a spirit level. You remember her charting the water table and the ley-lines. Quartering withered apples to feed the fell ponies over the garth wall. She had devices that hung in the garden to measure rainfall, air pressure, and wind speed, tubes that sang and gurgled, emptied and filled. Inside was her kitchen of pies and soups and breads, her known recipes, her faith in the ingredients.

You were once theirs, as Danny was theirs. The fertilisation of bilateral ova. Sometimes it seems unbelievable. That remarkable double spark. The celestial, genetic chance of you and he, playing thumb-wars in the womb, doing an amniotic slow dance, and making yourselves from the pattern they gave you.

You could probably tell them everything, about how you feel, or don't feel. You could say that your home life is deteriorating rapidly, that you are being unfaithful. You could say you can't work any more, that you can't even develop the last roll of film in your Leica because Danny is on it and you can't bear to see him, on the bench outside Euston with pigeons at his feet. You can't bear to be reminded that only a few months ago he was walking naked round your flat, showing Nathan some juvenile trick with his cock, making chocolate pizza to thank you for your hospitality, making you laugh. You could say to your mum and dad that you are in such serious trouble, in such decline, you are so unbearably alone and undefined, that you can't operate normally. You could say that without Danny you are imbalanced, you have no real identity, you are not really Susan.

Maybe they would tell you what to do, or who you are. Maybe they would remind you that you have always been the strong one, always wilfully yourself, despite the pronouncements of Dr bloody Dixon. They would say that you have control over your relationships, and that you are a professional artist. They would remind you of the time you sneaked into your dad's studio as a kid and applied some white acrylic to a painting he was doing. One rebellious brush stroke in the upper left corner. You waited a few days, braced for discovery and a row of epic proportions. But he didn't notice. All he did was rove about the house in the kilt he was currently favouring and sing in the bath and drink homebrew. Later you went back into the studio and the mountain had advanced in composition. The flat crescent summit appeared sturdy enough to support another world if one had been set down upon it. It looked like an authentic Caldicutt. Annoyed, you confessed. You didn't say you were sorry. You just said you'd done it. *Oh, bloody hell, sweetheart,* he said, *it was exactly the thing it needed.*

Of course they would sympathise. They love you. But they can't fix you, can't make you yourself again. No more than sex can shock your atoms, make them come alive. No more than Dr Dixon's therapy could make of you a first person. You are comprised of a million tiny locks. There's no master key to be found, encased in the plush velvet heart, no matter how desperately you ask someone to reach in and grope around. No matter how hard you try to find it.

You put the bottle away as the train began to move, and you watched the familiar old town slip away, its red masonry lost behind you, the river, the peel tower, the henge. You took out your mobile. Already other people were chatting to those they had just left or those they would soon see, oblivious to the Quiet Carriage signs. You scrolled through your list of contacts. You passed over Angela, Danny and Nathan. When you arrived at Tom's number you paused, then pressed the green call button. There were enough rings for you to guess he was finding a quiet room in Borwood House before answering. *Pronto. Are you coming back down today? I miss you. Can we meet? I'll come in. I've got something to tell you.* The train sped up and began to lean into its corners, the plastic bulkheads squeaking and wobbling, and the phone signal cut out. You drafted a text, telling him the name of a hotel and where to meet. You watched the country roll past. The hills and cellars of cloud, the flat, grey Irish Sea, then mill town skylines, chimneys, canals, and terraces, small back gardens filled with bin bags and scrap metal, prams and bicycle frames.

Translated from the Bottle Journals

I have not known Theresa to be a sentimental woman, but yesterday I found her weeping beside the tomatoes. A handkerchief was pressed tightly to her mouth. She was weeping with a terrible distress, as a parent might if their child stood before them with a suitcase in their hand, having taken a vow to enter a monastery. She was weeping for me. This morning we received a letter from the hospital. I do not know if it was solely this news that upset her or if Theresa was weeping with a private grief. I know, for example, that she misses her father.

In any case, we have been waiting for the news and the cancer is confirmed. It is not a surprise. I believe we all anticipated it, but Theresa is still a young woman and she is less reconciled to the inevitabilities of later life. I have been trying to continue with my work. I want to finish the new painting before winter. I am pleased with the arrangement of objects on the table. The measurements are exact, and the canvas is ready, but the easel remains unscrewed and turned away and I have stalled. Perhaps I am not immune to morbidity, as I would like to believe I am.

The sound of her crying in the garden was so unusual that I thought at first a bird was defending its nest from a predator. But she had left the house to grieve, trying to be discreet. Any compassion at my disposal is always tempered with an awareness of how absurd life can be. Theresa might have found more consolation in her work, for I am afraid I was not much use to her, and perhaps said the wrong thing. I wonder does she imagine me to be a lonely man? Does she underestimate the life I have lived and the pleasure I have derived from it? Of course I could not ask her simply to stop. A weeping woman has no desire for opposition; she wants only to know her sadness is correct on the occasion of her expressing it. All will be well, I said to her. Let us find some perspective on our little situation. In Spain this year they ran the bulls and twenty men were trampled. In Argentina penguins are swimming under the ice sheets instead of breeding. There are wars on the other side of the world and I am seventy-eight. She only wept harder. I said to her, come, my dear Theresa, we will forget our chores and retrieve our coats from their hooks and we will visit the aviary in the city. We will take the train like proud citizens of Italy! Today I am well. Today we will go. I pressed her hands between my own and she appeared to recover quickly, and I felt for the first time her hands made rough by continual work.

We spent an hour in the glass dome of birds, admiring their rich plumage. We strolled the conservatories and felt a welcome lightness of spirit. We gave new names to our favourite characters, as if we were cataloguing specimens in an uncharted land. We discerned the bolder personalities from those too shy to linger at the rails. Children tried to capture feathers from the green tails of the peacocks.

I mentioned to Theresa that I thought she was in fact a very good colourist and that I always notice the areas of the house where her arrangements are complementary and I thanked her for her years of good service. She shed her tears again and would not be consoled, and once again she sounded like a distressed bird, and I hoped that the exotic parrots might fly down and comfort her. We visited the church and she lit a candle – there were queues along the staircases so we did not go down to see the frescoes and the sacred robe. We bought pencils embossed with gold letters for her nieces and nephews, of which there appear to be several hundred now.

When we returned to Serra Partucci it was evening and she prepared salted vegetables, which we ate together at the table as if at a restaurant. I was of half a mind to read Ugo Foscolo to her but I thought perhaps it was too much and that she would once again break down. We sat companionably until the dusk arrived. Then, instead of walking her bicycle down the hill, which is her custom, she mounted it and I heard its wheels un-stiffening as she rode.

I had not truly realised her attachment to her position here, nor her affection for the stubborn old man for whom she caters every day.

Today she is her usual self again – that is to say, she has been banging in the kitchen and terrorising the house. We had a minor quarrel when she attempted to make me eat breakfast. I have no appetite, and the excursion yesterday had tired me. I wish to begin painting, but I have been too distracted. All I want to do is look out of the window at the view I love so much. A kestrel has been hovering in the air above the slopes, intimidating the mice and the larks. The ravens mock it, tumbling from the sky as if to strike a target. They fall suddenly, as if shot with a pistol, and then they recover. They are birds of the circus, trained for swinging on trapezes, and cannot balance on the tightrope of the hunt.

I read in the newspaper that on the greatest mountain in Africa the skeleton of an elephant has been discovered. It lies at an impossible altitude, as if the creature were seeking a path to the glaciers at the summit. Only God might know the reason for its journey. How slowly it must have moved, and in incomparable privacy, perhaps anticipating its fate. That animals choose their resting place speaks of a curious foreknowledge.

In the East, they believe the soul travels at the speed of a camel. Perhaps migration and meditation are close to the same thing. But stillness might also offer enlightenment. Outside, the kestrel perches in silhouette on the scorched branch of an olive tree, unmoving. It recognises the glimmer of coprolites in the rock and the wet-brown eyes of the voles. The contours of its head and wings are like those of the milliner's mannequin, borrowed by De Chirico to discuss the metaphysical. The kestrel achieves perfection in stillness.

I do not like to see omens in small occurrences, but a plague of dead flies has visited this room. In every corner there are upturned black bodies, balanced on dry wings, so it seems each ascends from the ground by a fraction, keeping in the death-pose a portion of that skill which they possessed during life. I prefer the shutters to be left open, even when it is chilly, so the house invites all kinds of little visitors. There are often scorpions on the steps. Strangely, these provide less consternation to Theresa than the lizards. The locusts have hatched from their tunnels now and have gone. The soft little phosphorous ones no longer illuminate the garden at night. Only the moths remain, drumming against the lamps. From inside the glass shades there is whispering. The moths are speaking of our prehistory, discussing the world before fire perhaps.

As a boy I kept a jar of dirt in which the traffic moved casually between the layers. Grubs and beetles got along together very well. I liked to watch the rows of ants scaling the sides. In this small condominium there would be the neighbourly investigation of items dropped inside – a Roman coin, sulphur, dough. Each fellow within the jar would attend to the object at its own speed and then return to its interval of soil.

I look out at the mountains, so dear to me. Their place on the horizon is utmost. It would be difficult to take them down and alter the sky around them; it would seem like an unfinished composition. There is sadness at the thought of leaving them, even while I rejoice in their presence. How can I explain the longing in my breast for what is present before me? I surprise myself with this melancholy. I have told them not to operate.

Tomorrow, Antonio is arriving. No doubt he will fuss and try to organise, and he will want to see the painting, which is unfinished. I have asked him to bring the official documents necessary for the transfer of the estate. It is all quite complicated. There is talk of creating a museum and there have been several requests for donations, which I must consider. Florio is also coming with a breathing mask and a tank. It will be impossible to drive up the hill in an ambulance; I do not know how he is going to manage it. The house will inevitably be too crowded. They will all buzz about and squabble over my chair and get under Theresa's feet, and everyone will need to be separated and calmed. Serra Partucci will no longer be a peaceful hermitage.

Often I tell visitors, who come and who sit uncomfortably in their city garments, to be heedless of the train timetables. I invite them to remain past the hour of their appointment, to take some wine and sit outside and relax. Take your hand from your wrist, I tell them, your blood pressure is not abnormal, you are not on the verge of disaster. Listen to this greater pulse, to the lowing of cattle and the beating of wings against the wind. The earth grunts as it dislodges and buds break open. Can you hear? The pulse will be there too in the place where you live, I say to them. Nowhere is exempt from the service of Nature. Perhaps the drains and cables between buildings are like stethoscopes, and you may hear the heartbeat of the city if you listen.

My visitors indulge me. They are charmed by my antiquity

and my devotion to this place. Later they walk back to the station along the road, and perhaps halfway they kneel with an ear to the ground. And perhaps they hear their own blood, and then the traffic in the town, and then a deeper rhythm. They get up, and brush the dust from their knees, and they continue walking. If everything seems lost, I tell them, trust the heart.

The Fool on the Hill

When he gets home the house is quiet. No one is inside. He walks through the kitchen and the sitting room and goes out the back door. Lydia is in the garden retying beanstalks, with oversized canvas gloves on her hands. She seems engrossed in what she is doing, intent on the binding. The air is very still around him but her dress is rippling madly against her arms. Her straw hat keeps threatening to blow off and, under it, her hair is snaking about, tying itself in knots. It's not the right time of year to be worrying about reinforcing the vegetables, but she has a sense for the turning of the weather and he can see that she herself is stormy, so perhaps it is all right. He waves to her. 'Are we expecting a gale?' She doesn't look up. She flops a gloved hand towards her hat, too late, and it flies off her head and into the distance. There is a shaved patch on her crown. She tautens a length of string, as if about to garrotte the beans. She bends down among the frothy green runners and disappears.

'Hey,' he calls. He steps over the lettuces and onions, and the row of stunted marijuana plants that have failed again. In the place Lydia has been kneeling there is a little plastic doll with bald genitals and empty sockets where the legs should be. A string has been wound around its neck.

Peter knows he is dreaming. Part of him is all too aware that he is lopped over on the wet rocks, his chin on his chest, awkwardly asleep. He can almost hear the owl, calling from the fence post above the Gelt ravine, almost feel the cold tightening around him, but he doesn't want to return to the harsh waking world. He would rather the surreal, disquiet of the subconscious, with its soft threats and lies. So he commits to it.

He's wandering round the outbuildings, unlatching the door of the barn and going inside. The barn is perpetually shedding its skin. Some time soon he is going to get a quote for replastering it. He is going to convert it into a gallery, and have people look round when they call on him, instead of traipsing through the cottage, leaning on the bookcases and fiddling with Lydia's bowls of sea glass. There is a distinct odour in the barn, a birdy, limey pungency. Strange light infuses the structure, admitted through the four narrow slit windows, between the bolts and slates and the open doorway. The walls are audibly crumbling. Flakes of mud and grout slough off and drizzle down. The floor is soft with feathers and sediment, years of debris. It feels pliant when he bounces on his heels.

Susan is there, in the corner. She is wearing her little purple jeans and her hammer-and-sickle T-shirt. She is small, perhaps five years old. She points down. 'We're on the back of it,' she says. He looks and it's true. The floor of the barn is soft fur: between the tufts there is yellow skin, a smattering of follicles. It is rising and falling slowly, breathing. The barn has been built on the back of a slumbering behemoth. 'Shhhh,' she says, 'it's going to wake and ride us away.' They hold hands and stand very still. Dust is in Peter's nose. He wants to sneeze. Every rustle and skitter of crumbling plasterwork sounds like the stirring of the Baba Yaga barn beneath them. 'Where's your brother?' he whispers. 'Where's Danny?' Susan grins.

He looks around. In the corner is the dilapidated agrarian equipment he rescued from the old farm down the road. There is a huge iron roller, which looks heavier than the world, and an apple-press with a broken handle, its pulping bucket full of bird shit. The rusty industrial frame of something unknowable, perhaps a thresher or a mangler, hulks in the corner, casting a shadow shaped like a bear. The massive slab of piebald marble he had shipped over from a quarry in Italy leans against the gable. Everything is moving up and down as the floor inhales, and exhales. There's the flap of wings in the rafters above, the slow warbling drill of a pigeon. 'Shall we go and find Danny?' he asks. 'OK,' she whispers. They start jumping furiously.

Blackness when he opens his eyes, as if he's buried in a rough stone coffin, as if his eyes are stitched closed and laid over with coins. Where is he? He hears oars in water. Someone's laughter. What is this hard thing beneath him? Ah, yes. He is here. In this hellish position, in the empty dock of night. The dark is so dark. Nothing will ever be created from it again. If he thinks too clearly he will ache from the twist of his hips, the strain of his neck, and the brace of his good knee against stone.

So, don't think of it, Peter. Don't go back to those tired legs, and that dry tongue. Don't enter the wakeful mind with its helpless honesties. Be kind. Come away. Yes. A sweet voice, so comforting. It is not his, though it is familiar.

The sky has a slight wash of green to it when he wakes up. The first streak, like a chemical development. After wanting dawn so badly, he was sure it would never come. There is stiffness throughout his body. Cramp in his side, a chill in the marrow of him, and pain. The very gift he asked for an hour or so ago is back in his ankle. It is good. Nice and sore. Nice and living, clearing his head, making him sharp. The night is draining and he feels rinsed of the panic and fear.

It is pain of a genuine variety, that's for sure, and competing with all the other pains he has experienced in life. Root canal infection. Bacterial meningitis. Hangovers. They were simply trials for this, the real thing. How much pain can a person withstand, he wonders? They used to saw off limbs on board ships and on battlefields. They used to hold folk down, dose them with spirits, then saw through shanks of bone with blunt unsanitary instruments. They used to cauterise the stumps with tar. Some of them survived.

An interesting thought now, and one that is surprisingly alluring: he could get rid of it. He could cut off the leg. If he had the little red-handled knife he uses for trimming the block of resin in his tobacco pouch, he could get to work. There are plenty of stories about outdoor types having to remove frost-bitten lumps of themselves. Plenty of farmers sever hands and arms in combine harvesters then, heroically, carry the mangled limb to hospital in hope of reattachment. Amazing what the brain tells you to do in an emergency. Amazing what is imperative.

He could do it. He'd go at it quickly, just below the knee, where things might be reasonably tidily separated. No hacking with the blade and making a mess, but carefully scouring through the flesh, and jointing the bones, like dismantling a rabbit. Yes, if he had the little red knife that's up in the car, he could most certainly do it, right now.

Howay! Of course he couldn't. Every fibre in him would revolt. There would be a mutiny upstairs and Captain Kneejerk of the *Black Amputation* would be made to walk the plank. Honestly, what kind of desperate lunacy is this? Lack of food and water and warmth is messing with his higher faculties. He has mentally buckled. The facts of the matter are embarrassingly simple. He has not been here that long. He has not been here long enough to contemplate mad acts of self-butchery. He will be found, eventually.

He's almost quite sure he told them where he was going. He thinks he can recall at least one conversation with someone in the family before leaving, that indicated he was coming to the ravine to work. Perhaps Lydia. Perhaps they rolled down the windows of the cars as they passed each other on the moor and he said, 'Hiya, love, I'm just heading to the gorge. Won't be long. If I'm not back for supper something is definitely wrong.' No. Blatantly false. Total self-delusion. How about Danny? Did he talk to Danny-Dando? Danny was in the bath, then the boy went to town on the bus, maybe with his guitar, but they didn't actually say goodbye. In fact he really only saw Danny when he was in the buff, passed out at the bottom of the stairs.

Then it was Susan he told, the disgruntled daughter. It was One of Two. Yes, it was definitely her. He can remember the exchange. He can picture the scene. He can rerun it again like a film and find the exact moment when he told her where he was going, which will be vital evidence in the case of the missing father. Rewind. Play.

It is two o' clock yesterday. He's in his studio, surrounded by clutter. On the desk, chunks of crystal, microliths, pen holders, papers. Under this tip, somewhere, his computer. He is leafing through ingots of loosely bound envelopes, letters bundled together year by year and secured with elastic bands. His fingers are walking up and down their edges to reveal geographical franks, recognisable or forgotten handwriting. He is considering the value of more shelves and drawers, though where he would put them is a mystery; the room is full to the gills already. He has been lost to his thoughts while searching. 'The spirits have lifted you, lad,' his mother would always say, peppering a herring, shaking flour over it and patting it down, while he stared out of the window on to Alnwick Street, wishing for what exactly he did not know. 'I wonder when the spirits will drop you back to us, Petie.' His mother, with her nylon pinnie and her tired eyes, beginning to forget things, saying, 'Where's Nev gone, why's he working on a Sunday? Has the pit collapsed?' Walking the street in her slippers and wetting herself. Oh, Dorothy.

Cut to the present. He is sitting at the desk in his studio looking for a letter to show the children. He can't find it, but he has turned up old first drafts of Donald's poems and some photographs. He has found his and Raymie's wedding certificate from the courthouse in San Francisco and, stapled unromantically to it, a receipt from the Justice. The staircase creaks. 'Hello Rumplestiltskin, where's your gold?' He looks up. Susan is standing there, a cup and saucer in her hand. 'Hiya, love!' he almost shouts, because he is pleased she has come into the studio to see him. He reaches round her bum and hips and squeezes her in a side hug, rattling the teacup in her hand.

She glances round. 'Looks like a bomb's gone off in here, Wilse.' He laughs. 'I'm looking for something to show you.' To illustrate his point, he continues to flick through the stiff envelopes. She raises her eyebrows, looks about at the rubblesome room, at her father's dishevelled hair, at the poor state of things generally. 'Right-o, well, here's a brew. I'll leave you to it, shall I?' No, please don't go, he thinks, and rises halfway out of the chair. 'Wait on. It's a really special letter, probably worth a fortune. It took years to reach me. Came halfway round the world! You've got to read it.'

She steps back. She sets down the tea and it ripples, as if a little stickleback has just swum across it. She crosses her arms and tips her head to the side, her brow lowering. Uh-oh. He knows that look. She's annoyed. The room's annoyed her. The fish in the cup's annoyed her. He's annoyed her. 'So,' she says. 'Whose letter are you looking for, Dad? Another famous colleague and chum?' Seldom misses when she aims, his daughter. He jerks his chin up and reaches for his pouch, pops it open. Yes, he knows this tone of hers. It says, 'Oh Dad, not this nonsense of yours. Ding-dong, let's humour you, shall we.' Doesn't she know, doesn't she realise, it's all for her? It's all just to impress her and make her smile. He's simply playing for affection, like Danny busking by the bandstand. What else can he do?

He slots a diff into his mouth and tosses the pouch back on to the desk. He spreads his arms wide, as if to take a deep, flamboyant bow. 'I am looking for instructions from the bottle man. Remember, I told you about him when you were little. Made completely out of glass. Glass hands, glass legs, glass eyes. Everything he drank you could see in his tummy. Wherever he went you could hear him clinking and clanking. Poor old fellow fell out the tower of Pisa and shattered on the pavement below. Terrible, terrible tragedy.'

God, he adores her. God, he infuriates her.

There is silence. His arms remain outstretched, mid-flight. She lifts her hand up to her face. She rubs her right eye, pulls out a stray eyelash and looks towards the easel. 'You're painting the gorge again,' she says.

Scene ends.

Green morning light. What a relief. In another hour it will be bright enough to see properly. It will be officially day – the right time for something benevolent to happen. Soon he can make a proper assessment. He can see if there's a puddle of red around the boulders. He can look around for a stick with which to crowbar the rocks apart. Maybe in one of the little trenches and gullies between stones something will have gotten caught. Maybe even now he can find it. There are always brobs lying about on the floor from the trees leaning out above the ravine. Yes, he's sure he's seen them, many times, hundreds of them, just waiting to be retrieved. If he stretches his long arms, he'll be able to tease one to him with his fingertips. He'll haul it out of its rock setting like King Arthur and bloody Excalibur. It will be there. It will be waiting for him. And it will be a beauty – he can picture it – a thick firm staff, not too brittle, not too weak, a holy rod, entirely suitable for digging down under the boulder and exerting more pressure than he alone could. Archimedes will save him, with his mighty lever. You are an absolute genius, Peter!

He begins to lean forward, reaching towards the ground. A spike of pain drives up the leg with such severity it takes his breath away. He yelps and punches his thigh. The head-rush, the pain whipping him, the urge to faint. He blinks and shakes his head, waits for it to subside. It hurts too much to move that way. It feels like he's aggravating it, tearing something open, forcing the bone through a loose flap of skin. So much for cutting the fucker off, eh, Nancy. When the queasiness abates he adjusts himself, squats down on his good knee, and gingerly leans backwards. OK – it seems do-able that way. He begins to grope behind, along the channel of the two big boulders. He feels shale, mulch, and snail shells. He fondles the wells and fissures, checking the holes like a fisherman stroking for eels. There has to be one here somewhere. Where? But already the mirage of the stick is fading. He grimaces, stretches a few more inches in his reverse crab contortion. He can hear Lydia. 'You should come to yoga, Peter, you know you're very stiff.' Yes, very helpful, love, thank you. He touches the corner cover of the sketchpad, which has slipped down off the rocks in the rain. It feels swollen and pulpy. He tweezers it between two fingers, tugs it out. The pages are damp and floppy, the charcoal lines have bled. All that work, wasted. Never mind, there are more important things. He sets the pad to one side on a rock. He tries the channel behind him again. There's nothing. OK. He'll just have to go forward again, slower maybe, so as not to trigger the fantastic agony.

He takes a breath, grits his teeth, and tips over. He tips from the waist as if attempting to clear his balls over an electric fence. A 'swan-dive' - isn't that what the extra-bendies call it? Bastard it hurts! He pauses. Come on, focus, man. Don't spew up or cack your trousers. Just try again. Turn the dial. He reaches down. Sweat breaks on his forehead, but he stays bent. The pain increases, eating through his cells. He tries to remain there. But some cautious auxiliary lobe in his brain is firing, and any minute now it is going to rescue him by over-riding the decision to self-harm. He can't. He can't do it. He lifts back up, his whole body weak and shaking. The walls of the gorge rotate past his eyes, grey stone, grey stone, and he feels himself carousel. He leans against the boulders, waits for it to stop. The walls slow. They slow and halt.

So. That plan didn't work. But it's OK. Not long now and it will be light enough to see. Then things will look better. Everything will become clear. He'll find a way.

The Divine Vision of Annette Tambroni

When Annette arrives home from the cimitero, the family is in a state of wild excitement. Uncle Marcello has acquired a television set. The owner of the electrical store, who has a small grove of olives next to the greenhouses, and with whom Uncle Marcello frequently plays cards sitting in folding chairs outside the brick office, has supplied it for half the ticket price. 'It's because I beat him at poker,' says Uncle Marcello proudly. 'It was either that or he put his hand in the till.' The family is standing in a gracious semicircle around the device, even Tommaso, who is sniffing and coughing with his summer cold, his upper lip red and crusted.

Annette's mother tuts. 'I'd like to know what we would have been liable for in this manly bargain of yours!' 'Just some compost. It was all very harmless,' says Uncle Marcello. 'But that is not the point, Rosaria. I did win. And now we have joined the civilised forty-nine per cent of the nation.' He puts his hand on her waist, twirls her round, and deposits her back where she was standing. 'This is excellent! Now I can watch at home in my slippers instead of going to the bar like a peasant and having people talk in my ear while the news is broadcasting.' Her mother shakes her head. 'Could you not have got a refrigerator instead, Marcello, or a new Zanussi?'

Annette would like to take hold of Uncle Marcello's hand and hold it firmly. She has walked home in a state of high anxiety and she would like to feel his strong, soil-lined fingers linked through her own. Or her mother's, or Mauri's. She would like to describe the terrible feeling at the cimitero, and the feeling all the way down the steps and along the road, that something was creeping into her. Her heart is curled tight and will not stop quivering. She would like to tell them all that a shadow has touched her. It followed her, and even though she turned the corners in the town sharply, she could not leave it behind. It seemed to crawl up inside her, and deposit its matter, like an insect laying eggs. She would like somebody to go to the window and tell her if there is a black shape at the edge of the courtyard. Perhaps, at first glance, a man dressed suitably for handling the body of the dead Christ, then, on closer examination, a man with horned cheekbones and a dog's mouth, running with bile. But her uncle is talking excitedly about the purchase of the television, and the family are talking to each other and over each other about it. 'Rosaria, this will be good for us all. We can play the quiz shows together. Tommaso will have *Carosello* before bed. And with any luck the Pope will give us a Western. Put it there in the corner, Mauri, move the table away from the wall.'

Annette slips towards her mother and reaches for her hand. But her mother seems too agitated, busy with the problems of the television and the rearrangement of the furniture, and she shakes her hand free. 'Be more careful, Mauri! You're going to smash something.' He groans. 'It weighs a ton! It's made of concrete!' Annette stands close to Tommaso. He is wrapped in a blanket and smells of camphor. He rests his head against her arm and she kisses his hair.

Once the television has been positioned and wired they switch it on. Uncle Marcello fusses over the settings, adjusts the dials and the aerial, and finally a rapid, trilling voice can be heard, carried on a flush of static. Then there is the pounding of surf. 'Aaaah,' they all say. Uncle Marcello claps his hands together. 'It is the Pacific Ocean! Look – they're surfing!'

Mauri clicks his fingers and begins to sing an American song. 'OK. We need some rules,' Annette's mother says, 'about how long we will watch, and when we will watch, and what is suitable to watch.' There are groans from the boys and Annette hears Tommaso blowing his tongue. 'Yes! We must limit our viewing to twenty minutes a day maximum, I think.' Her tone is firm, but she sounds pleased. Uncle Marcello snorts. 'Excuse me, let us see who the Stalinists among us really are by the end of the week.' Tommaso drops his blanket and Annette hears tussling and giggling. 'Netta, I'm riding Mauri,' he shouts. 'I'm surfing.'

And Annette knows, at this moment, that they cannot help her. They will not believe she has been touched somehow by the Bestia, and if she tells them a violation has occurred they will ask who else it was that did it, they will demand a name. She has no evidence. There is no stain against her skin, no wicked print soiling her dress, darkening her breast, for it would have been pointed out when she arrived home and the wire brush would have been taken to the mark. She cannot give them her word and ask to be forgiven. She will simply have to wear the impurity on the inside.

One by one her family take to the chairs. The television talks and hums, hums and talks, like an old aunt. Annette reaches for the table, to memorise its new position. After a while she sits beside the set and puts her hands on the casing of the garrulous new guest. It is a box, bigger than the radio, smaller than the oven. The screen bulges outwards, like a hard bubble. There is a little crackle as her fingers track over the glass, as if she has disrupted a strange hive. The carapace feels warm against her palms. 'Try not to dirty the screen, Annette,' her mother calls. 'I don't want to clean fingerprints off it every day.'

After the programme about the Pacific, Uncle Marcello sits Annette on his knee and explains the elements and workings and contents of the television set, as he would the tiny filaments of a flower under the microscope. She sits crookedly across his legs. She is too big now to balance there properly. 'This is what the social revolution has led us to,' he says with a chuckle, 'audiovisual propaganda, Vatican censorship, football and fashions on Sunday. It's not real.'

'Uncle Marcello,' she begins. 'Do you think we might be inside something like a television too? Can other people look in to see what we are doing all the time? How do we know what is real outside?'

'Ah, little one,' he says, squeezing her waist. 'I think you have more brains than the rest of us. It is an interesting philosophical question – we should speak to Kant. Perhaps he would say that nothing is real unless . . .' From the corner armchair, Annette's mother's voice chimes in to the discussion. 'That's quite enough. Tell her the truth, Marcello. God is the only one outside. God can see everything we do. God is always watching. That is the reality and the truth of the matter.' Uncle Marcello opens his legs and gently lowers Annette to the floor between them. His trousers smell musty, of vegetable roots and nutshells.

For the rest of the afternoon and into the evening the television is kept on, conducting its own theatre, talking and flickering, a mind warming in its shell. No perfume drifts from it, and it emanates no moods. The noises it makes are strangely remote and complete within themselves. And yet it seems to be casting a spell; her family is transfixed. They carry their dinner bowls to their chairs instead of eating outside at the table in the courtyard. 'For tonight only,' her mother says. 'It's just a novelty.' Their conversation loops around the conversation of the television. They talk about what it talks about. It is as if a dominant old relative is holding court in the living room, and they are all agreeing with everything she says. No, it is like a politician, like the mayor. Annette wonders what its capabilities are, whether it can recognise the scent of the roses it shows her family, or taste the beans it advertises. At times, high-pitched voltage escapes from the appliance, so elevated and intense it is almost celestial, but quite painful. Annette can feel her ears drums vibrating, and then she must get up and leave the room. She hears her mother worrying. 'Is it jumping too much, Marcello? Does it need to be re-tuned? Attend to it or we will all become cross-eyed.'

That night, as they prepare to go to bed, her mother covers the television with her special embroidered cloth, as if it is an antique armoire or a Chinese vase, as if they will presently be leaving the house for an extended season by the sea.

Later, Annette wakes to hear strange sounds. For a second she is filled with irrational fear. But it passes, and her heart slows. There are murmurs and footsteps. Someone is in the kitchen, perhaps getting a glass of water, and talking half in their sleep. If it is her little brother, if a bad dream has disturbed him, making him hot and panicky, he will need to be tucked back under his quilt and soothed. She sits up in bed, reaches for the handle of the door and opens it a fraction. Two voices are in intense and quiet discussion a few rooms away – not in discussion exactly, but certainly they are communicating. There are soft groans and whispers, which seem to imply questions asked and replies given, words in a language she cannot understand. 'Nah . . . ohf . . . coh . . .'

She turns back the covers, wraps her shawl around her shoulders, and goes into the hall. She pauses. The sounds are a little louder now, but still indistinguishable. There is a deep tone and a lighter tone. Now and then she can recognise a phrase: '. . . wait for . . . want to . . . oh . . . and beautiful . . .' She wonders if someone has forgotten to turn off the television. Perhaps the button has not been pressed firmly enough, or it needs to be unplugged from the wall. There is snapping and rustling, a hum like the hum of someone enjoying a mouthful of food, a grunt, and a scuff. Then, a bad word, which she has only ever heard Mauri and the men at the pork van use. A voice cries out, 'No!' Annette opens the door of the living room. Uncle Marcello calls from inside, 'Hey. Who's that?'

'It's Netta. Is the television still on?' She hears scuffling on the tiles, as if he is standing up.

'No. Yes. It's off now. It's OK. Go back to sleep, quickly.' His voice is hoarse, as if he is getting Tommaso's cold. 'Good night.'

'Good night.' As Annette makes her way back to bed, she hears, perhaps, though she cannot be sure, a very faint wail, as if a night creature, flying from roof to roof in the town, is calling to another of its kind.

In the cool back room of Castrabecco the following morning, Annette prepares the cuttings. She binds them with twine and loads them into the back of the flower van. Mauri does not say much as they drive through the old walled town. 'I have things on my mind,' he tells her when she asks if he is feeling unwell. 'I have personal matters to contend with. I have inner conflicts. You are a girl. You would not understand.' She wonders if Mauri is in love. Perhaps he is thinking of joining the army, as he did once before, when Vincenzo left for Argentina. It made their mother furious. At the citadel, he forgets the lug of the wing mirror and it cracks back against the side of the van. She hears a telltale chink as the glass cracks. Her brother curses and punches the steering wheel. Annette flinches. He drops her at the pitch, puts up the canvas stall without ceremony or performance, and then leaves without kissing her cheek. There are no jokes about killing their mother or joining the Foreign Legion. There is no teasing about adoration unrequited or his virility. Perhaps it is Maria from the cinema, Annette thinks, who all the young men are passionate about, or Romana who works at the information cubicle of Civitella, who has notorious flaming hair like the mistress of the mayor.

In the hot sun the flowers begin their mysterious olfactory elicitation. 'Buy us, buy us, for reasons of marriage or seduction.' There is the usual bustle and weekend gossip. Elemme tells her there is a new antique stall set up in the market to attract the tourists. It sells clocks, angels made from bent coins, old postcards, photographs and glassware. In old crates are religious wooden icons distressed to look ancient. 'Most of it is junk,' says Elemme. 'Not worth spit. Just rope and springs. But everyone is over there looking for ceramics and Venetian goblets. I'm bored. Do you want some Coca-Cola?' Her castanet shoes click quickly down the stalls, her heels slipping in and out of the leather hulls as she goes, and the beads in her hair tick-tack. Annette pictures all the people walking past, sipping coffee or eating *porchetta*, carrying baskets, pausing to fix a stocking, scoring a line through a list.

As she waits, she wonders about the new television set. She wonders about its productions and what happens when it is turned off. Programmes are still being fed into it, but what does it do with them? Uncle Marcello says the device is simply a magic box of light and signals, a shrunken cinema in which people might act, but she can't help imagining all the people it contains lying down to sleep when it is turned off, or going on with their lives in privacy. Perhaps this was the case last night, when she was woken. But do they know that they are being watched? Are they oblivious to their capture and their shrunken size, or do they know they are captives, that it is their duty to jump up and act whenever the silver switch is pressed and the tuning wheel turned? Do they take their cues by walking up to chalk marks scored on the television floor, like school children in the religious plays? And if they are unaware, do they still feel the gaze of people watching them, like an intuition, as she feels the leer of the Bestia?

A breeze passes, bringing with it the scent of peach and pork fat. A woman stops to buy a little posy for a sick friend. The friend has had a hysterectomy, the curse of eight deliveries, the woman says. Not that she agrees with the doctors overseas, practising termination – bless the poor babies. Annette is distracted, she does not follow the conversation. She knows her mother would not approve of such rumination over the television set. She would consider it a vexing realm for Annette to have strayed into. She would prefer it instead if Annette contemplated Good Works. When the two of them become engaged in difficult conversations often she has wondered whether Annette might be better suited in a convent, where life is simple and virtuous and repetitious. 'You are walking into a maze, daughter,' her mother has often said. 'Just how do you think you will get out? Where are you trying to go with this?' And yet Annette cannot help but think how she thinks, the world being as full of puzzles as it is.

Perhaps the people inside the television might hate being looked in upon, as her mother despises pedestrians in the street casually glancing into the lower rooms of Castrabecco. Perhaps the television dwellers fear the moment when the silver button is pressed to the OFF position, because they will be left in complete darkness, knocking on the walls of the television and bumping into each other, banging foreheads and stumbling over each other's feet. They will be locked up inside the bubble with all the creatures and crimes of the television's world, and the whole roaring Pacific.

Her head begins to ache a little. This is the real problem. What if the people in the television were watching other people on television, who were in turn watching televisions? How many television worlds could there be? Could the worlds of television be endless, like the windows in the Dutch paintings, revealing places with yet more windows? Could there be a long glass hole in the universe consisting entirely of television screens?

Elemme returns with the Coca-Colas, which are so cold she cannot hold the bottles. 'Quick, take it! My fingers are stuck!' The two drink their drinks under the flower-stall awning. Sweetness explodes in Annette's mouth, it fizzes and stings her sinuses. Elemme pats Annette on the shoulder. 'Listen, we should untie your hair. It's so pretty. It's a shame always to have it in braids or hidden under a scarf. Here. I'll arrange it for you.' She unties the fastenings and gently begins to unravel the long, crimped strands. 'Do you have a television at home?' Annette asks as she has her hair combed. Elemme grunts. 'No, angel, we cannot afford it. And if we could I would prefer a dishwasher. That would be the very best thing. There are too many men renting our house. Not one of them knows how to turn on the kitchen tap.' She tucks a strand of hair behind Annette's ear. 'There! Tomorrow I will bring a little conditioning oil and we'll shine it. Maybe I'll even open a styling shop, since no one is buying my buttons.'

As Annette finishes her cola, she imagines herself trapped in the static factory of the television. Inside it is not like a womb. It is not like a wardrobe. It is claustrophobic, even though Annette is shrunken. It smells of nothing, or perhaps it smells of singed flex and burning dust, like the iron when it gets too hot. She gropes for a trapdoor, a window, or a loose seam, but there is no way out. If Elemme were inside a television set she would surely be able to find a doorway or a plastic chute next to the wires at the back, and open it, and slip out. She would immediately know where she was and how to get her bearings. She is practical like that. In the un-drying paint of the Deposition, the Bestia also knows how to work the release mechanism. He pours out of the composition and emerges bright and terrible, his horror bleeding everywhere.

The most frightening thought of all is that she, Annette, would not even realise her position if she were stuck in the oubliette of the television, and then she would be forgotten. She would not be the real Annette. Once this thought has occurred to her, she finds it very hard to cast aside.

When Mauri collects her in the afternoon his mood has improved considerably. He calls to her. 'Rapunzel! Rapunzel! I am here to rescue you!' He climbs out of the van giggling like a schoolboy, and scoops up Annette's loose hair between his fingers. He bends her backwards in a dancing dip. Elemme calls over from the thrifts, 'Hey, Annette, I think your brother is drunk.' The stall is carelessly packed away, flower stalks are snapped, and Mauri drives very slowly and very badly to the greenhouses. Occasionally there are small swerves, as if he is avoiding objects in the road. 'Is something wrong with the van?' Annette asks. 'Yes, it's not a Ferrari! It's not a Mercedes!' He dissolves into laughter again and she begins to think he has been drinking as Elemme suggested.

At the entrance to the gardens he stops the van and leans over and puts his arm around Annette. 'Did you take your hair down just for me? You do love me after all. I'm sorry I was angry. Give me a kiss. Everyone else is at it.' She turns her face to kiss his cheek, but finds his mouth waiting instead, like a supple wet fruit. His lips are damp and loose as they press hers. Up close there is a bittersweet fragrance to his shirt, a scent with notes of almond and detergent. For a moment she feels a slight flush of dizziness. Is this how a real kiss feels? Mauri releases her. 'Oh,' he says. 'No touching tongues at the greenhouses. Not unless we want a visit from you-know-who!' His tone is neither playful nor serious. He is not tormenting her, but Annette is not certain he is joking.

The van recommences its weaving journey and brakes suddenly outside the little brick office and the engine stalls. Mauri opens his door and jumps out, his boots thudding on the ground. Annette's door is opened by Uncle Marcello, who takes her hand and helps her down. 'I'm sorry, I shouldn't have let him drive. But look at you, with your radiant golden hair. Are you going to photosynthesise our plants?' Annette takes hold of her uncle's elbow. 'I think Mauri might be unwell.' Uncle Marcello sighs. 'No. Unfortunately, your brother has become stupid with toxic vapour. It's on his sleeve but he won't change his shirt. He's such a clumsy fool. He spilled chloroform everywhere. Now he is killing his brain and he thinks it's hilarious.' Her uncle sighs again then calls over to Maurizio, who's humming a waltz and shuffling his feet by the pomegranate tree. 'Go and walk around, idiot boy! Get some air into that stupid brain! Go and dig or do military jumps, I don't care!'

When she was seven, Annette was given gas at the dentist for the extraction of four back teeth. The dentist placed a mask on her face and the gas made it impossible to feel anything inside her mouth or to be sensible. The procedure seemed only to take a few seconds, though her mother said it had been longer. The gas had bent time. When she came round she was violently sick into a bowl that her mother held. 'Will Mauri be OK?' she asks. Uncle Marcello places a hand on the back of her head and strokes her hair. 'Yes, princess, but he's going to have a very bad headache. And you? Did you feel all right this morning, after your restless night? I'm sorry if I disturbed you.'

They proceed into the office. Annette can feel the breeze passing through – the two tin-framed windows have been wound open as far as they will wind. She can smell the bitter-sweetness again, a smell that gets into her throat and pads it out with cotton. Under this is the smell of soil, worms, and fertiliser. She hears a metal bottle cap being screwed, the quick wash of liquid as it is upended against the neck. 'I'd better put this somewhere safe where your brother can't get at it.' The wind in the cabin flutters the papers stuck to the wall. Annette wonders if the little English fairies on the postcards are drowsy too.

The battle against the greenfly has been a success, her uncle tells her. The ones in the trays have been destroyed, and their larvae poisoned. But they will have to wait to see whether the flowers can withstand such a harsh measure. Her uncle gently takes hold of her face and kisses her, once on each cheek. He sighs. 'It's a difficult balance between salvation and harm,' he says. 'We should always try to move forward, but sometimes that upsets everyone! I just hope we've done the right thing, Netta.'

Translated from the Bottle Journals

As predicted, there has been much commotion today. I have three nurses and they do not accede on matters of care. Theresa believes most ardently in the restorative power of soup; Florio, rest. Antonio sees that I wish to work and tries to defend my position, but the other two have interpreted his motivation as financially beneficial to himself, taking, as he does, a percentage of any sales. They do not mean to be unkind. It is simply the tension of the situation. Finally they have all agreed on the virtue of fresh air. They have moved an armchair into a square of sunlight on the veranda. I have been here all morning with a blanket on my knees though it is still very warm. The radio sits on a small table nearby and a bowl of fruit and my cigarettes. There are sunshades clipped to my spectacles. From here I can see the mountains. I have my tobacco and some books and it is quite a haven, or it would be if it weren't for the continual disturbance.

Theresa visits my little oasis every fifteen minutes, as if it is a watchtower. You are missing your holster and your pistol, I say to her. Why don't you go and patrol the garden? She fusses. She adjusts the blanket. She brings more soup and suggests I take a nap. I do not want to sleep through midday, I tell her each time. I am not a Spanish restaurateur. Antonio has gone into town to make some telephone calls. I suspect he is escaping the relentless dominion of Theresa. Florio is adjusting the pressure of the oxygen tank. The intention was to bring the device here twice a week for treatment, but the struggle to get it up the hill was so great that the doctor is leaving it at Serra Partucci for the duration of my illness. Perhaps I should rephrase – the duration of my life. Poor Florio. He does not have the waist of a young man any more. He brought the tank on an upright barrow, but the wheels ground into the path and we could hear him cursing and kicking the frame on the ascent. Antonio went to assist. When they arrived Florio was purple in the face and mopping his brow. He could not speak but bent over and flailed one hand until Theresa provided him with a glass of water. I thought he would have a stroke and expire at my feet.

I took some oxygen. It made me very light-headed for a while. There is a triangular mask that fits over the face and is secured with a band. The valves hiss when they are open. I am uncertain of the benefits. The cancer is inoperable and it is simply a matter of time. But Florio insists it will prolong things and grant me some relief. Theresa, though, is now convinced of my dementia. The initial flow of gas was too great. After inhaling it, I believed I saw Benicio lazing in the garden, his head on his paws. He turned and bit his tail as if biting fleas. I was overjoyed to see my old dog and I called out to him. Theresa crossed herself and then put a hand on my forehead. Florio is making sure the gas exits the tank more slowly in future.

They believe me to be optimistic in my outlook. And I am content, except for the fuss. The discomfort is permanent, and the symptoms are invariable. I cough. I wheeze. I move as if lamed and cannot clear my throat satisfactorily. I lie through the night, awake. But it is tolerable. My mind is a little looser I suppose, as befits such a condition. This world is coming to a close. Perhaps, after all, it was Benicio's phantom I saw. He was always the best of guardians.

* * *

I have crept away and closed the door of the bedroom, saying I will rest for two hours, but truthfully I want to try to work. It is my habit to wait until the last possible moment before applying paint to the canvas, and I know that this period of meditation is long, often taking weeks, but then the image is always quick to produce. I am a little impatient now for the commencement. Even when commissioned I have never felt myself to be limited in this way. My thoughts are elsewhere. She is in my mind so often. There will be two interviews this week. Antonio is keen not to exhaust me, so he has selected the most reputable journalists and then I will be left alone. We all understand the significance. I know they will ask me about my life and the meaning of my work. I know they will ask if there are regrets, and I do not know what I will tell them.

Dina wore a white lace corset for our marriage, the waist of it drawn tight enough to grind pepper. Lace from the South, with its pauper's history, its deliberation of stitches. This is a country of bitter and lovely traditions. She was veiled and underneath her hair was like burnt vines. I mourned for Christ on behalf of the congregation and asked for our union officially. I was ten years her senior but I felt young. Her smallness beside me in the church was startling. I imagined she was standing barefoot, her toes on the cold stones, as if in crisis. It was in 1934 and Fascism was noble and Mussolini had not yet told us anti-Semitism did not exist in our country. We were married in the Catholic tradition. She was among the faithful and gave up her ring to the Fatherland after ten months.

She thought me romantic for eventually confessing to her that I prayed every day for the jewel in her hair to fall into my wine, so that I might have had reason to solicit her attention. I told her I had longed to place it back in its dark setting. She thought me avant-garde because I was a target for much debate in the café, but it was not truly so, nor was it my ambition. In one journal I was called the Italian Le Corbusier, and she asked me about this and whether she might visit my studio in the Accademia. I was nervous for her to see the work, but she was kind and not disappointed. When she first sat with me, it was the moment I knew myself to be visible to all the eyes of the world. Her perfume was violet. She was too beautiful. I could not hold her gaze. Instead, I studied the pattern of the tablecloth, the red and blue squares. It was she who courted me and I who was ridiculous.

Our first apartment was in Bologna, close to the stadium, and I was teaching etching. My income was not high. The apartment had two rooms and loud pipes, and the bathroom was communal with no lock, so at first we were too afraid to use it. We would make sure to wake before all the other residents and then turn on the taps and sing while we bathed. We felt like operatic fugitives. There was no room to paint as well as cook, so I worked in the bedroom. After a successful exhibition, there were several patrons. I was able to sell more work and we moved to a better apartment on the Via Fondazza. But I remember her laughter in the old place and the beautiful sound of her singing and the dripping of the taps. I remember the sighs of our lovemaking against the roaring of the crowds in the stadium when the ball was taken towards the opposition. By then ill feelings were beginning to come into the country, but we paid them no heed.

Perhaps I was sombre in my middle years. I was so earnest about my work and could not express myself. How must I have appeared to her? Perhaps not fully developed, but solvable, so she would try all the time to make me smile. I could not convince her of my happiness though I felt it daily. I felt it in the strands of her hair left on the basin, which I jealously collected so that our fellow bathers would not wind them around their fingers. It was my wife's habit to imitate those in power and the police captains, and often she would dress up in my hats and pencil a moustache, and this theatre brought us much amusement. I look back on this and it was harmless. Yet Europe's terrible legacy has left traces of paranoia in my mind. Perhaps we were too casual. Perhaps oblivious to the dangers.

Sometimes Dina would try to unlock me. She would deprive me of sleep, sitting for hours at the window in her nightdress, asking questions, and imagining ways to cure me of the reticence from which she felt I suffered. Once she told me that my silence was able to break the spirit of all the things around me, the spirits of the fireplace, the washstand, the bowl of almonds and the photographic album, even the spirit of the womb. I do not know if she truly believed me capable of this. I blamed my age for our childlessness, but after seven years our daughter was finally conceived. Her name was Elizabeta. Because of the misalignment in her mother's pelvis the delivery was difficult and she was born with broken bones. From birth she had no appetite and gained no weight, though she lay perfectly against the blanket. She lasted five weeks in this world.

I seldom dream. I would gladly accept dreams of my daughter or my wife. I would buy them if I knew the currency with which to do so. Perhaps dreams are the bonds of a frugal God. Or perhaps they are mirages that the thirsty soul falls upon. But I would walk each desert of the world to see Elizabeta. I would not hesitate to give my own life in exchange for Dina's. I would have given up my country's patronage and its protection in those dark years, if it meant she could have been saved. I have thought this too many times to count.

No sun was brighter than the love Dina possessed for our child. Even the surgeon's prediction did not convince her that her maternal involvement would be temporary. After the birth we sat together outside the hospital looking at the designs of Erba, and those carved angels seemed vile to me. Their eyes were deeply recessed and empty where the chisel had struck down, deep holes, which were the lair only of the stone-worm. We took Elizabeta home, though it was not recommended.

After the baby died a mania came to Dina. She went from room to room looking for her. She lifted the tablecloth. She opened bulbs of fennel. She was alert to any possible hiding place. At night she heard noises in the alleyways like the mewling of a newborn, but it was only stray cats singing to each other across the roofs. Once she broke the bones of her hand looking for her small bundle in the awnings of the café. She was as lean and hungry as the wolves on the lakes of ice, scratching at the doorway of another world.

She visited the new synagogue on the Via dei Gombruti in the years that followed, until it was damaged in the bombing, but she seemed to find no comfort there. During the war there was much fear and suspicion. The prayer rooms in the Jewish ghetto were often closed, and the faith could not be practised openly, but it was only when a Jewish man was shot on the Via dell'Inferno that Bologna the Learned began to take the threat of intolerance seriously. Perhaps it was Dina's faith that exposed her during the occupation. She was a proud woman. The Resistenza was fierce in our city, and I have no doubt that she knew many members, but we were careful and our friends were loyal, and the priests and servicemen did their best to offer shelter. Nevertheless, one night I came back from the Accademia and the doorway of the apartment was standing open. A neighbour told me that the building had been searched, and the old medieval heart of the city had been raided and cleared. I ran from room to room but Dina was gone.

I had sold paintings to a man in office at the time. I

238

contacted him and begged him to help. He made an appeal to the German security police, but there was little else he could do. Later, he found her name in the transport records. I remember sitting with him in an empty café in the district of the Two Towers, where Dina had been a child, as he gave me this, the only available proof. I remember him taking hold of my sleeve as I stood up to leave. This is not our great system, he said, this is not what we conceived. And I said to him, no, but neither will we be forgiven.

After she was taken, I understood how it felt to reject what is known to be true. I understood Dina's desperation on those nights when she had heard our baby crying in the alleys. I understood sorrow, sorrow that is inestimable and unfinished. I should have walked with her when she scoured the streets looking for Elizabeta. I should have picked up a rifle.

In the last few years the money offered to Antonio for my self-portraits has tripled. They are rare, and they are felt to be the best clues to the enigma of identity. I have outlived tragedy; that is all. Much has been made of the descriptive accuracy in the paintings, the facial expressions, and how unlike the still-lifes they are. The last self-portrait was completed over twenty years ago, the year the war ended. It is not heroic.

As if to cheer me from my sad memories this afternoon, a postcard from Peter has arrived. He is in America, and has a wife! Here is such joyful symmetry. We should not look for signs, and yet how often they present themselves. Peter describes the Pacific as 'terrifying'. It is so vast. The policemen ride horses as large as the Elgin marbles, he writes. He has spent five nights in a terrible hotel with torn sheets and bodies sprawled in the corridors. He has seen the Pan-American Unity mural. It is all a great adventure. It is 'mind-opening'.

I am fortunate to receive correspondence from friends in all the countries of the globe. Though my life is one of reclusion, I have received many exotic gifts over the years. A tsuba from Japan, black pumice from the Antipodes. Antonio once sent me some antique woodcuts from Bavaria. In truth, I had hoped Peter might choose to come to Italy, to tour Florence and make notes on Fra Angelico, and perhaps even visit me in these humble hills. With what great enthusiasm we would have shaken hands! I would have enjoyed making him some coffee and showing him the objects in the studio. Here is also a lesson in today, in now, such as that found in the Odes of the Augustan poet. Last year, I was sent a gift of coffee from Louisiana. There are still a few black grains, enough spoonfuls left in the tin to filter. It is blended with chicory leaf; the taste is sour and interesting, and I have been saving it for no reason. We will have the last of it today when Antonio returns from the town.

The Fool on the Hill

The last few hours have been restless and uncomfortable, but the dawn is here. Early morning mist lies in austere banks along the valley floor and the boulders drift. Peter can see a weak, low sun through the white reefs at the head of the gorge. It must be almost seven. The hour of rise-and-shine, when civilisation restores itself. There is hope to be had. There's the small road up above on which his distinctive old banger is parked and which will soon be carrying locals and a few late tourists. His car is a give-away, if anyone is looking for it. Some walkers might come this way, having strayed down from the Roman wall – the day looks as if it will set fine. He'll hear their voices up above. He'll hear the squeaking of the wire frets on the fence near the mouth of the ravine when they step down on the dividers, the pulse and rattle as they lift over, and he'll know they are within earshot. No one has answered his shouting yet, but he does not feel so alone.

There's a chilly relish to the air, and the aroma of the new season: damp notes of wood-rot, mushroom, mud. He can hear a bull blaring away in its pen nearby, objecting to its enclosure. The bugger could probably trample straight through the dry-stone walling if it chose, its beady eye staring off into the distant past as it heads for the cows in the pasture. But it keeps on calling, *noo-oo*, *noo-oo*, mired in its own behaviour, as if it's the protest that matters. 'Right on, fellow. Right on.' Sometimes too, the bells of St Andrews can be heard, conducted by the mist, iron-clad, out of key. He is not so far away from everyone.

In the cottage his wife will be up. His side of the bed will not have been slept in. Nor will she find him passed out on the couch below, gin bottle gripped in his hand, drooling on the cushions. Out in the garth, his car is gone; only her Beetle will be there. She will register the void from the landing window as she goes to the bathroom. 'Oh, Peter, what are you up to?' she'll whisper. The usual routines will apply. She will notice the new cold and so light a fire, and the crows will step down off the chimney as the smoke begins to ascend.

The kids will get up – Suze first. There will be a conversation over cups of tea and wholemeal toast. 'Still not home?' 'No. Not like him to say nothing at all.' 'On a bender, you think?' 'Could be.' Then they might rouse Danny. 'Did Peter tell you where he was off to yesterday?' And the three of them might troop out to the gate to see if he has driven home pissed from the pub and stalled somewhere in the lane. There'll be no sign. Just an oily patch on the cobbles of the garth where the Daf is usually parked. They will consider ringing round. 'Hello. The wanderer is on the loose again.' But Donald won't have seen him. The Jerry will say that last night he wasn't in. And perhaps they will begin to worry then. Things will seem too quiet. Instinct will prickle. They will smell something out of sorts in the misty autumn air. They will see a buzzard with carrion in its beak, and the entrails will be readable.

What he wouldn't give to be there in the fray, toasting some coffee beans in the range, boiling an egg and buttering a scone. He'd give his right arm. His left foot. Ha-ha.

It was a much livelier habitation before the kids grew up and (partly) left home. Something was always going on – chatter, band-practice, odd little art projects. Friends of Susan and

Danny's were always staying over, camping in the garden with their sleeping bags and bottles of cheap cider. 'Mr C, have a glass of Bucky. Mr C, fancy a bit of hot knifing?' It was fun. It made Peter feel young. At one stage the cottage was like an animal refuge centre. There was inevitably some furry or feathered creature parading around the gardens, a ruckus of squawks or grunts or whinnies. There were at one time or other goats and geese, rabbits and guinea pigs, a pig, a chinchilla, and even tame sparrows in eggbox nests, which had clocked their heads on the windows and stayed stunned long enough for the kids to bond with. Christ Almighty! The earnest dissection of worms on the chopping board!

Dan went through a spell of keeping weasels in a chicken-wire shelter. They used to dig their way out or gnaw through the barbs. He had a harness for walking them and he would sometimes try to sneak them into school in his gym bag, slipping them into his shirt between the buttons, like an old farm-hand, so they bulged in a ring around his waist, scratching him with their claws and getting him sent to the nurse for flea bites. Once the school phoned up apologising for not noticing Danny's 'condition' before, saying he could be excused from showering after cross country. The pet-shop rabbits always escaped, too, and had orgies with the local population, leaving a legacy of sorrel and red eyes in the burrows.

They all needed to be fed, successively, on a diet of vetch, potato peelings, slugs and snails. The goat had an industrial appetite; he remembers it eating car parts, wing mirrors, upholstery (not quite enough to fully dispose of the aban-doned vehicles, which would have solved the scrapyard problem). Once it took the door trims of a Maxi. It was a bugger to wrestle away when it started chewing anything; it fought the rope and grunted in protest, glass tinkling crisply in its beard. The place was surrounded by sprout buckets and jars of pellets and compost bins. They were always on the hunt for dandelion leaves. It was great. It was a happy time.

Peter liked the geese best. He liked their orange webbed feet flopping on the ground and their matching orange beaks. He liked the way they reared up and flapped their wings, nodding and honking when he arrived with a pail of vegetable scraps, as if saying yes, yes, we're hungry, hurry up, Peter. Their proud white breasts. When they were mad about something they hissed like snakes.

The scruffy fell ponies still come up to the wall when they're passing through. Lydia still feeds them.

The mist thins. A modest warmth glows from the bare sun. His clothes are only damp now, not wringing wet. He needs to unstiffen though, and move out of this awkward twisted position. He needs to run some life back into his arms and thighs and think about looking for that stick again, now he can see the ground. He has taken off the tourniquet. It was far too tight. It was this that probably cut off the feeling in his leg for a while, before the rain slackened it and the ache returned. Florence Nightingale he isn't. There's no red stain below – not that he can see. If he's bleeding it probably isn't too serious. He's a little dizzy, yes, but it's likely just tiredness and hunger.

There has been no sound of traffic on the road above. He thought he heard a dog barking, but when he yelled only his voice in the gorge echoed back. He will have to try moving again. He will have to confront the pain. He will have to run headlong into it, like the proverbial buffalo into the storm. He'll have to face down the ripping febrile sensation, take anguish square on the chin, stand up to it like a man. The damage is already done – he will simply be acknowledging it fully, the way you have to acknowledge such things before you can ever move on and recover. Recovery. Is it possible?

He doesn't often agree to think about her. When his mind goes there, it isn't with his consent or because it is something he ever wants to air. He keeps hoping she will vanish, that, one day, he will have a blank in his memory where she has been, and she will be gone. Sometimes it seems to be finished. There are long periods of no disturbance. Then, all of a sudden, the comfortable absence is broken, and without warning she is there, as she was in the bathtub yesterday. She is there singing 'It's Me My Love', and asking: 'Why don't you ever help me, Petie?' She is there lying provocatively on the floor, or untying the belt of her orange silk dressing gown. She is there slumped over the table, blue-mouthed, and violated, exactly how they found her.

And this now – this trial being held by a higher power with a shitty sense of humour, this meaningful little opportunity to reflect on past crimes, and wonder which it is he is being charged for – this is when treachery and blame can really rain down on him. If it is punishment, if it is divine penalty, then it's not for the minor offences and the negligible sins, his flaws and foibles: booze, pinch, grouching, thievery, filthy language. It's not his escaping of class, putting too much salt on his spuds, inflating his business expenses, or even screwing over Ivan. It's her. She is the reason, isn't she?

Raymie could last a month on a packet of beef jerky. She ate almost nothing else, but she had a thing about protein, thought it would keep her ovaries healthy. And that was her solution – dehydrated saddle meat. He never understood it. The stuff was awful, as chewy as desert leather. It was days after eating it before he could go to the toilet. But it was cheap and she was convinced it would option her health later in life. He never understood the renouncement either, but it was popular for those trust-fund kids to go rough, to slum it. He'd always been skint, as a boy, as a student, even with his scholarship and the supplementary wages. But she was from money, she had access to accounts, she could have bought a loaf occasionally.

There was seldom food in their apartment kitchen in San Francisco – a little fresh tomatilla salsa in the summer, packets of cereal now and then. The indigestible, desiccated jerky. Sometimes, Raymie would make a show of making butternut soup from scratch. Seeds all over the joint. God, it was manna; it felt like liberation! He missed pastry, dripping, battered haddock. He used to dream of banquets and fairytale feasts. They lived like French fucking symbolists, meanly and fashionably. But, there was a narcotic accessory for every occasion, for every gathering of friends, every gig attended, and their wild assisted sex. Some such thing was always produced from her little case, and if not by her then by other struggling, landed artists. There was even a little green ampoule for the enhancement of their marriage. Love made bright, so they could taste its colours, so they could kiss every poor surprised Chinese on the street as they walked back to their apartment. He liked to drink and he liked to ride, but she was bloody fearless. The first Mrs Caldicutt. Raymelia Coombs. Her nerve was awesome. She terrified him. It was the power she held.

'Those were the times,' he's said in interviews, to students, and even to his own kids when they got interested in his herb pouch. But what times were they really, when he was sour with liquor and developing ulcers? What times were they, when her body at intervals was barely human, her breastplate corrugated like a prisoner of war's, the flesh inverting off her pelvis, when she was emaciated enough to stop menstruating? Protein to keep her ovaries ticking for a baby, eaten strictly like medicine through the week, even while she smoked her gums up off her teeth and blew angel dust through her receptors until her vision went blue and she couldn't feel him moving inside her.

The truly messed-up thing was that though she was skeletal, she looked so heavy, like iron or pewter, like a piece of classical sculpture that wouldn't be lifted. 'Hey, nothing is wrong with my body, sweetheart,' she would say, stepping a heel on to the chair like a screen vixen. She was breathtaking. For all the passing out, the skipping of meals and vomiting past five mouthfuls; for all the hair growing thick on her arms and legs, she still had him convinced she was A-OK, in charge, beating the odds. 'Chill out, Goldy,' she would say, when he commented she'd only had one bite of her homemade soup. 'All I need is Larry to fill my prescription.' A blind spot – is that what he could call the relationship? A disaster, out of his range of vision?

And Dyas loved her too – that much was certain. There would be no recompense for winning her away from him. Though Dyas had had other feisty madams in the college, though he was the great Mersey seducer, it was Raymie he wanted, Raymie he left his wife of twelve years for. He and Peter had been so close for that first term, and it was like getting another father. He had found Ivan Dyas behind one of many sports papers in the Roscoe Head, where the carpet was sticky, the tiles chipped and the ceiling fag-stained, but the ale was good. 'Ah, now then, Petie, this your watering hole too, eh? Sit down, and we'll have a jaw about the RCA. Which of the lovely ladies have you got with you? None, oh, that's a shame. I tell you what, why don't you make a little venture to the bar first and ask Blanche for my usual? You can save me from my wife's casserole. Spot on.' Six months later, the man's bags were packed and he was hooked on the beautiful American who had come to Liverpool because of Stuart Sutcliffe and hoping to meet Lennon.

They had travelled about, the three of them, to Glasgow, Leeds, and to the capital, in Dyas's Sunbeam Talbot – now that was a car to drive, that was a classy motor! The trips were supposed to be educational, extra-curricular. They would debate loudly for the first hour, Raymie challenging them on all things repressively British, and Ivan swerving across the corners as he gesticulated. Then they'd switch driver, and Ivan would snore in the passenger seat with the road atlas open on his lap. She had no licence and insisted on using the outside lane. Dyas knew people everywhere it seemed, and all of them were moderately famous. The Hungarian glass sculptor. The cockney actor. The poet laureate's beautiful cousin, who had been one of his regulars before true love reformed him, who was put out to be hosting the new girlfriend and not at all interested in Peter as a replacement. There was always a camp bed or a futon, a mattress or a pallet, in some hip city flat, and a gathering last thing at night where gay patrons, musos, and teenage prostitutes mingled. There was always an invitation to an exhibition opening. Peter was out and about. He was circulating, being current. He was going to be a painter and he didn't mind saying so. It was the decade of having an attitude.

'What is your accent precisely, darling?' agents would ask him at parties, straightening his collar for him. 'Ah. The North Country. Well, there seems to be ample talent up there these days. Here's my card. We're not, if I may be blunt, interested in landscapes at the moment. But if you've anything hard-edge, keep us in mind.' Across the room, Dyas and Raymie would be mooning, and blowing into each other mouths. Once or twice they had shared a room in the motorway lodges and he had pretended to sleep while they whispered and giggled. Her eyes had flashed in the dimness, looking towards him as she moved.

He must have been jealous. She was watchable, flirtatious, she dressed like an aristocratic homosexual with cravats and velvet coats, she told a good joke. Her eyes hunted for him in the darkness while she sucked her lip and rode. She knew what she was doing. There was nothing to do but let his lust impact, while he got angry at other things. 'That stuff in there says nothing to me,' he would inform Dyas when his tutor came out and joined him for a smoke on some West End balcony. 'It's mindless.' And Dyas would agree, naturally, then tell him to knock off the sinister act and get back inside pronto. He reckoned Hockney was about to have a brawl. 'If you want to see two boys clinging, Petie, best you get a shift on. Come on, relax. Stop taking everything so personally. Let's get you laid.'

Then, one night, after spending an hour looking at a window covered in smudged faeces, with the creator standing alongside saying it was the best medium with which to describe human anguish, the tension finally broke. 'It's shit,' Peter heard himself say, unnecessarily, and out he stormed. Raymie followed, intrigued by the sudden loss of temper, and they found a club nearby. They drank. They danced. Her body was against his, then apart from his, against and then apart. It drove him crazy. By the end of the night he had lost his mind. Ivan was unconscious on the floor of the place they were staying, and Peter was holding a hand over his girlfriend's mouth, forcing her against the wall, trying not to slip out of her.

The Mirror Crisis

On the hotel bed he raises your legs on to his shoulders. He moves your hips back towards his and holds your thighs. You feel your tendons pulling tight, the depth increasing. He is straining not to come. He is saying *are you, are you* but the question cannot be completed. There is enough unity, enough collaboration between you, for the timing to work. Your abdomen fills with heat. Your stomach pulls inwards and the spasm takes over. The quiet screaming in the room is the sound of something coming into the world, or leaving it.

He moves the damp hair off your forehead. His hand is shaking; he is a little clumsy. You have twenty minutes, and then you will both have to leave. He is collecting his daughter from nursery. You have to continue preparing the exhibition space. The hotel is close to the station where an overland train can be taken to the heath. You share a glass of water. *How is it, with Danny?* he asks. You shrug. You rest your head on his arm. After a moment he says, *Susan, I have something to show you. It's really exciting.* He lifts his bag on to the bed and unbuckles the straps. *I shouldn't take it out of the gallery, we're not insured, but if I get mugged I'm sure they'll go for my wallet first.* He takes out the diary and flicks through the pages. There are paper markers tucked between the leaves. The handwriting is exquisite. *Here,* he says. *Listen to this.* His eyes are bright with tears.

The meetings between you are more regular now, and the

exchanges at the gallery are more daring and insistent. The building is shut for a few days while the new exhibition goes up; there are no milling strangers to hide behind, no distractions. He leans close to you when he passes by. He strokes your spine if he sees you have taken off your jacket, touches your breasts through the thin material of your blouse. All the while his wife is close by. You wonder why she cannot see it, why she does not notice the atmosphere, and the heightened musk of her husband, for it is as if a rich substance has been released into his cells. You can smell it under his skin, this tropic nectar, which passes through his ducts and arteries, condensing into sap near his groin. His body exudes invitation, reeks with it, and his eyes seem to confess infatuation, even while he is talking about his work on the journal, even when he is speaking professionally to you in front of Angela.

You treat the presence of his wife like foreplay. Her being there at the gallery simply increases the anticipation. The affair is shot through with risk and would be called pitiful, abject, and vile, by anyone who knew about it. When Angela goes out to collect their daughter from playgroup, he moves you on to the desk, sits in front of you. He lifts your skirt and moves his mouth along the seam of your underwear, then pulls the material aside. Your dress rides up against your hipbones, the stitching tears. The sound of the front door opening and closing is thrilling. You go to him. You press your thumb along the stem of his prick, feel the hum of blood in the thick vein. You move him towards the back of your mouth. In the bathroom he washes his face, checks the material of your dress for damp marks. You both act with the swift confidence of the damned, brazen with obsession. But it is he who recovers slowest, remains unlaced and casual in his furtiveness, he perhaps who wants to be caught, or would confess.

* * *

You lean forward, reach behind and pull him between your legs. He raises you against the wall, the tight friction tearing your fragile skin. Then you take his full weight on the bed. You are late for the train now and will have to catch the next one. He will have to take a cab to collect his daughter in time, or call and say he has been held up. But in these moments you can forget about everything else. You are not bereaved. You do not feel disconnected from yourself, or uninhabited, as if you've slipped accidentally from your cage of bones. When you are with him you are here, inside yourself, behind the calcium plates in your chest and pelvis, which rise and move against him. He marks your frame. The delicate meat of you contains him. You clear away his milky substance from your skin.

You wonder how it will be possible to continue working at Borwood House. You are, no doubt, a monster of some kind, bloodless and reptilian. You watch Angela and Tom together to see if there are any distances opening up between them. You watch to see how much of an effect you might be having – you, the mistress, the adulteress, his new love. At the gallery they are professional with each other, the relationship is workable; arguments are never carried out in front of you or visitors; there is conviviality, discreet affection. You wonder how they connect at home, whether they function smoothly, whether there are accusations, resentments, frigidities. You wonder whether Tom still tries to fuck her, or she him. This is not something you and he have discussed, but you think about it. Do the fumes of his body still arouse her, or is she now immune to him? Does she know what excites him most, and have they tried it? Has she pulled the bed sheet tight across his face so that he cannot see or breathe? Has she been gently inside him, has she let him taste everything? You wonder whether he can hold their daughter now without imagining she will shatter in his hands.

When you arrive at midday the two of them are engaged in their separate tasks. Between them they mind the baby, or the baby is left with a sitter, or deposited at the nursery. Like most of London's working families, their choreography is tight and slick. How does he manage to slip into the city to meet you, or linger long after she has gone home in the evening? How has there not yet been any substantial damage to the stability of their home and business environments? Perhaps he tells her he has meetings with publishers or agents. Perhaps his lies are adequate, delivered convincingly.

Each day you walk into the gallery alert to the possibility of discovery, sure a reckoning of some kind awaits you. You will have left a mark on him, unmistakably congressional, or she will find something incriminating in his pocket, a book of matches from the hotel, a phone bill, your earring. She will smell the sex on his clothing, the salt and ammonia. You hold your breath, hang up your coat, turn on the computer, slide open a window. When you leave one room and enter another the hairs on your arms and neck rise. You know discovery could happen at any moment.

And you know there will be no forgiveness for this atrocity. Life does not work that way, in love, in betrayal. There is always hurt, directed exactly into the central chamber of the heart. This is the worst possible scenario. You imagine her walking in on you as you press against him. You picture the disbelief on her face. *No, it isn't true, it couldn't possibly be. Say you haven't.* You picture her striking you, leaving a gash under your eye from the tall stone of her engagement ring. You think of her distraught, hunched over with the baby in her arms, her hand covering the fontanelle, the skin there delicately beating. And her phone calls to Nathan – torrid discussions where they become bitter comrades. *How could she do it? Because of her brother. No. The bitch has no excuse.*

You will have no defence. You imagine Nathan's torment. Nathan, who does not deserve such treatment, who knew straight away he wanted to marry you, and hung in when you said no. Nathan, who is kind and considerate, whose proximity has transposed, inexplicably, into something not precious enough for you to cherish.

The grisly cinema plays through your head. You catch Angela watching you, and you hold your breath. *Are you OK, Susan?* she asks. *You look a little queasy. Are you feeling sick? Oh darling, I do wish I could help you feel better through all this.* It's perverse, but you wonder, just for a second, whether she knows everything and it does not matter, whether she has, during this time of catastrophic loss and descent, generously loaned you her husband.

You try to concentrate on preparing the exhibition space. The maple floors have been polished to a gleam, the walls whitened. The artefacts have at last begun to arrive, delivered by courier, and accompanied by their verification certificates. Carefully, you've investigated the containers, delving down through polystyrene chips for the frail, bandaged lumps. You gently lifted them out, each one, and unbound the strips of cotton wool and tape. And there, in your hands, were the relics of the great artists who have always been in your life, in your father's books, in his stories and boasts, in the lecture halls and essays, and in your own early compositions. A crippled man's bed slippers. A Russian violin. Eyeglasses. There was an almost electric charge to each item, a faint pulse, perhaps your own, or perhaps just the poignancy of knowing to whom they had belonged, and by whom they had been used.

There you were, holding the damaged leather case that had

held those corrective spectacles. There you were, unzipping the pouch and removing the hinged frame with its one chipped lens, its wire ear hooks. And, quite unexpectedly, you were moved. You phoned your dad. The phone rang in the house and the answering machine clicked on. Then you remembered he had a doctor's appointment. You set the glasses on the white column, the wire arms folded, the frame leaning against the case. Next to it you put your father's bottle.

It's now apparent that *In the Artist's Shoes* is going to be a success. Already there are media requests, the culture shows have booked airtime, the guest list for the preview is full, and, looking about at these curious little artefacts, you know people will come to see them, and they will be intrigued. They will connect the historical dots; give each item importance. They will recognise these familiar items not just as precursors to their modern-day cousins – smaller, denser, bolted and pinned, sprung and stitched, unmistakably crafted – but as vital salvage, things that have been touched by genius, preserved by families and servants, and saved by museums. In them they will recognise their own humanity, just as you have. And it will astound them that a human being, such as they are – short-sighted, overweight, weak-boned, an addict – could produce those definitive works of art. You were wrong to ever doubt the idea.

The chattels suit the domestic interior of Borwood House. It is the best exhibition yet, and will be personal, and intimate. Nothing will be encased under glass. You are affixing signs to the walls. *Many of these items are delicate. Please do not touch.* You think about Danny and his metal angel, the sound of her ringing through the V&A, and you know that human nature is an innately contrary thing. People will always touch that which is forbidden.

* * *

You went to their wedding, however many years ago it was. About the same time you were hooking up with Nathan actually. The ceremony was in a little blond church in Suffolk, in a well-kempt village with nodding rose bushes and thatched roofs: Angela's old territory. You were too busy with Nathan to care much about what was happening. You remember drifting about the village the day before the ceremony, having a drink in the pub early, feeling tipsy and a little sore from the prolonged, exploratory sex at the bed-and-breakfast. You barely knew Tom. He was handsome, dark, almost forty. Angela seemed smitten with her Italian writer. The next day, in the church, he showed you to your seat. He shook hands with Nathan and held up a palm to you. He was wearing a three-piece graphite suit, a pink cravat, a pink flower in his lapel. His hair was cut in military style. The groom's side of the church was thinly occupied. There were some friends from the publishing world, including a well-known author, and one ancient, weeping aunt who spoke no English, and looked far too frail to have travelled from the continent. She remained in the church while everyone else went to the reception.

He was, more or less, a stranger. You had talked pleasantly a few times in smoky moments of privacy at events and parties, and from end-table chairs at restaurants. There was no obvious attraction, though he was good-looking and quietly sociable. He talked interestingly about translation, the marvel of the apostrophe. Later, when you were renovating the gallery, he told you some stories about his mother, about how she would go to the local bookshop and black out any swear words she could find in the texts. He laughed and said she was mad, that she used to write letters to women in prison asking them to repent. Then he sighed and said she was probably just depressed, but he had had to get out of there. He said the family was unlucky. And you felt as if this was an intimate conversation to be having.

256

You were stripping the old wallpaper together with a steamer, peeling it away in great damp bolts from skirting board to ceiling. His T-shirt and jeans were flecked with paint. When you got to the small snug room at the back of the building, he said, *We should leave this paper in here, the condition is excellent.*

While you were decorating the two of you accidentally disturbed a wasps' nest that had been built behind one of the old window shutters. It was a hot summer. The windows were open and one or two wasps had been drilling about the place. Then Tom found the grey, cindery pocket in a wall cavity, and, thinking it was disused, he began to chip between its seal and the plaster. Suddenly the air was swarming. For a moment he was paralysed as the insects rushed and scribbled above the nest. *Gesù Cristo!* He picked up a decorating sheet, threw it over the two of you, and you stumbled from the room, slamming the door closed. *Are you stung? No. Nor am I.* Underneath the sheet he smelled of sweat and dust. You could hear the wasps as they flew against the other side of the door, rapping softly like fingertips.

He does not speak ill of his wife. There are no complaints, no unkind sentiments. At your neck, against your thigh, he speaks only of wanting you. He makes breathless erotic pleas. *Can I take this off? Please. Tell me what to do. Tell me to stay still.* Only once, when you were dressing yourself afterwards, preparing to leave the hotel, and you could not find your other shoe under the bed covers, he said, *She is not you. You understand it, don't you? You know what it does to you?* You know nothing of his love for Angela and their daughter, or his habits at home. You have not yet read anything he has written. But you know the events of his childhood, what he has seen. You know the haunted space he is looking into when he moves against you.

You know that he comes using his full body, his ecstasy straining to get out, the seizure seeming to break apart his every atom.

Angela puts her hand on your shoulder. *Really, you don't look well. I'm going out to get you something to pick you up a bit, OK. Maybe some peppermint tea?* She shrugs on her cardigan, collects her purse. *The place looks great, Suze. Really great. You've worked so hard. I know it's been difficult.* On her way to the door she pauses. *Hey, you don't think you're pregnant do you? I felt like shit when I was pregnant with Anna. I wanted to collapse all the time.* You smile, and shake your head, but something inside you splits, and you feel half of you subside along a fault line running from the base of your skull down your backbone. Angela shuts the front door and is gone. The building ticks, listening. For a moment you sit still, waiting for something. Something. Then you go to the cloakroom and look in your bag for your organiser. You can only see your phone and your wallet.

When you open the door the snug is almost in darkness, but for the glow of the screen, and a weak table lamp. The curtains are drawn. Tom is wearing headphones. He cannot hear the traffic on the main road, the birds in the trees next to the heath, or the hustle of the city beyond. He doesn't hear you come in, and it is like that first time, when you found each other and it all began. Behind him, the erogenous red paper left on the walls three years ago, as if you had both dressed the stage for the exchanges that would follow. His back is turned. You walk towards him, a shadow in the room. On the desk next to the computer is a pad of paper on which he has written columns of words. His diary is open to this week's page. You stand behind him, calculating.

In a moment you know he will turn round. He will glance

past you to the door, which is open. Then he will look at you and his eyes will flicker with excitement. You will take his fingers into your mouth and put his hands under your skirt. You'll feel him stroke your legs, and move you on to his lap. He will pull your buttocks apart as if separating pieces of a fruit. He will rub you wet with his thumb, open the fastening, and move the tip of himself into place. You will hurt yourself slowly, your legs either side of the chair, and he will continue to open you outwards as you move.

In a moment he will turn round and his eyes will flicker.

The Divine Vision of Annette Tambroni

The following week brings high temperatures again. The earth cracks open. Taps wheeze and trickle. It is the season of floating pollen, sticky arms and abandoned arguments. It is the season of wilting peonies and calendulas. Beekeepers have brought their produce to the market, jars bright and slow with their gorgeous orange contents, and then returned to their fields with swollen wallets. The professional cyclists have passed through the town, pushing stiffly up into the hills through the cheering crowds, gathering speed around the chicanes of the downhill slopes, and flashing away down colonnades of aspen and barley. Young birds have become confident about leaving their nests. The pavements ripple with heat.

A week after the purchase of the television, Annette is no clearer about its governances and possibilities, but the rest of the family are fully committed to its charms. Uncle Marcello believes absolutely that he could win *Lascia o Raddoppia*. He has dispatched a letter of application to the competition. He will write one a week for the rest of the year until they accept, he insists. If he wins, the business will be sold to another family and they can all retire to Argentina. Her mother is uncertain about this proposal. Argentina is the Land of Forgetting, in case he has forgotten, and there they could lose their heritage and their patriotism. It will be too hot in summer, too cold in winter. And besides, Vincenzo will not want them; he writes so infrequently it is as if all thoughts of reunion with his family have vanished. 'Then a world cruise,' Uncle Marcello says optimistically, 'if it pleases you more, Rosaria.' There has been a miracle reported on the news. Near Naples, a girl has levitated. Witnesses say she was surrounded by heavenly rays and cleared three feet at least. The Vatican is investigating. Maurizio complains that his favourite advertisement for nylon stockings has been discontinued. If the skirt was too short and broke the decency codes, then why was it made in the first place? he asks. He shakes his hand when Mina Mazzini steps past the piano to the microphone, and Annette can hear his fingers slapping against each other like fresh-caught fish in a bucket. Their mother re-tunes the channel.

Tommaso is less enthusiastic about the buzzing, twittering box of pictures. He is engaged in riding up and down the hills, between ruined towers and ripe vineyards, and even up the steps of the cimitero di campagna. 'I have to build up my thighs,' he says, when Father Mencaroni asks him why he is leaving tyre tread on the sacred masonry. Sacrifices have to be made if he is to produce a gold medal for the country, he informs the priest, and off he rides, leaving a small cloud of dust to settle on the priest's cassock. Father Mencaroni shakes his head.

Either the mignonette honey, or the television's distraction, has saved Annette's mother from her weekly migraine. She is busy watching the religious programmes, instead of lying down in her room with a camomile head-wrap. When Annette leaves for the church, her mother does not say anything about her returning home safely, or minding the potholes in the road and the troglodyte Southerners. Nor does she insist that Mauri and Tommaso accompany her to mass, for mass has been brought to her. She watches in a headscarf, her long dress arranged in drapes over her knees, and her hands linked, exactly as if she were sitting at a pew in San Lorenzo.

Annette gathers up some peonies for her papa and for Signor Giorgio. She counts the number of flowers on each. They are uneven. It cannot be helped; sometimes nature makes unlucky patterns. Their globes are full and heavy. The petals froth and their scent is balanced delicately between mountain air and frankincense. Concentrating hard, perhaps she can just see a border of red, an echo of red near her hand when she holds up the stems. Sometimes red can be seen in the world because it is so vivid. But sometimes the colour is simply a trick of blood lighting the discreet hollows of her eye sockets. She is nervous after the incident with the shadow last week. Though she has bled, she does not feel as if what went into her has been brought back out. She does not feel cleansed. She finds Tommaso pumping up his bicycle tyres and asks if he will come with her to the church. 'Why?' he demands. He has already been excused and he does not wish to be recommissioned. 'I just like your company, little one,' Annette tells him. Maybe he will come later after his training, he says.

She collects the little rosemary spirit-stopper from her dresser and steps outside into streets as warm as an oven. On the way to San Lorenzo, people amble by and greet her pleasantly. 'Hello. Good day. Not with your brothers this week? Regards to Signora Tambroni and to your uncle. Stay in the shade!'

The church smells as it always does, of sacred wood and the white talcum gloves of the old brides of Christ. Today they are to consider Abraham, so devoted to God that he would sacrifice his son Isaac. Such a difficult story for us to comprehend, Father Mencaroni says. What price is there for loving God best among all our loves? Imagine it. To hold a knife to the throat of an innocent. To be prepared to slice the artery as one would a festival goat's. Is this not trust, absolutely? Will we not be rewarded in heaven for such devotion? he asks. On Annette's lap, the uneven peonies nod their heads imperceptibly. She thinks of the weeks after her sickness. There was a game she had played with Mauri, which he had invented to help her recover, and which had developed from the object-holding game. He would mix special pastes and concoctions in the kitchen, combinations of anchovy and pomegranate, fig and salt, and she had to open her mouth, receive the spoon, and describe the mysterious mis-combined contents. If she recoiled from the test Mauri would object. 'Trust me. Imagine I'm St Luke.' The game's tonic qualities were never truly apparent to Annette, as her taste buds had not been affected during her illness, but she continued to play it until Mauri lost interest.

While she is receiving the sacrament she does not lift her head up towards the Deposition, with its jostling pyramid of mourners and the brutish creature no more than an arm's length from the green-tinged Christ. But she knows his face will be staring out between those of the disciples, casting and recasting itself. She does not want to attract his attention or antagonise him. Perhaps if she remains cowered and small he will not follow her along the road and up the steps to the cimitero. Perhaps he will not even notice her. She thinks of the artist in the madhouse, slipping a blade in behind one eye, beginning to cut away the soft globe. Father Mencaroni lifts his hand towards Sebastian on the wall of the church. He asks the congregation to think for a moment about suffering. Then they are reminded not to use water unless strictly necessary – the region's reservoirs are running low. The service concludes. The congregation sighs, leaves the basilica, and everyone begins to fan themselves in the sweltering heat. All thoughts turn to dozing behind closed shutters.

The gates of the cimitero are open when Annette arrives.

She closes them behind her. They do not creak; they have been oiled. Climbing the marble steps she has made a resolution. She will not be afraid. If the Bestia is there, if he has leaked once more from his ornate frame and moved undetected through the town, and if his shadow begins to seep into her – into the canals of her ears, between her legs, and in through the pink eye of her belly – she will trust God to protect her. She will trust him, and the little glass vial of rosemary in her pocket. It will be a test of her courage, and her faith.

She steps into the stone garden of departed citizens while the sun burns furiously overhead. Carafes of wine have been left to fortify and evaporate in niches. She can smell plums and dry incense. The pathways through the memorials are worn smooth. She goes first to the photograph of her father. She touches the laminate panel, perhaps where her father's hat is tipped back off his head, perhaps where his moustache is shaved so finely against his lip. She touches the figurine of the Madonna. A spider's web has attached her to the corner of the alcove, as if the Holy Mother has been caught in a net. Annette removes it, and removes last week's desiccated offering. She places the peony stems in the metal canister. Three blooms. Five blooms. 'Papa, I remember your polished shoes,' she says. 'We have a television now. People are talking about a drought. Don't worry about the flowers; Uncle Marcello has barrels of rainwater collected.'

Next she visits the chamber of her old tutor. She passes through the private gate, whose hinge has also been oiled, into the shady recess. It is quiet in the tomb, like a stone lung without any breath. On the wall a brass plaque shines dully. Pale insects with wings like oat husks crawl in the fissures. Annette empties the blue bottle of its dry stalks and flies, and delivers the new flowers with their five erupting red blooms. The light in the glass hull reflects the entrance of the chamber and the little crypt window, which looks out towards the beeches. It reflects two figures: one is a girl who is no longer a girl, and the other is squatting in the corner of the chamber in the darkness, like an animal. Now, after all, Annette can hear that the room is breathing. There is the sound of air travelling the length of a nose, into the well of a throat, and down into the chest. Air rushing back up the throat's tunnel and blowing from two nostrils. She holds still.

Now there is the sound of swallowing, saliva moved from the tongue to the gullet. Now, the sound of something stirring in the corner. The hairs on Annette's arms and neck lift, as fine as the filaments of a dandelion clock. The air is pulled away from her and it is difficult to breathe. There is the dry crackle of heels, like the sparking of matches against the sandpaper strip of a matchbox; the figure is standing slowly. A footstep. The gate of the tomb closes. The air breathes. She tries to speak, but her mouth is cracked and dry, like the earth in the centre of Italy, and words will not grow. In the pocket of her skirt, her fingers curl around the little glass vial. In her mind's eye, she pictures the abundant rosemary growing in pots outside Castrabecco, and her uncle grinding oil from the green spines to keep her safe. She thinks of the blessed, humble rose-mary, whose flowers turned blue when the Virgin hung her laundered robe on the bush as she travelled into Egypt.

There is a deep sigh, like the growl of an animal guarding its prey. She could clap her hands sharply, one-two-three, like clapping stray cats away from a dead pigeon in the street when they squabble for its plush entrails. She could call out for help, though the cimitero is empty, and the town is apathetic in its long summer state. She could rattle the gate, release the catch, and run down the steps – she knows the way – but she has made a promise not to be afraid. She has made a contract with God to trust in Him so that He will keep her safe from harm.

The breathing continues through the damp internal passageways and catacombs, through the holes in the face. Finally, he has come. What does he look like? She wants to know. Has he the lumbering back of a boar, with hair so coarse it cuts through bark? Does he move on all fours to slaughter sheep, like the Lobos dogman Vincenzo has written to them about, gore smeared about its mouth? She finds her voice. 'Is it you? Is it you?' A smile perhaps, the wet cracking of lips. Then there is silence. It is a silence so cavernous she could fill it with everything she knows and imagines. She could fill it with impossible bouquets and tropical fruits, exquisite hybrids spilling in eternal suspension. She could fill it with memories, of Signora Russo's white baton conducting the anthem, of the tomb of the wolf's bones, of Signor Giorgio's suspenders, resting tight against his bloated chest. And of the eyes of her father, as green as the river, and of her mother and her uncle kissing, and of her brothers, with their chestnut skins and pouting mouths. It is a silence so big it might never end.

She lifts her face. Behind their lids her eyes are rolling and fighting the impediment. She raises her arm, reaching out. She thinks that when she touches him his hands will be flat and ringed like hooves, or with nails as long and barbed as porcupine quills. When he brings her palms up to his neck there will be a mane alive with lice, and plates of reptilian armour. His mouth will stream with spittle, the lips torn to shreds by the many serrated teeth. His tongue will wind around her wrist like a snake; it will be hung with hooks and barbs, attaching to her skin like thorns, and it will drag her to him. And when he tips back his head and roars, it will crack the stone of the tomb, and shatter her into pieces.

But when he touches her, his skin is soft and warm, and his hands are the hands of a man. And when he lays her down there is no thrashing tail, no soft underbelly, like the belly of a dog; no loaded jaw against her neck. He has been transfigured; becoming human, with smooth legs, and muscles in his arms. He lifts her skirt gently above her waist, but he does not open her abdomen with the blade of a horned thumb, nor is there the pinch and tug of her liver being taken. There is dripping on her forehead, two, three anointments, and salt on her mouth that she tastes with her tongue. She says to herself, 'I am washed clean in the blood of the lamb. I am washed clean in the blood of the lamb. Heavenly Father.' Her mouth is carefully opened, and the braids of her hair coiled inside. He pushes her chin so that she will bite down on the dry cords. He is breathing harder as he pulls the skirt higher, above her head, arranging it around the contours of her face, like a veil. He begins to remove her underclothes and she stirs, tries to shift away, but he secures her wrists. He is patient. There is rustling, the clinking of a belt, and then the force comes, to her back and hips and up inside her. She cries out but the sound is muffled. She bites her hair, coughs as it touches her throat. There is a red piercing, and a flame licking into her. It is like the pain of the mystics, the pain of St Theresa. She is being opened like the heart of the beloved. She is being burned alive.

The Bestia does not howl loudly in the tomb and break her apart, but groans and chokes, and the pressure lifts. His shoes scrape against the floor. The wetness spills. She is thinking, now I know who you are. Does he hear her think it? Is he afraid? He is holding her down. He is pushing against her chest and it is hard for her to breathe. He is tightening the skirt across her face and she cannot spit out the braids, the hair is in her throat. Small fireworks detonate inside her skull. Her legs kick. Her eyes feel as if they will break like yolks. The fit throwing her body up will snap her ligaments and break her spine, but she cannot stop it. There is one last flash in her head, and then she calms, and her feet still. She can smell the bitterness of candlewicks blowing out, a hundred thousand candles being extinguished all at once. Then she is falling away, falling down through the stone mausoleum, down among the roots of the hillside, past the two-headed worms and the blue-black beetles, down into the darkness.

Above, the swallows are also at rest. They have swung in among the great brown girders of the viaduct and are roosting along its iron belts. When a train from the city rattles the metal joists, they will spill out like a bag of dirt shaken from a balcony, performing great spinning arcs in the air before returning once more to the black vaults once the carriages have passed.

Annette is dreaming. She is dreaming about walking the road home. As she walks down the steps, the ice in her eyes begins to melt. She is beginning to see again. There are colours and depths, and edges are slowly emerging. As she looks out over the town, she can see everything at once, in all directions. The courtyard of Castrabecco, and the summer theatre, the narrow citadel, and the tower of San Lorenzo. Citizens and children. On the tables are figs baked with polenta and roasted lemons, uncorked wine and pecorino. In the alleyways, old women are sitting in the shade, their legs crossed at the ankles, holding canes in their hands or kneading dough. Laundry flaps on the lines between buildings. At San Lorenzo Father Mencaroni is unfastening his belt and removing the wafers left on the plate, eating them one by one. Annette sees her mother weeping over the photograph of her papa, while the television hums and crackles, rearranging particles to make another world. At the gardens, Uncle Marcello is conducting a ceremony; he is naming his beautiful new lily Rosaria. Beyond the citadel, the green water of the lake is languid. Underneath its surface, fish doze between reeds, oblivious to the lures of the fishermen, and the eels are asleep under stones.

Annette can see all this, and see past it. She can see beyond the solid world of bricks and chair legs and telegraph poles, through the heavy substance of the houses and the bodies of the trees, and behind each is a little glow, a bright twitching ember. An emerald shines next to the cypress, a pearl translucence shimmers in the clouds. The spirals of the iron gates contain the orange spirit of the foundry. In the old town, cats are curled on the hot tiles, their sleek golden essences beside them. In the long meadow grass, Maurizio holds up a magazine picture of a naked woman to shield his eyes from the glare of the sun. Tommaso rides his bike along the unmade road towards the cimitero di campagna. He passes a man running whose face he will not be able to remember. Her brothers each have a heart in which love blooms like a red flower. Annette sees everything twinned with light, everything immaculate.

The Fool on the Hill

For a while the two of them carried on in secret, and they carried on being part of a strange freewheeling threesome. He was caught between obsession and friendship, and both were impossible to walk away from. Regardless of the guilt, of which there was plenty, he loved their company, and loved their lessons: Ivan's in craft and composition, Raymie's in slippery reversals and dog styles. He loved the nights out in town, the long drives on new motorways. He felt that everything was coming to him, that he was part of things. He was in the scene. He was eating up life. It tasted rich and bloody.

The European exhibitions were the best, unquestionably. The work smelled serious, of paint that would take aeons to dry. There was still some old code of integrity at work on the continent. The wine at the viewings was better. Gatherings were more civilised. Even Dyas would shave with more care, so as not to leave red blotches on his chin, and he would pack a linen jacket and shirt instead of travelling with just the clothes he'd pulled from the washing line. Raymie would flex her Italian and French, which were surprisingly good. Dyas adored the middle-aged female agents who directed the shows. 'Have you noticed,' he would comment, 'they always seem to know where the light switches are. It's very impressive.' In the warehouse bays of the museums there was no hint of cheap packaging, no suggestion of discount carriers. Carpenters had been employed to crate the paintings separately, sheathing each one like an artichoke.

The Italian exhibition at the National was their last. Peter was sick with something and Raymie was making a fuss, saying they shouldn't go, while he was delirious (though the night before she'd still managed to get him to turn himself loose in her, in the bathroom of the Why Not). He'd palmed a double dose of aspirin, curled up on the back seat of the Sunbeam and fallen asleep, leaving them to bicker in the front. By the time they'd reached the city his temperature was in the low hundreds. He'd woken up alone, parked on a back street somewhere in Soho, the upholstery slippery with perspiration. Some kids were peering in at him, making V signs and fart noises under their armpits. He'd hauled himself out of the car, taken a painful leak in the gutter, and made his way to Trafalgar.

At the ancillary door, after an altercation with the security guard, he'd been let through. Inside the gallery, Dyas was in polite conversation with a small dark-haired man in a three-piece suit, and Raymie was standing to the side, casting her eye over a portrait. Dyas gestured for him to come over. The room was wobbling. He picked up his dead feet. 'Ah,' said the dark-haired man, as he approached, glancing over Peter, 'this is the student of great renown. He looks the part, no? Molto bohemian.' Peter realised he was sporting two different shoes and had failed to tuck in his shirt effectively. The man in the suit took hold of his elbow. 'Come with me. I'm going to show you something as a special favour. Ivan has told me you are an admirer and have written to our great master. Come, signore.'

He followed the agent into a vault below the east wing, past the guard who looked at him with no less suspicion or distaste. The man removed his jacket and gave it to Peter to hold. He delicately turned back his cuffs, brought a diminutive frame out of the stacks and leant the painting against the wall. Then he backed away. '*Vetro cuore Italia*,' he said. 'Please, enjoy.'

The painting was nothing for a moment, and then it was everything. The blues and browns shone, and the dust on the glassware was dense, like velvet. The signature was inscribed almost vertically in the lower right-hand corner. Peter sat himself opposite and looked at it until he felt his head clear. When he turned, the agent had moved off to another part of the storage room and was checking dockets. By the vault doorway, Dyas had hold of Raymie by her shoulders; he was shaking her, and then putting his arms round her, but she was not crying. Ivan looked over at him and smiled, and for a still, luminous minute Peter had thought everything was going to be OK.

Then there he was, an ordinary boy from the North-East, getting married in San Francisco. And then spending Christmas in upstate New York, entertaining his wealthy new in-laws after they had insisted on flying them out, while his wife stalked brattishly about the mansion. Her father, the owner of a chain of hardware companies, had pumped his hand up and down, grateful perhaps that he wasn't like any of the previous boyfriends, had married her at least, while the mother, razor-thin and heavily pearled, had been several degrees removed. They thought he was Scottish, asked him to recite Burns. With her family, he quickly found out, Raymie was ugly as sin. She stole their prescription medicines if she thought they looked interesting, slapped her mother when she discreetly handed her a psychologist's card. Her older brother had died in Indochina. His ashes were on the mahogany mantel. Raymie said he was the lucky one. There had been spells in school abroad, but she had never fitted the mould. She had wanted to work in Paris: Liverpool had been a compromise. He felt sorry for her, though he could see she knew how to work the switch in men, using their instinct to assist her, if she acted the victim. But that was the attraction. Beside her pale long limbs and the shirts unbuttoned to her navel, beside her obvious careless talent and fashionable, chemical liberalism, the distress was fascinating. He felt good, auditioning to be her saviour.

She was a genius, almost. Her work was hideous and unique. She collected the extracted teeth from dentists' surgeries and sewed them on to teddies. She stuck chicken bones and fingernail clippings on to dolls. Dyas had once said she was the vanguard of a folk revival, that this was outsider art. But there was no ambition, no reason for her parents to have paid the college fees. She simply dabbled. Peter relentlessly encouraged her. 'Why are you being a flunkey? You're better than the rest of us put together. You have ideas. Why don't you paint something instead of messing with that stuff?' She'd snort and draw out a cigarette. 'It's easy for you, Pete. You don't have the inhibitions and the stiffs for parents. You're the capable one, remember. Every time I try to find my own anatomy I'm obstructed by blood, like fucking Leonardo.' The click of the lighter at the base of the hookah. The glitter of her black, black eyes. She gave up showing her work, began modelling for other up and coming artists, Brylcreemed and panty-less, a cosmetic blush applied to her labia.

It wasn't that he tired of trying, or tired of the way she arched her spine to the ceiling when orgasm hit her. It wasn't the mess she made of the apartments, the ashtrays, syringes, the intimate waste, or her decision that sobriety was an unbearable state. Not her voice calling, 'Peewee, Peewee, pass me some Lysol for my bad arm.' Calling, 'Please, honey, pass me some ice, pass me some cold. Shut off that bulb, it hurts my face.' It was not finding the masticated lumps of jerky wrapped in little bags and hidden in the corners of the freezer, or seeing that she didn't care enough to clean herself properly, when she reclined on the futon, angular and filthy as a coal-town bridge. Where other users ran the course, then left handbags full of needles on the counter for their Wall Street fathers to discover, Raymie did not want sponsored therapy. Nothing stopped her. Not the volcanic nose bleeds, not the miscarriage – they hadn't even known she was pregnant, until the toilet was full of pink slurry – and not even the incident with the kitchen knife when he had to hold her down to stop her cutting out the red-eyed locusts, which were hatching in her veins.

He was accepting, concerned, protesting, a good husband. Yeah, he was probably OK. What sent him home wasn't falling out of love with her. He loved her, loved her desperately, this haunted girl, this hungry ghost. And he would tell her so, holding her slack, puking head and whispering in her stinking ear, or shouting it across the street when she pulled away and walked towards PCP Larry. 'Hey there, officer, got any candy for me?' It reached the point where he begged her on his knees to stop. It reached the point where he knew nothing he could say would prevent her. One day, during that second New York winter, he just knew he had to go. The weather was so cold, cold enough to freeze the piss pot in the bathroom, and she was sleeping underneath every blanket they owned, maybe not sleeping but unconscious, and he, missing the way it had been, missing the calm smell of paint, went out into the blizzard. He walked all the way to the Met through the snow, without his coat, and then sat on a gallery bench for an hour in front of a now priceless painting. *Nature Morte*, 1964, the very last in the series. He'd known then that he couldn't watch her do it any more.

It would make a great story for the kids. And the journos and the critics. The beautiful destructive wife. The sixties casualties. The peace signs. What he couldn't tell them about coincidences; what he couldn't say about meaning and fate. He could confess it all, every intimate detail, pouring out his big loose heart. They might even believe him for a change. But he hasn't told anyone, not even Lydia, not when they lie together at night, not in anger, not for absolution. The truth is that truth has no grand story. He packed his suitcase, borrowed money, and took those planes back home, hop-scotching from Boston to Gander to Shannon, and finally to London, from where he hitched north, migrating home. He left her to her noxious spiral. He left her to sink into oblivion. Within three months she was gone.

Old pain – that's how it feels now. Pain that has been accommodated, and is familiar. Life goes on, and the pain hangs around. He can live with a bad leg and a limp. He can live with no leg if that's what it comes down to. But one thing is certain – he does want to live. He wants to go home. Over his shoulder he can see the landscape now, out beyond the ravine, gorse and moor grass, rowan and elder, and the summits of the blue and yellow fells. In front of him is the dark face of the gorge. Something has to happen if he's going to get where he wants to be. And what choices are there really, other than to say, I am this, and I am here?

He takes a breath and leans forward as far as he can. The pain is immediate and blurs his vision, until saltwater drips from his eyes and he can see clearly the rocks below. He reaches down into the crucible, between the stones, to the point of compression. He reaches further through the agony, and touches the leather of his boot, which is trapped in the narrow shaft between the boulders. His boot that is wider than the foot inside it! The light epiphany arrives. But pain in his leg is speaking directly to his brain, wanting to shut him down. He claws at the laces frantically, tugs at the fastening until the struggle is too intense. He rises, puts his palms down either side of himself, and hunches his shoulders. He shouts. His head bows. He is crying and laughing. The sound is broken and grateful and helpless and determined. Sorry, Peter, sorry. There is a world, un-chosen, and in it is a bastard lot of suffering, before you get to joy. Come on. Try.

He bends again, shouting into the granite stadium, and the noise echoes back at him. 'Fuck you.' 'Fuck you.' Again he reaches to the laces. He picks at the knot, loosens the binding a fraction. Again he rises, shouts, again he bends. Five more times he goes down into the torment, yelling, dashing the water from his eyes, fighting the threshold. He undoes the double knot, pulls the laces from the metal eyelets, loosens the tongue.

There are days when he comes home and stands at the cottage door for a moment, worrying that everything inside has disappeared. He imagines the floor has dropped out and nothing is left and no one is there and he is not who he thought he was. He has to tell himself that, when he opens the door, Lydia will be sitting in the blue armchair by the range, keeping it alight. Her hair will be loose or knotted in a bun at her neck. Next to the chair will be her embroidery bag, the one she collects sloes and elderberries in this time of year. The one she used to carry the twins about in when they were tiny. He simply has to trust, now, that she will be there.

He takes hold of the leg with both hands and pulls as hard as he can.

Translated from the Bottle Journals

The rain has been keeping us indoors by the fire, but this morning the weather has broken and I am able to venture outside. I try not to dwell on my condition but I am asked frequently by the doctor and Theresa and Antonio to describe my discomforts. What can I tell them? Yes, it is uncomfortable. I have no appetite. I am thinner. Something dark consumes me from inside; it has multiplied and has entered the lymph system. There is no miracle. Everything has slowed – my writing, my movements, the paintbrush. I am full of sorrow for the loss of delicate fragrances. I can no longer smell the herbs or the rain or cinabrese. Even my old friend paper is too subtle with his cologne! But I am noticing other things more sharply. A cherry stone darkening on one side while the other remains pale and lit, like this remarkable planet. A piece of coral from the shelf is uncomfortably crisp to hold, as if baked almost to desiccation by salt kilns. I make these observations with a sense of wonder, and am only roused when Theresa comes into the room and asks what it is that I have forgotten or am looking for, and why I am stalled.

I am kindly forgiven for wearing this old robe, with ragged cuffs, when visitors arrive. Antonio limits the time of anyone wishing to call upon me, and now refuses to let me give interviews. This is a relief, and I am thankful. The newspapers are already commemorating my life, it seems, though the speculation about the motifs continues. More reporters would like to come, but the door of the studio is closed to them. One day one of them will write a simple sentence.

I must fortify myself and commit myself to putting the studies and canvases in order. They lean against the walls every which way and are not in series. Antonio is doing much lifting and carrying; he goes beyond his call of duty. The accounting has been done. The papers have gone to the solicitor. I know nothing of archives; needless to say, I am no clerk, and I leave much work for them to do! The house is to be left to my wife's family. They will have to excuse its gardens. There is a sense of preparation here at Serra Partucci, and it is strange to think that I will not need luggage, or even a hat upon my head, for my departure. I strongly feel that I should fold my clothes, press my shirts and polish my shoes.

I have begun several letters to Peter. Each sounds too conclusive and too imperative, and each has been discarded. I have no wish to depress him, nor should I press upon him any methodology for working. I wish only to say his correspondence has given me great pleasure. He will find his way, I am certain. I was schooled with Nelo Ungaretti, the great mathematician and architect, a man of such vivacity that all who knew him were certain he would prosper in his field, and though the war sadly robbed us of him, he was indeed triumphant. I believe Peter has Ungaretti's qualities.

I have sent my best wishes to the children in the school, and to Signora Russo I have donated many books. Upon my request, Giancarlo brought his small dog here and permitted me to stroke him. He has proved to be a good forager. Giancarlo and I talked fondly while the dog ran about, sniffing in the corners of the house. Theresa was nervous throughout the meeting and kept her hands tightly linked. Perhaps she thought our discussion would move on to politics or that I would embarrass her with praise. I have made small provision for the family in the will but I have not mentioned this in case they will not accept it. The doctor has given me a small supply of morphine for the coming days. I have not yet taken any.

My mind reaches back into the past. Today, as if finding a lost charm or trinket, I have suddenly recalled the infant nickname my mother gave me. Gyri. I have remembered my mother's voice calling from the orchard of Via Lame, calling to me now, sixty years after she passed away. I recall the woven basket she wore over her shoulder with its red scarf under the strap, the pop and rustle as each fruit was snapped from the branches and placed without bruising into the container on her hip, and the pollen shaken down into her hair. One does not question God. One does not question a life beyond this. We cannot understand or predict. But if such a thing should exist, and if the beloved remain there, then how willingly I am gathered.

The voice calling is not my mother's; it is Theresa's. She has arrived early. She is keeping kind hours. She has rested her parched bicycle against the gate with its pedal between the railings. She has come into the house and has begun to prepare breakfast for her patient. I must extinguish my cigarette!

Now there are medical procedures to be endured, for which I need her help. I will pause and resume after.

The painting of the blue bottles is almost finished now. I am pleased with it. Standing at the easel is difficult, as I have less strength. I have tried sitting but it is an uncustomary position – the canvas is tall and awkward, as the artist must have been all his life! I am committed much of the time to my bed, and it is a comfort to look over and see this composition nearing completion. The bottles on the studio table collect and empty their bright tides as the light of each day arrives and passes.

What can be said of them finally? I do not know. They are not consolation, but they have always been sufficient.

The artistic efforts of men are indicative of our human openness, our inquisitiveness, I think. When we attempt to evaluate, or to obviate, we seldom guess correctly. Our minds are born nervous, in darkness. We are subterranean beings. We must learn by the senses and continue to be instinctual, to use the antennae. The oils of lavender bring sleep when we apply them to the pillow. Aniseed stirs us. In the museums, we must believe in the Dutch trick, the red deer, and the monk beneath the vast sky. We must look at the reality, and then look again at the illusion. We must see beyond. For what shakes the eye but the invisible?

Theresa is calling for me to come inside and eat. I must obey her or there will be unrest in the house and the broom will come out. I cannot be responsible for the decimation of our lizard population! But the view from the veranda is marvellous, and I linger.

I abhor catastrophe in all forms. There has been much I have wished to retain and repair. There is so much still to order. Yet I wait for the snow to arrive on the mountains.

The Mirror Crisis

You hold the thin plastic device in your hand, watching the strip for a blue line, which may or may not appear. The bathroom door is locked. The blinds are drawn. Opposite you is your reflection. Nathan is in the kitchen – you can hear the gonging of pans as he lifts one out of the cupboard, the hiss of the tap, and the bowing of water as the metal hull fills. The lid of the toilet seat is cold on the backs of your legs. There are small hexagonal tiles under your feet, the edges of which you trace with your toes. This is a scenario you were never sure you would experience. You have always been ambivalent about children. But here you are. You've followed the test instructions with clinical precision. The box tells you the percentage of accuracy is high. You are in the hands of trustworthy science. Science will scout out the correct hormones, distinguishing them, or declaring their absence. The tiny portable laboratory in your hand is, at this moment, going about its business.

It should only take a few minutes, and then you will know. The world will arrange itself around this information. It will make way for another temporary pulse, or it will retain its position, adjusting the count elsewhere around the world as people pitch in and out, headlong, hundreds of them by the second. The indicator paper is clear and prepared. You think of bromide emulsion, light sensitivities, of waiting for a face to develop in a photograph. It's like waiting to know if the image has succeeded or failed. The device is a viewfinder, an observatory. And in a few minutes you will know who is or is not there.

You feel no discernible emotion either way, and you are not sure what you will feel when the result comes in. Terror? Elation? Disappointment? Or something in between? You will have to wait and see.

The funny thing is, you've been thinking so long and hard about death that you've lost sight of its fraternal twin, its obverse pole. This is the prerogative of grief you suppose. There have been times you've not realised you were crying, until you put your hand to your face and it came away wet, until you noticed that someone was looking at you curiously, the concerned stranger on the train, or the woman in the supermarket who offered you a tissue. You have been so consumed that you've almost forgotten about the other side, the affirmation, the positive stroke. Life.

What is it really? A term. A condition. A state of being, for a while, animate. A state that is no longer radically felt, perhaps, that has no hard mortal slap, day after day, no jeopardy, nothing hanging in the balance – at least not in this safe little bolthole of the globe. There is no requirement to kill, no murdering for the scraps. Even the bloody bookends of birth and death are dulled with morphine, epidural, euthanasia. The occasional reminders of what it is to be anatomised, what it is to be made of particles, neurons, nerves, and senses, what it means to be homo sapiens – the car accident, the toxic oyster, the bolt rattling out of the rollercoaster – are few and far between. Ecstasy and agony are now on sale. Pay for the ride, pull the parachute cord, pop the pill, there will be insurance of some kind, a safety net below. The brain fires but the true biological impetus, of pain and desire, of hunger and fear, is missing. Because human beings can't be given happiness, after all. They have to fight for it, sprint for it, get close to the edge for it. They have to rut for it, permit the striking of those dutiful, savant gametes. So you go on, in abstraction, until something wakes you up – a bomb, an accident, a close miss. So you fuck him, not for love, but because you both understand that death equals life. Perhaps.

In a few minutes you will know. You will know the consequences of your actions, the result of your programme to fulfil yourself, the primitive attempt to establish your presence. Here you are, waiting for a sign, waiting to know something more about yourself. What you already know is this: you reside at a privileged set of coordinates. You have a partner who loves you, employment, a house. You have parents, talents, a salary, a vote, and firing synapses. Hitherto your body has not let you down – breasts, cervix, eyes, ovaries, cerebral functions, immune system, lungs, and heart: nothing has yet malfunctioned, no dire failure has occurred, beyond the gentle degradation of ageing. If you choose to, you will live. And in your hands might be another life.

When you came home from the gallery an hour ago you thought about telling Nathan everything. You thought about telling him that you are no longer you, the woman he knew and trusted, that you are a different person now, capable of the worst possible damage. You thought about confessing, telling him about Tom and your dark obsession, the hotel rooms, the test kit in your bag, everything.

You took out your key, opened the flat door. Nathan was home, of course. *Hiya, love.* He came out of the kitchen holding a glass of wine. *Not staying late tonight then?* He passed you the glass stem, kissed your cheek. *You have this. I'll make dinner.* You shrugged off your coat, sat on the couch. You looked around the place. Everything was familiar, the

Victorian fire with its trivets and tiles, the flax-green walls, bookcases, furniture, your photographs, hanging in meaningful series, all of which you had chosen, all of which you could leave.

The door of the second bedroom was open. Sitting on the corner of the table was your Leica, and a folder of contact sheets for an overdue commission. Steam was coming from the kitchen, the smell of garlic. You put your bag on the couch beside you, took a sip of wine, reached for the remote and turned on the television. On one channel was a film set in the Australian outback. An aboriginal woman had had her child stolen; she was beating her head with a rock. On another was a programme about trepanning; people were drilling into their foreheads, blazing in towards the tender frontal lobes. They thought it would bring them wisdom. The hundred sexiest music videos. A hospital drama, someone's hand about to be amputated. *You can't do it, you can't do it to me,* the patient was screaming.

You kept pressing the arrow key on the remote, passing up through the channels until you reached those that were blank. In the corner of the screen was the word *scrambled*. You wondered if this was what Nicki saw behind her eyelids – a dark visor, a projection of nothing. You wondered how her life feels. Like an endless intermission perhaps, a continuation of those forty-five airless minutes on the moor, lying in the winter snow. The nurse once told you her muscles are so wasted that if she woke she would not be able to use them. *Imagine a moth carrying a tractor on its back*, she had said to you. You turned off the television and thought of Nicki's hair, kept glossy by solutions of proteins and minerals dripped down into her, and by the brushing and brushing of her family.

You thought about going for a run. You imagined the cool twilight slipping past you on the heath, the city rotating under your soles. You drank your wine quickly, stood up, and went into the spare room. The phone was flashing red. The console told you there were three new messages. You picked up the rangefinder, dusted it off. Inside the heavy case you knew Danny would be sitting outside the railway station surrounded by birds. His arms would be stretched along the back of the bench. He would be smiling. You shut your eyes and thought about his first bike, the one he'd had when he was a kid, the one with the long handlebars that had rattled over potholes on the farm roads and flung him off into the thistles when he hit a ditch on the moor. You thought about him laughing, even as he lay there getting stung. Danny.

Nathan called from the kitchen. *You've got a few minutes, I'm just about to put the pasta on.* You took the film cartridge out of the bottom of the camera, worked the casing open and drew the thin plastic strip out into the light. You laid it on the studio table, where it re-curled, set the Leica down next to it and went back into the lounge. You took the paper pharmacy packet out of your bag and locked yourself in the bathroom.

You hold the plastic device in your hands. It weighs almost nothing. The floor tiles are small and cold. In the bathroom mirror your reflection is returning your gaze. London is outside the window. The streetlights are coming on, making the sky orange, and the traffic is continual, planes and helicopters passing overhead. Either side of this building, millions of people live, and millions die. The world can accommodate your situation, as it accommodates all situations. And your body will keep explaining to you how it all works, this original experiment, this lifelong gift. Your body will keep describing how, for the time being at least, there is no escape from this particular vessel. These are your atoms. This is your consciousness. These are your experiences – your successes and mistakes. This is your first and final chance, your one and only biography. This is the existential container, the bowl of your life's soup, wherein something can be made sense of, wherein there is a cure, wherein you are.

You look down. In the window of the test there is a faint blue line. You watch it grow stronger and darker. Outside the bathroom door, Nathan calls softly. *Susan? Susan?*

Yes, you say. *I'm here.*

How to Paint a Dead Man

We shall next speak about the way to paint a dead man, that is, the face, the breast, and wherever in any part the nude may show. It is the same on panel as on wall: except that on a wall it is not necessary to lay in all over with terre-verte; it is enough if it is laid in the transition between the shadow and the flesh colours. But on a panel lay it in as usual, as you were taught for a coloured or live face; and shade it with the same verdaccio, as usual. And do not apply any pink at all, because a dead person has no colour; but take a little light ochre, and step up three values of flesh colour with it, just with white lead, and tempered as usual; laying each of these flesh colours in its place, blending them nicely into each other, both on the face and on the body. And likewise, when you have got them almost covered, make another still lighter flesh colour from this light one, until you get the major accents of the reliefs up to straight white lead. And mark out all the outlines with dark sinoper and a little black, tempered; and this will be called 'sanguine'. And manage the hair in the same way, but not so that it looks alive, but dead, with several grades of verdaccio. And just as I showed you various types and styles for beards on the wall, so on panel you do them in the same way; and so do every bone of a Christian, or of rational creatures; do them with these flesh colours aforesaid.

The Craftsman's Handbook by Cennino d'Andrea Cennini
Translated by Daniel V. Thompson, Jr.

Acknowledgements

Thanks to the following people for invaluable help with research: Simon Webb, Diego Mencaroni, Paul Farley, Dana Prescott, Philip Robinson, Teana Newman, Lani Irwin, Alan Feltus, Tobias Feltus, Joseph Feltus, Dr Richard Thwaites, Dr Sarah Laing, Dr Charles Fernyhough, Neil Rollinson, Anthony Hall and Jonathan Hall.

Thanks to the following people for editorial advice, critical reading, and general feedback: Jacob Polley, Lee Brackstone, Clare Conville, Jennifer Pooley, Lisa Baker, Helen Francis, Jane Kotapish, Damon Galgut, Rebecca Morales, Christobel Kent, and Elizabeth Hall.

I am indebted to all those at the Civitella Ranieri Foundation, the staff, friends, and fellows, for the extraordinary gift of a residency in Umbria in 2007. Grazie!

Lastly, thanks to Peter, on the hill.

ff

Faber and Faber – a home for writers

Faber and Faber is one of the great independent publishing houses in London. We were established in 1929 by Geoffrey Faber and our first editor was T. S. Eliot. We are proud to publish prize-winning fiction and non-fiction, as well as an unrivalled list of modern poets and playwrights. Among our list of writers we have five Booker Prize winners and eleven Nobel Laureates, and we continue to seek out the most exciting and innovative writers at work today.

www.faber.co.uk – a home for readers

The Faber website is a place where you will find all the latest news on our writers and events. You can listen to podcasts, preview new books, read specially commissioned articles and access reading guides, as well as entering competitions and enjoying a whole range of offers and exclusives. You can also browse the list of Faber Finds, an exciting new project where reader recommendations are helping to bring a wealth of lost classics back into print using the latest on-demand technology.